Buddhism
for Western
Children

The Iowa Review Series in Fiction

Harilaos Stecopoulos, series editor

Buddhism for Western Children

KIRSTIN ALLIO

UNIVERSITY OF IOWA PRESS | IOWA CITY

University of Iowa Press, Iowa City 52242
Copyright © 2018 by the University of Iowa Press
www.uipress.uiowa.edu
Printed in the United States of America

Text design by April Leidig

The University of Iowa Press is a member of Green Press
Initiative and is committed to preserving natural resources.

Printed on acid-free paper

ISBN 978-1-60938-596-5 (pbk)
ISBN 978-1-60938-597-2 (ebk)

Cataloging-in-Publication data is on file
with the Library of Congress.

for Luc, Declan,
and Michael

Buddhism
for Western
Children

BOOK ONE

Bellwether

CHAPTER 1

Dear ones!

Listen to Me!

My miracles are not sentimental shit,
they have nothing to do with eating the Christ-fish
that walked on water.
They are not miracles to commute the sentence of death,
not miracles with cheap
psychological endings.
Not: I have not found love
but I am okay not finding it.

Do you hear Me?

You come to Me with your human monkey junk,
your station wagon story, you come to Me
looking for yourselves, for God,
for your next drink, people.
You complain to Me that you exist
in the void of boredom,
you are dead already,
but you keep waking up
with a bottle for a pillow,
a demon monkey form licking up vomit.

Listen.

Once you know Me,
you want to be completely inherited
by My love, you people.
That is certain.

Well all you have to do is open!

All the doors have always been open!

Daniel's parents listened to the Guru on cassette tape all the way down to Maine from Halifax.

Canyon stripes of browns and grays whipped by like banners out the window. As they got farther south there was yellow-green in the blur of bushes at the bottom.

His dad, Ray, set a plastic milk jug of drinking water on the floor of the back seat, and it was Daniel's job to pass it up when Ray got thirsty.

Early spring when they arrived—the ground was still frozen beneath the sponge, and the bay was a dark oil stain. The first thing they learned was that the Sanctuary was closed to lay-disciples. The Guru was in a period of retreat after exposure. The rental house up the road from the Sanctuary was a tall, stark, unadorned Colonial, the half white of old snow, porcupine quills like pine needles around the foundation.

Dad Ray, Daniel's new name for him, was eager to show off how that same foundation had been neatly wedged and split by the roots of maples so that the floorboards peaked at the seam that divided it: the two halves of the house slanted away from each other.

Daniel went right up to his new bedroom. From the back window, he could see the fingery salt rivers that fed the bay and the exoskeletons of marsh grasses. The stairs were on rusty springs, and the front door stuck so he had to throw his whole body at it. He stood against the chalky front of the house and watched hoarse gulls drop blue mussels on the road to get the meat. His mother, Cleary, wandered outside with toast in a napkin. Soon they would learn that bread was worldly. She saw the cedar fox before he did. No bigger than a housecat. It crossed from one woods to the other.

They hoped to catch a glimpse of the Guru.

He watched how his parents began to form half-secret, self-proud smiles: they claimed to be astonished by the sudden, strange revelation of being in love with Avadhoot Master King Ivanovich, the Guru. Ray said there was this feeling like being plugged into a wall socket. But that was the old language. The new language? In His world-weary and His crazy-fool and His divine fury, this guy was a madman who was mad for them. His crazy-madman love redeemed them.

Cleary adopted the manner of other devotees of not answering Daniel's questions. That was part of sadhana, the Practice, not answering stupid questions. In no time at all she had assumed a cloud wall, total serenity.

He set out exploring. The garden site behind the house, abandoned by previous tenants, was full of dog ticks and spiders. He poked around an old chicken coop choked and buckled by blackberry. It would make a good hiding place.

That same evening, John Hartshorn, the Guru's lieutenant, leaned against the bare wall in their kitchen with his hands crossed loosely over his privates. The Guru couldn't stop laughing when He found out you were from Canada, he started. His nostrils flared but his mouth hardly moved, thought Daniel.

His parents did not protest.

The lieutenant angled toward Ray. Did you say you were a carpenter? He cleaned the corners of his mouth with his tongue. The Guru is always renovating. He wants to know what you can do with that chicken coop.

Daniel dropped his eyes to the floor as his ears caught fire.

Chicken coop? Ray echoed.

Coop of grace, said the lieutenant. It was like a tic how he cleaned his corners.

They watched—and waited till the lieutenant hit his stride. Back down the road toward the Sanctuary.

Shall we? said Ray, and Daniel followed him out through the garden to look for the hovel.

Ray let out a hoot when he got a glimpse through the tangle of bare bushes. Jesus! There were little bi-leaves of maple in the loamy roof. But he had no trouble wiggling the door free and then banging it up and off its hinges. They peered inside together. There was still sawdust on the floor, and a chicken ramp with shims for treads to the nesting boxes. There was still chicken shit.

It took a day just to get through the blackberry. Look at that, said Ray, the runners were already macho, ready for summer. The rotten wood fell apart like stringy beef. Underneath, porcupine again, and the smell of cat piss in carpet.

Ray and Cleary said His withdrawal wasn't unusual—rather, nothing was usual. Whether He was extroverted or elusive, spontaneous, subtle, paradoxical, or silent. This is the Way that I Teach, the Guru would say, referring simply and universally to His Being.

Daniel sat low in the driver's seat of the station wagon where Ray had backed it onto the grass to unload lumber. There was that startling pleated sack where the emergency brake originated. He'd asked about going home and Ray said, The Guru is a really important Teacher, Daniel. Really one of the most important in modern times, and his eyes were glistening.

Still, Daniel imagined they were on the road back to Canada. He felt guilty excluding his little sister from his game, and she seemed to float around the car, waiting for him to come out again. He looked in the rearview mirror. He had to admit his hair was not quite black. It grew raggedly over his ears. He had a spatter of freckles that stood out like markings on an animal. He squinted. His sister had dropped out of view to adjust her sandal. Who was he, really? That was the big question. It consumed his parents. It warped toward the stars. What superpower would he have if he could have one? He was ten. His T-shirt hung to his knees. Wasn't he growing? His knees, under his shirt, were like faces. Who was he?

The Guru was supposed to know the answer.

Penny Del Deo, their spiritual sponsor in Halifax, had tipped her shapely head to say that there was a chance Ray and Cleary MacFarland were emerging from their own Kaliyuga, twelve thousand years of subhuman vulgarity. There's a chance this guy really is God, you know, said Penny, and Ray sat up straight and said he liked how she made it sound like there was a chance He wasn't.

There's no dogma, said Penny.

Wait till you hear Him on the piano, she said, a little smile playing on her lips after a private moment.

Word came that the Guru emerged from retreat and would give a concert to which all were invited. The Guru was a classical musician—a serious person. The heart of the Sanctuary, they heard, was the Concert Barn, its back to the blue hemlock forest.

Dad Ray could fiddle, but couldn't read music. They went single file down the road to the Sanctuary, Daniel hoping that no cars would pass them. There were scabs of late ice in the farmyard, and the snow in the shadows was like pumice stone, gray and porous.

They took their shoes off at the door, all those empty shoes like dogs waiting for their owners. Daniel saw his sister staring at two of the Guru's wives in long white skirts and white blouses, flowers in their hair that made them look like American hippies. This was something to tell his classmates at home in Halifax.

The stalls and the hayloft had been knocked out like teeth, and devotees had built a simple raised platform for the Guru's grand piano. Zafus were arranged on the floor in rows, enough for the whole sangha, community of disciples. Ray was awed: he whispered that the Concert Barn could hold two hundred people. There were space heaters on frayed extension cords, kerosene lamps in tin houses corroded by salt air hung on nails.

His parents were to sit apart, the men's side and the ladies'. Ray put one arm around him and one around his sister as the three of them split off from Cleary.

There was Craig R., who they'd met already, poet-devotee, he'd called himself, with two freckle-colored horns of beard and his own canteen of water: you had to hydrate the husk after sitting meditation. Happiness is cutting the strings to happiness! he greeted them. He snipped an invisible cord over his bald spot. Red hair, holy clown behavior. Suddenly his lower back seized and he put his hands together and bowed testily saying that he might have a hernia from sitting meditation but the body was the rag of the body.

Craig R. pointed: What's your name, Daniel's-sister?

Violet, she mouthed. She lost her voice when she was frightened.

Next time she should sit with the ladies, said the poet.

Incense sifted through the air, nag champa, Daniel could taste it. A girl with a round face the color of rice was up on her knees looking at them openly. Her black hair was downy but wild. He accidentally caught her eye and out darted her snake tongue. He saw that when she waved to grownups in the audience they beamed back at her. He watched her push her fingers into backbends. Her fingers touched her arms as if they were boneless.

Suddenly there was a shared shift and rustle as people turned to watch the Guru's procession. First came His child-sized page-turner, Dorothy (later they would learn that she hated children, like a small grown dog can't abide a puppy of a larger breed); next, a slim page in a Nehru collar, Arthur, the jikki jitsu, meditation leader, who Ray would claim looked like a young Bob Dylan.

Daniel caught Violet changing her legs from lotus to knees to see better. He saw Craig R. push his face up to capture radiance. He tried to follow his breathing up and down, as he had been instructed. His breathing began to triangle. What was wrong with a triangle? Then it went in a square, and he couldn't seem to stop it from making the shape of a stop sign.

He gave up. He fixed his eyes on the lid of the piano, open in half flight, a crow's wing, jet and lustrous.

A bell cleared the air of its last feathers.

And then there He was, He who was called the Uprooted Center of the Cosmos. Daniel couldn't help staring. He was huge, as tall as Ray but twice as broad, full of caloric life energy. His huge head was cabbage-shaped, white-tufted, and as a child in the Soviet Union He had strolled Moika Embankment pulling sweets from thin air for His sweet-toothed mother.

Ray had warned that He might not be, at present, in His body. His body was not Him, Ray had explained. The laws of the universe were only props for mortals. Why should the Guru abide by the body? Daniel had no answer.

But He slid His incarnation out along the piano bench. He smoothed His great thighs and closed His small dry eyes as air expanded His belly. He was sat-chit-ananda, Happiness Spreading. He tilted His head back in private rapture.

Ray spread his buttocks out on the zafu. There was the gong, and the nasal voice of the jikki jitsu: Let go of your stuff, you devotees of the Fully Realized! Let go, devotees, of your big-muscleman breathing!

Surrender the mindform
into the renowned current,
yield the spirit,
the aggravated subject-body,
into His heart-fire,
say His name, God.

The music started. It was surprisingly gentle. Pebbles and water, bells and chimes overlapping. It wasn't hard to listen. The separate sounds made a long cradle. Before he knew what was happening Daniel was inside the cradle. He did not have to act to listen. His sister closed her eyes beside him.

Or a boat. It was music that could take you. Drown your thoughts and tune your mind to its own vibration. There were so many notes at once—how did He do it? How did He know so many different voices?

The Guru stopped abruptly, and Daniel felt the loss almost like nausea. His throat was tight as if he had to cry. He watched the jikki swim forward to reach the Guru's feet, which they would learn were prodigiously expressive.

Even My feet are lovable! cried the Guru, laughing. Everyone laughed with Him. Daniel heard Ray's familiar baritone.

Dear Ones.

Just like the cassette tape. Ray leaned in and whispered that this was one of His Open Letters. Some people called it poemform, spontaneous recitative, the Guru Himself had said that it might be inspired garbage.

Have you seen the mudden hives
in the eaves of My farmhouse, people?

His hands were huge and curled on top of his knees like lotuses. His feet were bare, His legs were open. When devotees received eye contact, they took the impact to their soft centers, they smiled through their tears, their hands moved together in prayer position. Daniel tried to shrink behind the shaking back of the man in front of him. Was the man crying?

Swallows swing between us.
And yet it has always seemed to Me
that the birds are scattering,
not flying,
around you, people.

The Guru leaned forward. He was suddenly grinning, and Daniel saw that Ray was grinning.

Have you seen My chickens?
My coup de breasts,
My henhouse?
Chicken shit can't help being what it really is!
This is the fundamental life!
Were you looking for some other kind of truth, people?
Fundament comes from ass!
The ass of life, the great rumpus!

He barely gave Himself time to finish before He was laughing again, laughing so hard He had to hold His belly. Devotees took their cue, they doubled over.

Through His laughter: You are all so fixed on separation! You think you are separated from your own source of happiness! You think I am rejecting you because I don't move you up a Level or I don't praise your posture in the zendo or I give a concert and you're not invited.

But you are not separate, do you hear Me?

You are with Me now!

Wiping His eyes, He looked around at each and every one of them.

And by the way, people, happiness does not depend on so-called happy experiences!

He turned back to the piano.

When the silence had lasted forever Daniel opened his eyes and looked sideways at his sister. He saw that with her eyes closed she no longer looked like a worldly child, fearful and self-consoling. For a moment he imagined that the Guru's music had moved her organs from one side to the other as if they were caught at low tide between giant rocks, her heart in streamers like seaweed.

CHAPTER 2

THE GURU'S FIRST WIFE met them at the sandy lip of the road for a formalized tour. The Sanctuary didn't have a gate or a flag or a sign or anything.

It's like the Practice, she breathed. It just starts. Out of nowhere, each moment. She had oval, hooded eyes, a long sallow face with painful-looking moles the color of ketchup.

Ray said later there was something Virgin Mary about her. Something All the World Shall Be Taxed. Although she was too skinny to be pregnant.

Her name was Kai. She had purchased the Sanctuary for Him in old farm form, she told them, tear-down condition, hillocks of shingles between the bay and the woods, rocks on the shore gray as gunmetal. But soon after the Guru took possession He discovered a small colony of chickens, and a rooster, thriving unpastored in one of the shoulderless teepees of shingles that had once been an outbuilding. This was a sign that a sangha would arise, said Kai, a community of practitioners; and this was also the reason the Guru collected birds on the Sanctuary. He named them in His native tongue, Russian.

The main road made a tight curve around the farmhouse. Ray said he'd seen worldly neighbors rubbernecking. Kai said they had glassy eyes. They wanted to see, without believing.

You can't see Me as I truly am, people—the Guru's constant admonition—until you believe that I love you.

He had already loved them forever. Worldly neighbors didn't

know that when He slid off His skullcap, His crown glowed and a halo rose and tilted like the ring of a planet.

We can't glom onto Him, Kai warned them.

Did they know that guru was an Indian word worldly neighbors found sheer babble? There were plenty of worldly rumors about Him. That He'd skinned a live cat to harvest a psychedelic found only in the shallow feline lymphatic. He'd been seen in a skullcap like a Jew, and the floppy diaper of a renunciate.

One of the Guru's favorite words, lymphatic. Kai let out a little burp of laughter. Daniel glanced at his sister to see if she'd noticed.

The Guru lived in the every-which-way farmhouse. Ray said it looked like it was all elbows. The big dirt lot was the farmyard. Descendants of the first birds mirrored devotees' issues and constrictive ego-serving behaviors, said Kai, parading like repressed farmhands, harried divas, childish parents. She gazed mildly at Ray and Cleary.

Catpaws of moss grew between the shingles of the dormered farmhouse. Kai said the storm door banged of its own accord, as the ghost of the Guru's favorite cat, Bob, went in and out constantly. There was an outsized pole barn with a corrugated pewter roof. Ray sized up a badly faded tractor. A cluster of single-story sheds appeared to be molting paint as dirty as a seagull, but there was the smell of more exotic fowl: the Guru's birds were imported like hothouse flowers.

The Guru's nine wives were Kai, Sita, Zoya, Tamsen, Dovorh, Jyoti, Amina, Heidi, and Piti. The Jersey cows in the pole barn were Masha, Pasha, Sasha, Dasha, and Irinka. The Guru was good with names. In the Soviet Union, murmured Kai, He had studied exclusively music and literature.

She pointed out a shed clad in rough-milled, yellow boards, the new banya with a shiny stovepipe.

The one-room cabins scattered throughout the Sanctuary had beautiful names too, according to the Guru: Lupine and Ozera, Columbine and Kitezh. Morye Odeyal, which was Sea of Blankets. Kai said, Does anyone speak Russian?

Ray stood with his mouth half open and his hands clasped in front like a choirboy. Should Daniel say they didn't?

That high-pitched whine was a table saw. If your ears recovered you could hear a series of growling, guttural explosions down low: the knotty waste being devoured. A quarter of a mile down the dirt track toward the bay was the woodshop. Spruce trees, scrappy and stiff from salt spray, were culled from the lacy hemlock of Kishkindha Forest. Their resinous boles bit the blade and they kicked out violently. The sawdust on the floor of the woodshop was buttery, thought Daniel, like cake crumbs. He bent to take a handful and Kai fell completely silent. The air was charged. He tried to let the sawdust go but it stuck to his sweaty fist, between his fingers.

Kai ran her hand along the top of one of the picnic tables that devotees sold in Topsfield Fair, near Boston. She checked her palm for splinters. The profitability of the woodshop showed that the Guru was practical despite His early training, a farmer-yogi, in the mold of the Tibetan teacher Marpa. She paused, Do you know Marpa?

We have so much to learn, breathed Cleary.

To cover the remaining expenses of the Sanctuary, said Kai, there was tithing. She picked up a rusted blade like an old aluminum pie plate.

Ray whistled. Lost any fingers?

Kai smiled indulgently, and Daniel noticed that her big teeth were streaked with metal.

There was an awkward silence.

How long have you been here? Ray tried again, attempting to

sound natural, but he hadn't had years of practice speaking to the wife of a Divine Being.

As long as my Beloved.

Daniel thought, a stupid question. There was a farm barn circa the early 1800s; a work crew was kicking the old scab of cedar shingles off the roof but they quit when they saw the First Beautiful. Ray gawked up three stories and wondered aloud that they hadn't been corrupted by asphalt. The scarecrows waved down.

Shudra Service, said Kai. Her hands had disappeared in the folds of her tunic.

Violet turned to meet a dog who'd snuck up behind them, and Kai changed her tune crying out, Vash! My Vashik! She reached down to rub the dog's axle shoulders. Vash's Leela, she declared, is that he showed up hungry.

Dad Ray wasn't going to let her get away with it. He said, Leela? Cleary pointed herself in the other direction.

His Leela is how he found us, said Kai. A tiny, precious laugh: His whole dog deal.

At last they followed the First along footpaths through the holy forest to the zendo, not by-the-sea at all, as Ray had regaled them on the car trip from Halifax, but still, it appeared to float in the pool-like clearing in the forest.

. . .

Zendo-by-the-Sea—Ray thought he was teasing the whole world, but the only eye he caught in the rearview mirror was Daniel's. The joke was that the zendo would be just like one of the turquoise-trimmed motels they stayed in along the way to get there. Ray steered with one tall knee. One loose arm around Cleary.

Well what would he miss? Ray proposed. Daniel was silent. Ball games?

Very funny because they were headed to the country that invented baseball.

Cleary drifted out the window. Daniel had noticed she had a crosshatch of lines around her eyes that made her look wise and wistful. Her hair was the color of raisins with a few early grays, she called them. He'd caught her pulling one out in front of the bathroom mirror. The pop it made was the death sound.

She stretched her hand back to rest on the knee that always butted up against the seat back. (Violet sat curled in the window.) You'll miss your friends, Dan, she said gently, returning to the question. Ten-year-olds with stencils of dirt where the socks ended.

Trying to be funny like Ray, he said that he wouldn't miss *school*. Cleary turned to smile at him with a mix of relief and exasperation.

He had listened to their grownup talk, registered their excitement, got wind of his grandparents' disapproval. He had heard them say to each other that perhaps they really had located God, in the form Ivanovich.

He hadn't thought God would be a person. But was the Guru?

They stayed in seaside fleabags with vending machine breakfasts. One evening there was a traveling circus in the parking lot, and they watched a showman escort what could only be a bear, marveled Ray, into the room next door to them. In the morning, Ray sidled up to a fellow gauging the tires of one of the circus trailers. Could my son here see Smokey?

The showman burst into tears right where Ray confronted him. Without warning he seizured into hysterics.

Later Ray jerked his bear-colored eyebrows up and down in the rearview mirror. He was a dancing beast with chain sores and a trembling lower lip, although the real suffering was endured, he said grandly, by that traveling showman who drove the bear and fed it dog food.

It wasn't that God was distant from people. Ray had laid it out for them: it was that people were all fear and rhetoric. It wasn't that God was inside now, after centuries of being a dichotomous old bully. It wasn't that there was no more clash between beefsteak and doe-eyed vegetables.

What was it? Ray said the original juxtaposition was God and Human. But you didn't say God anymore. What replaced Him? Some combination of self-improvement and the supernatural.

Ray was like the younger brother of the world, asking his own questions. Answering them. He believed in reincarnation, UFOs, vitamins. He had read about meditation, sat cross-legged (he was tall and loose-jointed with a thin nose and a wavy beard—it was cold on his balls on the floor, though, he confessed to Daniel), and watched his breathing roll out like sea surf. He wasn't sure if his obstacles of thought were unique but he had read that a spiritual teacher could break them down like the mineral deposits of arthritis.

Cleary had met Penny Del Deo through some talks at an alternative bookshop. Penny was not content to go willy-nilly through her days on an outside authority—the dominant culture, she said, or for that matter Jimmy Carter—that advised over loudspeakers hidden in trees, Store-bought bread and Coca-Cola! She told them it had been two years since she had eaten from a supermarket.

There was a new language to explain that Ray and Cleary had spontaneously opened. Penny warned that further opening could feel like fear. Fear was just a farting old guard dog. Guarding fear. Guarding the empty chest in the empty chamber in the empty temple. Emptiness itself was bandied about as if it were something, Ray offered.

It still echoed: Tell your schoolteachers you're finished with cave painting, Ray announced one evening.

There you go! He walked his fingers. Moving up the ladder of spiritual evolution.

Liking something was not happiness. Not liking something was not unhappiness.

Daniel was small for his age, with what Penny Del Deo claimed were sable eyes, to flatter Cleary.

. . .

All summer long Dad Ray cut shingles for the chicken coop temple in undulating patterns. He framed a tricky round window that he was especially proud of, sanded the floor on his hands and knees, and used the rough edge of his thumb to whisk off the dust and administer the final polish. He laid down tatami mats that smelled—he declared—like grass, at the moment grass decides whether to dry like hay or molder.

Daniel watched, and helped a little, but mostly he was left on his own, he and his sister.

Ray had just made his last trip to the lumberyard when the lieutenant arrived unannounced to pick up the station wagon. Apparently Ray had signed it over.

(Soon the Guru would have what looked like a used car lot behind the woodshop on the Sanctuary. His bumblings as a mechanic would endear Him to some of the men, He was so dear to them in this incarnation.)

The lieutenant opened the driver's side door and sat sidesaddle. Ray stood back and hitched up his loose pants. His hair stood in a ridge as if even his skull had gotten skinny.

It's so simple, you people, said the lieutenant, looking out at them. At your Level. He too wore baggy pants, and a small sweater. His hair swerved around his bald spot.

Daniel saw him glance quickly toward the chicken coop, but he made no mention of it. Ray had worked till ten o'clock some evenings, Cleary holding a flashlight. His parents were susceptible, hopeful, loose, watery.

They left before dawn to sit in the zendo. Daniel felt timid at first about getting his own breakfast. Getting his sister's. Ray went directly from the zendo to his Service. Cleary came home, at once flushed and lightheaded, and washed their bowls out.

Ray expressed wonder that there was no embarrassment meeting the Guru face to face. Not like with a palm reader, he said, the way you were afraid to catch her eye and see her disdain for you for falling for her in the first place. Phew, said Ray, eyeing Cleary. Anyway, this Guy doesn't give a hoot about your fortune, or your future. Here is a Guy who really lives in the moment. Here is a Guy who blows His breath straight into your breath so your two stinking breaths mingle. Here is a Living God, said Ray, swollen with admiration, not just a long story.

Ray ordered the kind of textbooks and workbooks for children who were ill or at sea, he said, and if he wasn't mistaken they could do two grades in one year. No little Canadians slowing you down, eh Dan? No educational industrial complex?

Two grades! What would he tell his friends?

After that could they head back to Halifax?

You're acting like a baby, said Cleary. She never said that to Violet. He was almost too old for baby teeth. Violet was seven— tall and weedy like Ray, with cool blond hair whose individual strands Daniel had recently discovered were translucent. She would have still been expecting visits from some fly-by-night, as Ray said, operation.

But wasn't the Guru something like the tooth fairy? If you wanted Him to be a real guru, you had to believe in Him. You had to love Him, thought Daniel. His existence depended on belief and adoration.

Two grades, said Daniel, pushing his luck, but then what? He couldn't stand lentil sprouts and shredded carrots with tamari, turds of dried fruit. The fresh, raw milk tasted like skin. Kai had warned that the Sanctuary wasn't always on dairy.

And then what? Ah, Ray smiled, answering himself, though he was pledged against rhetoric: And then your spiritual education.

What about the milk? Daniel persisted dangerously.

A devotee wore an old-fashioned farm yoke hung with two buckets. He hauled the milk to the bay in a hundred daily trips. He poured the milk in salt water, which had no effect whatsoever on the ocean.

Milky sea, Sea of Blankets. Ozera was lake in Russian, and Kitezh was the village of master artists that sunk itself to the bottom of the lake of the ocean, leaving only its outline in foam on the placid surface.

He woke when Ray crept up to his bedside and sat down, pulling the blanket so tight that his arms were crutched to his sides. He knew Ray didn't mean to.

Hey Daniel?

He tried to free his arms and betrayed himself.

You know we're in the company of indisputable power. He's really something. I don't know how much you pick up on—

He wished he weren't on his back, a mummy.

When we resist, or when we do our egos—think of a wave trying to go against the ocean. Good luck to you, wave, Ray said, rueful.

Daniel said nothing. Still his dad sat there, thinking.

He was in the shallows of sleep when Ray pushed off—he heard the door in the distance, and then he was free, floating.

CHAPTER 3

IT TURNED OUT that Penny was a real favorite. She had her own cabin in Kishkindha: Rika, which was river. Ray peeked in a window and reported back that it was a jewel box. There were waxy yellow leaves on some of the less-favored maples in September.

Penny had suggested to Cleary that they increase their tithe while the Canadian dollar was strong, and Daniel overheard Ray laugh incredulously when Cleary told him.

What's tithe? asked Daniel, and Ray whinnied, tithe was their lack of transportation.

Craig R., the poet, paid them a visit. He said if they had their gas turned off they could tithe the money they saved on utilities. He said several other families were doing this. The kitchen smelled like gas, strangely. Craig R.—they would learn there were no other Craigs on the Sanctuary yet "R" was the insight of the Guru—stood staring at Ray and Cleary, holding court in the kitchen. The lieutenant slipped in, and Craig R. said showily, The Guru's not going to let you come all the way from O, Canada just to sit on your asses, yeah people?

Daniel saw him burrow in his redfox beard to find the nubby pink scar in the middle.

Cleary was straight as a flame. When the phone rang now, she wouldn't answer, as if it would make her more mortal. Less inner life, less Guru.

The lieutenant backed his elbows onto their kitchen counter. His hair was thin and charcoal, Daniel noticed, without really having any gray in it. His ears were very neat, well organized. He wasn't really listening.

Gratitude, said Cleary. Such gratitude for this visit.

It sounded like a Christmas carol. That was the old language.

There's no problem with telephones, the lieutenant said coldly. There's no renunciation-in-His-name here, Cleary.

She looked stricken. Should he go to her? Not in the lieutenant's presence. The Guru is East-West, said the lieutenant. He's Mystic-Musician-Saint-Farmer.

Dad Ray was nodding as if he were primed for any wonder.

Listen, said Craig R., changing keys suddenly. Violet's invited on the Sanctuary.

What? Ray was already laughing in disbelief, jogging in place, overgrinning, chewing up his own scenery.

The lieutenant was trying to weave a loose thread back into his sweater.

Daniel looked at his sister. Her mouth turned down when she was shy. Being tall for her age had never endeared her to the type of grownups who "understood" children.

Ray: Do we send her with you? His laughter couldn't find a natural ending.

Jesus, Ray, said the lieutenant, pushing off the counter.

Craig R. said, You're really stimulated.

The black-haired girl from the Concert Barn was Noa, and it was she who had invited Violet. Her mother was Kai, and her father was a Japanese roshi who lived in Kyoto, where the clouds swept up from two sides of the sky to make a cloud pagoda.

No wonder Noa looked like a little Buddha from the fifth century, said Ray later, planted in the raked gravel garden by the zendo. A half God, Ray whispered.

The wind was almost wintry, and papery leaves skittered and circled inside the farmyard. Daniel followed at a distance: Violet looked strange walking alone, as if the whole rest of the planet were sleeping. But the sun shone brightly, even brighter on the Sanctuary, and soon he felt its warmth in his core instead of outside him.

In a Children's Talk on cassette tape the Guru had predicted and described this sensation: sat-chit-ananda, and now Daniel understood it. Happiness Spreading, as far as the inner eye could see, leveling like water. When he closed his eyes he saw light—black light, holographic schisms, Ray called them. Surrender to your cones and rods. Ray had tried to explain optics.

He heard the screech of the saws from the woodshop.

Up ahead, Violet paused uncertainly. A peacock brushed her like a walking bush. Daniel thought the bird took pains to pretend it didn't notice her.

It has its third eye on its tail, remarked the Roshi's daughter. Where had she come from? As if to mock the bird, Noa was fanning herself with a spray of peacock feathers.

They took off their shoes behind Noa in the farmhouse entry. The half mortal called it the narthex. She just had a regular voice, a little bit slangy. Violet placed her shoes neatly and inconspicuously beside Noa's zoris, even though they looked like thongs you could pick up at any supermarket in Canada. It was dark in the narthex, and it smelled meaty, like feet. Was there something cooing in the corner?

Noa pointed a broom at a lumpy gray bird that might have been laying. The bird was not intimidated. It blinked repetitively, mechanically, without feeling.

That's a lyrebird, she said when she'd pried it out of its corner. He hatched it.

Incense hung as heavy as pollen. Violet dropped to her knees, then her belly, at the threshold of the Guru's Own meditation room. Devotees called it the presbytery.

I call it the throne room, Noa informed them.

There was His altar. It gave Daniel a lump in his throat. He felt the pressure building, not sadness but capitulation. He watched his sister sink down and rest her forehead on the dull pine floorboards. A full prostration was three breath cycles. When you rose up your blood felt solid, your eyes were starbursts, and when you could see again, you had a headache.

Don't stay down so long, Noa chided.

As Noa backed away from the altar, she scooped up a fancy cellophane package.

Outside once more, they stopped beneath a tall, sparse pine tree, more like a flagpole than an evergreen. It had bare spikes for branches, a crest of dark green at the very top like one of the top hat roosters that jerked chestily around the farmyard.

Here's where His parrot Gautama proved it had nine lives, said Noa. Even though it's only cats that are supposed to. Have you ever seen parrots climb? They use their teeth. Noa bared hers to show them.

Nine times, she insisted. She reached her arms out. His wings didn't open. Her eyes were on Violet.

She uncrinkled the package. Four bulby chocolates. She placed three of the candies between the big root-veins at the base of the pine tree. She gave the fourth one to Violet.

There's a chance I'm a lama, she said. Reincarnated.

Violet nodded. Lamas have to die, too, said Noa.

In Tibet or Mongolia. In Colorado or California. There was a saint—Daniel had noticed Ray and Cleary said sri now, which sounded less Western—who wandered around India pulling confections from the atmosphere. Ray had been to Goa, tasted the candy, but that didn't make him a roshi. In India, candy was called milk sweets. Ray had seen old men with jackal haunches in India, squatting to shit on the beaches. He had eaten off banana leaves, swallowed fire, taken snuff in the front seat of a Taj Mahal tour bus with the red-eyed driver, red-toothed, he had explained to Daniel, from betel. He had bowed to long-horned cows and bicycle rickshaws garlanded with rotting jasmine. One frigid purple morning he had hiked above Darjeeling to see the white plaster mountainhead of Kanchenjunga.

Noa paraded them back to the farmhouse. Kai bowed very slightly to her daughter when the three of them passed her. She walked like a skeleton, her hips and knees wobbled in their ball-and-sockets. Her small head in a crocheted skullcap looked like a beanbag.

They followed Noa up the stairs to the bedroom she and Kai shared along a pitching hallway. Outside the door sat Monju Bosatsu, guardian of wisdom. There was another gargoyle like that at the zendo's entrance. The little room had low, slanted ceilings. The dormer window faced the curve in the road, where cars were forced to slow whether or not they were curious about Buddhists.

There was a cardboard box under a heat lamp in the corner, and Daniel wandered over. Don't breathe on them, said Noa. A guinea chick, she pointed, a really rare duckthing, a crane with purplish eyelids, fragile as a bubble of blood. She leaned down into the sweet-smelling wood shavings. He cuts their wings with fingernail scissors. He alone can hatch them in any season.

She pressed the pad of her longest finger on each bird's head in turn, and each baby bird squeezed down and then rose back up again. She pinched the tiny, soft crane out of the box and palmed it underneath the heat lamp. Her breathing was gusty and rapid.

Daniel could smell something fatty, like French fries, beneath the smell of wood shavings. He took a few steps backward. Outside the glowing circle of the heat lamp, the bedroom was suddenly freezing.

Then there was another smell, faint at first, like burning hair. Bird skin as delicate as the flying-dust on a butterfly. Noa swooped the crane chick around and around the bedroom. Finally she landed it on the stormily unmade futon.

The sun was a spike through the dormer window. The crane vibrated with a force that could not have come from its own scrap, and Noa stood back triumphantly, eyes flashing, That's the Life Force.

He couldn't take his eyes off the bird. Had Noa had put a spell on him? Needles in his palms. Was this his own Life Force? Then with no notice, Violet was flying across the room, and before he could think he bolted after her.

He caught her skiing down the back stairs, and he nearly slipped in his socks behind her. They were both forced to stop short at the bottom before the screened porch, where sanghists were gathered in heavy sweaters and blankets, hands wrapping stoneware, discussing a parable or a precept. It was forbidden to discuss koans. They couldn't just cross the porch and disturb the grownups. Daniel watched his sister check her pocket. The chocolate stolen from the Guru's altar. It was fudge now, and it would make a brown stain as if she'd had an accident. She gathered her breath and made a dash for the farmyard.

He jumped slicks of bird poop, mud puddles with floating feathers, behind her. If you looked up, you would get tinsel in your eyes. The Teachings said the whole world was a tapestry woven in thread that could fit through the eye of an atom. He could believe it. Violet glanced back once and then slipped into Kishkindha, the hemlock forest.

He was wary of the paths—he'd been reprimanded harshly for marring the groomed gravel. It had been raised in Children's Talk that there was a real lack of attention, and Craig R. had instructed them to put their hands on the smalls of their backs—their smalls—and bring the bright there: he put his own hands on his chronic sore spot to show them.

Daniel skirted behind boulders and hemlocks now, pausing every few seconds to listen. Then the path came into view, and there stood the Guru, as big as God, opposite his sister. The Living One, the Live Wire, the Lamb, the Lion, tearing the lively meat, full of the knowledge of human suffering. He must have been coming from the zendo.

His nose, thought Daniel, was the same purple as the crane's eyelids. But even His shock of hoary hair was enlightened. Light shone through His gray eyes when He locked your gaze—Daniel had heard Cleary—drew your stuff to the surface. Violet managed to bow before she crumpled. Her knees would be wet, the earth smelled tonic, like sap, and water. The Guru rose above her. Her back would be getting warmer and warmer, as if under a heat lamp. There was the sense that in His presence you would cave inside, devotees said you would atomize.

He demanded love, that's what Ray said. Not that He could read their minds, but He must have been able to read the universe with its sudden absence of a hatchling crane, the mauve pinfeathers would have come in a week later. What would He do? He would shout in someone's face, Karma, dharma, farm-a! Nonsense, per-fect sense. Someone asked Him about dogma and He said, Cat-ma! God's leetle pet name, eh people? Are you God's leetle pets, people?

His Russian accent. There was nothing benevolent about Him. He smelled like sandalwood, but also the briny woodsmoke from the faulty stove in the zendo. Smash the hall of mirrors. Torch the theater. He would kick the wandering fowl when He was cross—

that same lyrebird crouching in the narthex had performed on mounded earth behind the silver fan of its own tail feathers until the Guru, in a rage, charged it, all flushed neck and shoulders.

But Daniel could see now that He was beaming down upon Violet. A smile of such brilliance, such overwhelming love, that you would forget your fear as you were transported to the shores of light that were the inside of the Guru's great cranium. It was on cassette tape. You were, at once, resting, and very, very active. You could feel yourself shiver as you basked in the source of all happiness. The Guru said time was a prism. Prison! Devotees understood He was greater than time, and they understood greatness.

The Guru began poking Violet in the soft spots of her ribcage. Daniel saw her stiffen. He could tell it didn't tickle. The Guru was wiggling His toes around her barrel. He slipped one foot out of His zori. A small foot for such a big man. When He got old, very old—did a Guru?—He would totter.

The earth smelled like an old porcupine. From the cassette tape: All you have to do is open, dear ones! All you have to do is receive Me, people!

The Guru's love was real. Wood. Spit. Skin, muscle. His love called forth their love, had they ever loved before this? A million pale maggots that could turn a fallen tree trunk into jelly. Love turned death to jelly. The Guru flexed His toes and grunted as He shoved her.

She was love and she was spirit. Did He want to roll her over?

Then He kicked hard, with the blunt head of His heel, as if He were suddenly impatient. He wouldn't break His short toes on her.

Daniel's entire body tingled, and the oatmeal of wet dirt was dense in his passages. He felt spacious, his blood was sloshing. He couldn't control the urge to start shaking.

The Guru pressed His foot between Violet's ribs, and she began to vibrate.

He must have felt her shaking travel up His leg bone.

She wouldn't have been able to see anything.

Facedown, the length of a full prostration, she was long for a girl, where were her pinfeathers? The Guru was Shiva, was all the names of gods that sound like babble. He was the Only True Embodiment of Power, He had said it. Power attracts you people. So I have to make Myself attractive.

The Guru's phenomenally attractive leg was shaking and kicking. He jiggered with kundalini. Violet was the demon nest of roots, the Guru could split her like a log if He wanted.

And Daniel?

He could have jumped screeching onto the wide shelf of the Guru's shoulders. He could have sunk his teeth in.

He was about to, when the Guru saw him. The Guru winked and headed off into His forest.

CHAPTER 4

THEY GATHERED in the Concert Barn, and it was only after they were all sitting, quiet, that He revealed Himself at the back of the hall in the shadows where, it was whispered, He had been meditating on them for hours.

He moved through the crowd. He wore a blue silk lungi and an undershirt: great heat was His prerogative. He touched their scalps and He paused behind this one or that one to rest His knees against the absurdity—as Dad Ray was now saying constantly—of shoulder blades.

He settled Himself on the piano bench before them but—they had been forewarned—this would be a dry darshan, no music.

You know Milarepa, people?

There were murmurs of *Ah*. They knew Him like a lover.

Capable Father Repa,
and the blocks of stone, people?
Are your hearts blocked, people?
As the Jesus-den?
Well, listen.
This is no common song,
no ordeal of resurrection, people.

Milarepa sought out Marpa.
Old Marpa received him: You think you want my Teachings?
Teach me, venerable Marpa! cried Milarepa the murderer.

To you I dedicate all accomplishments!
So build me a big house of stone, said Marpa,
and you can have my Teachings.

Milarepa dug stones from the ground
and carried them on his back.
What a house!
Nine levels!
Finally he was finished.

Now Venerable Marpa said, I must have been drunk
when I told you. Put those stones back
where you found them, idiot.
You want to leave big holes
all over my property?

So the teacher trumps the student.
Milarepa toiled—
he built and demolished one hundred stone houses,
do you hear Me, people?

There were whimpers and small moans, ladies with the tendency to utterance.

Will you go back to your temple-
building tomorrow, dear ones?
Have you listened in the least?
Form and void,
over and over.
You lazy Westerners
with your tractors and your powersaw,
with your King Ivanovich,
easy as a whore,
telling you all His secrets.

Well I am the Self-Buddha, people,
I arise spontaneously.
I turn the holes you make on My Sanctuary
into one hundred holy grottos.

Daniel was back in the woods, Kishkindha. He closed his eyes, he couldn't help it—the Guru towered over Violet. Was this what He was up to?

. . .

In the spring the Guru led Walking Meditation again and Cleary was asked; word came, subtle word, that He was curious about Cleary. The local woods were like broken ladders, thought Daniel, but Kishkindha was known to shimmer with self-consciousness, each leaf and needle waiting to be framed by a human eye, full of the knowledge it was an ongoing exhibit.

The Guru stopped to show Cleary a stiff owl of a pinecone, the swath of a dark green bough, like eyelashes, blue sky clipped out behind it.

He turned eleven and he began to figure they were staying, and it seemed like another life, the morning they'd left Halifax, a coarse-grained fog, clouds that smelled like seawater. The spirit of the age, he remembered Ray spouting, to take a whole week driving down the coast—but maybe, Daniel thought now, Ray had sensed they would lose the station wagon to the Guru when they got there.

Tithe was the new language. The Guru consumed everything.

He stood watching Ray take apart an old mower stood up on its end in a circle of greasy parts, wrenches that looked like puppets.

Ray dropped to the ground, caught himself kneeling. His laugh sounded hollow. I can't do this on Kalma, he said, to no one, or Daniel. I'm lightheaded like a lady. He let himself over and out on his back. As quietly as he could, Daniel sat down beside him.

Kalma, the raw diet. A spring fast, said the lieutenant, before a hedon summer. There was Divine Silence before a Period of garrulity. He could be so generous, the lieutenant continued. He could speak so freely in poemform, His love was entirely free, His Teachings were wild.

Ray put his hands under head, which made him look less deathbed, thought Daniel. You finished your schoolwork already?

Daniel nodded, cleared his throat: I'm in Grade 8 now. They both laughed. There was talk about building a school on the Sanctuary. Ray MacFarland had proved himself a carpenter. But Daniel had adjusted easily to the homeschool curriculum. Ray praised him when he put aside his own work to help Violet. Hers was like coloring books, Daniel had said once, as if he and Ray were in this together.

No one cares if Noa has school, said Daniel now. It was a problem, she was always distracting Violet.

Ray looked startled. Then he was up on his elbows, unstoppable, brimming with explanation, Who needs school!

That was the old language! And by the way, happiness was no longer bound to the material! Their mailbox, bashed in overnight by worldly neighbors—Ray gave a good squint, a baseball swing—sure, but how about those silly gifts they had received as a matter of course on birthdays and Christmases, those toy recorders and tin robots? Chimeras of desire! Desire was just another manifestation of emptiness.

Shake out the gauzy sleeve of false happiness! Walk away from your own garbage! In Halifax, where they were opponents of themselves, worldly people, they had a toaster on the kitchen counter. Now they had an altar. There was a mandala of acorns and curled petals, a postcard of Japanese brushstrokes like stick fences. Ray sat up and bowed to the caps and purples. To the horsehair calligraphy.

He bowed to Daniel. He started up again: Worldly people were sluggish and guilty! They shouted at their children! They buried happiness in pleasure. Raccoons easily raked apart their plastic bags of garbage.

Worldly neighbors did not know the zafu like a little fist or the taste of dates rolled in coconut. They did not know that what they had was false and what devotees had wasn't. Followers of big dairy, they were all cheese and butter. They were all wheat and sugar. They did not know rice or umeboshi. They shouted at each other over the noise of TV and radio.

Ray stopped to catch his breath.

He was gleaming, overcome, he'd moved himself, thought Daniel.

Worldly neighbors hated starving Buddhists. Shy-of-life Buddhists.

In the bay air it wouldn't even take a season for rust to edge the new crater of the mailbox.

· · ·

The Third Wife, Zoya, let China and Meenakshi loose, and they trailed Daniel in Kishkindha until they grew bored and began throwing pea gravel at him. It didn't hurt. All the Sanctuary Children were younger than he was.

Tamsen, the Fourth, the former Catholic, formalized Children's Service. She swam in the bay like a knife: he'd seen her stumble out, exhausted, shedding bay water. Her small breasts were round and hard as her biceps. Maybe she was athletic, but she found it painful to sit in full lotus and asked the Guru's permission to kneel. He laughed lustily, and Tamsen scuttled backward.

Why can't you laugh with Me? said the Guru, and His gargoyle turned cranberry.

Ray said Tamsen had an advanced degree in religious studies. All in Leela. She had been in a mission and saved runaways. Now she was saving herself, joked the Guru. She lurched off, furious. How could she save herself if she was supposed to eradicate herself? Erase the self to achieve satori.

When she came back He grinned broadly and broke down her Practice: show the children all the Walt Disney classics. A rooster posted as if it were on a carousel pole behind them. Mirror, mirror, on the wall, the Guru goaded Tamsen.

Daniel lugged a fertilizer of kitchen scraps and farm manure in a wheelbarrow, the stink of the earth was Children's Practice. He dumped the compost around Kishkindhan hemlocks, tamped it with his feet, and finally, with his fingers, massaged the muck into the loamy soil. Noa and Violet moved anthills with teaspoons, picked leaves and duff out of moss beds, snapped individual twigs that the Guru had specified via Tamsen. Sometimes Noa played pied piper, pack leader of the Sanctuary Children, but mostly she and Violet were twinned up, stuck together.

The forest paths converged, and a stylized curve of dun and silver pebbles gave way to a sudden view of the zendo, set in raked white sand, floating on foam, cloud, smoke from a dragon.

Bow to the zendo, bow to the humanoid gong at the zendo's entrance. The jikki jitsu struck the gong with the side of his thin, bare hand where the hand bulged with a corn-yellow callus. He pushed out his white lips like a blowfish when he sat meditation. He pissed outside Sava, his cabin, rather than hike to the outhouse. He didn't use his fly and his buttocks were just like his lips, white and swollen. Interminate graduate student Arthur, said Ray in the wondering voice, the voice that deemed it all remarkable; the Guru was Arthur's new institute.

He saw Noa and Violet standing together on a stump to peek through the porthole of the cabin's single window. Noa and Violet: Craig R. called them No Violence. He was, after all, a poet.

Then he heard the girls begin to trill, *The jikki never sleeps, the jikki never sleeps, hi-ho the dairy-o* . . . until they lost their voices to laughter. Swishing monk's robes, Arthur in costume. Violet fell off the stump and stamped her feet to the song in the soft needles. Had they ever managed to scare Arthur out of his cabin?

He wandered down to the bay when he'd finished his Service. The water looked dented in places around rocks, and out in the middle it was as hard as pottery. Half a mile up the beach was a turnout above a cove where worldly neighbors parked to watch the sunset. Old lilacs ringed it. He started out along the wet gravel like chainmail, his ears ringing. There was a weak place inside him like another belly.

When he reached the cove he made himself climb the punky cliff to the overlook. His sweater snapped a branch of lilac. His heart laddered up, but there were no worldly cars parked or idling. No baseball bats rolling back and forth on the floor of the passenger seat. (Every time Ray fixed the mailbox back to its pole or tried to beat it back into shape, those damn yokel vandals came by for a repeat performance. The year of the mailbox. Daniel was twelve now.)

It had been formalized that to counteract fear he should begin chanting.

I was a hidden treasure
(I was a hidden treasure)
I loved to be known, so
(I loved to be known, so)

I created the world
(I created the world)

But when he closed his eyes he could see devotees in covenant, faces boneless with happiness, lips like fat gills all opening and closing together. Genitals on the gravelly sand. He quit chanting. Suddenly the lotus was sickening.

A truck scooped into the lot behind him. The radio trailed the engine. The doors clapped shut—when the Beautiful Wives clapped, their elbows made devotional curves like jug handles. He understood that his fear had materialized worldly neighbors. That fear was perverse did not surprise him.

Remember that fear is the excessive reality of worldly life, said the Guru. Fear is the false hope of death, people!

He watched worldly neighbors stroll to the edge of the turnout. A few rocks were nudged loose, and they took lumps of sea cliff with them. He held his breath and made his squint a skipping stone across the water. That fear was worse when you succumbed to it did not surprise him, suddenly. Children were charged with overcoming fear, children were told this constantly. His heart was in his temples. As if fear were the definition of childhood.

He felt his fear could walk on water. It could turn one thing into another. It started at the base of his spine and it gripped the back of his neck and shoulders, spasming like kundalini. He closed his eyes and tried to imagine himself lighter and lighter, lighter than fear itself, which could walk on water.

Still, his stomach felt translucent. He could almost see the blurry bags and tubes, and his palms smelled sour.

He caught a whiff of cigarette smoke. He opened his eyes and saw worldly neighbors lighting up, leaning on each other, laughing.

Was it possible they hadn't seen him?

The wind was lively, changeable, and it carried tails of their banter.

The Guru was the enemy of formulaic banter.

Of inanity and shittiness!

If he became the rock at his back, worldly neighbors wouldn't see him. If they didn't see him he wouldn't be caught out holding fear to his chest like a baby. He was a baby, and fear was a naked, shitting baby.

He pulled up short. All the old daydreaming about going back to Canada—he still held onto it. But how could he go back now that he was afraid of worldly people?

The wind changed again, the bay smelled iron and clammy.

Perhaps there was a solution. Death would make him invisible to worldly neighbors.

Not dying, but not being afraid of it.

Why was he afraid of it?

That was from a Children's Talk on cassette tape.

He tried saying it under his breath. Afraid of death? Maybe he wasn't. He was his own call and his own response. For a moment he was persuaded. For a second, enlightened.

He crossed up the lawn to the farmhouse and there was Dovorh, Fifth Beautiful, gliding out to meet him. When she smiled she looked sad, and it made him sad: her deep-set, spilling eyes, like sunlight through rain, said Cleary. Like all the wives she wore a white Punjabi tunic, leggings tacked in at the ankles. Leather sandals, sandalwood mala, bright red tassel. She had a forest of dark, crimpy hair, and a very light body. Once, during Dark Breakfast, midnight fruit and tahini, she had made space for him on the lawn beside her. She'd put her airy arm around him when he got tired, which made him shy and happy.

As she came closer he saw that her green eyes were laughing, darting nervously, and he remembered Ray saying, Why does she always look guilty?

And Cleary, Please don't comment on the Beautifuls.

Now she ushered him hastily toward the summer kitchen where Sita, the Second, stood impatiently on the doorstep, the diaphanous screened porch behind her. The Guru called Sita a peasant, with her large brown feet, broad cheeks, hard eyes. The Guru said she was the one with the Spanish hair, He caricatured all of them, He was forever playing Disney. Sita opened the door for them without speaking, but she, too seemed excited.

Daniel followed them inside and then ducked back out and hid his shoes behind a bush. They were five times their normal weight, sneaker sponges. The stench of the bay was in his hair too, and in his snaggy sweater. It didn't surprise him that fear had a smell. He balled his damp socks in his waistband.

There was a pyre of flowers. It was really joyful Service. The petals should be separated from the stalks; later Sita would burn them to make an ash as fine as silk. She reached over and plucked a leaf out of Daniel's pile. It's important to have a lot of beauty around the Guru, said Sita severely. Rich food and flowers can lead to ego-tripping, but He simply was not a monk in this incarnation.

His favorite flower was calla lily:

the crimson rod
still fleeced with pollen.

Now they worked in silence, but Daniel felt the wives were jittery, and they seemed to be eyeing him more than usual. He wished Sita had let him stand beside Dovorh. She was all alone on the opposite side of the table, smiling through her tears, flickering like a candle.

He watched a housefly drive up the wall. It looked like it had been rolled in sugar. Another one, its engine all revved up, beat itself against the window.

Dovorh dropped the shears by accident and Sita startled. Dovorh! Why can't you pay attention?

Sita was such a hardline. Daniel had heard Ray and Cleary say it. Sita's big bones were eardrums. She never looked at anyone but Him if she could help it.

He'd heard Ray speculate boldly on which wife was the Guru's favorite and Cleary shush him. Zoya, the Third, was doing the yogurt. It was incubated on rough shelves against the south windows.

China and Meenakshi dashed through the kitchen. Identical heads of parched blond hair and the same tiny pink noses. The Guru had chosen Craig R. for Zoya. The girls came racing back in again. Daniel saw that Meenakshi, the younger one, was trying to keep a cat in her arms. The cat yowled and Sita exploded, You are so unconscious of your unexamined instincts, Zoya! Your whole strenuous motherly!

Zoya drained back. The girls had already vanished.

That kind of love is all polarities! cried Sita. Fluctuation and disappointment!

He didn't like being in the middle of the ladies. Sita's outburst seemed out of proportion.

Dovorh bowed even lower over the irises she was trimming.

As if she could no longer contain herself, Sita announced, Put your flowers to the side, Daniel.

Now Dovorh and Zoya were lightning rods of attention.

Today is a very important day for you, said Sita.

Dovorh hurried over to help him cover the floating petals with a damp towel, sweep off the surface.

You're to come with us now, said Sita briskly, and they led him outside, across the farmyard.

Birds do-si-doed like folk dancers.

I can walk home by myself, he said, behind them, when they started up the road. Dovorh turned and reached for him—her fingertips pecked the air—and he gave her his hand even though he was too old for it.

The lieutenant was already there, and they hung back and watched while he slipped out of his zoris as if he were Kyoto-trained, and the Guru had said that these were the days of sockfeet as soft as dogs' testicles. Instinctively Daniel put his hands there to protect himself.

The lieutenant nodded stiffly at Sita, and Dovorh dropped his hand. For a moment he felt naked.

The silence was self-conscious. Who was supposed to say something? Then the lieutenant nudged him through the door, and there were his parents waiting in the kitchen, practically trembling with expectation.

Gratitude for this visit, murmured Cleary.

I'd like to sit with Daniel, said the lieutenant.

Extraordinary gratitude, said Cleary.

He followed the lieutenant into the meditation room. Heavy drapes tamped down not only light but all the senses. The tar-colored floor took footprints. The altar was laid with censors, salt, oil, dates, an Indian brass bell, and the murti.

Some people said that meditation was a dark cocoon inside of which you were pelvic floor and sits bones and knee knuckles. Some people got worked up about it. Some had problems with twitchy legs, others made lists of chores. Others experienced emotions rising like therapy. Still others went to sleep: once when a lady hit the deck, Daniel saw the jikki bundle her out of the zendo.

When Daniel sat now, he imagined his head as big as a hot air balloon. His little body was the dangling basket. The walls of the world were cloth and orange light shone through them. It was difficult to relax with the lieutenant. He tried holding his breath for as long as he could—then breathing seemed miraculous. He attempted to move his littlest toe independent of the others. The little toe was not independent. The little toe had nothing and everything to do with enlightenment.

Finally he felt the lieutenant's hand on his shoulder and his eyes popped open in the votive darkness. The lieutenant leaned forward and dipped a finger in the blue bowl of water at the altar.

He wetted Daniel's forehead and Daniel understood it was anointment.

He rang the brass bell and in that moment, Daniel knew he had been chosen.

He knew that he was known, now, and that he was as guilty of self as anyone.

Praise, said the lieutenant. The lieutenant's other hand was on his small, pushing firmly. Head to heartwood. A full prostration.

When he came up again, the lieutenant had drawn one knee up to his chest in the favorite asana of the Guru. The lieutenant had big showy eyes that glistened with devotion. Now Daniel saw them as moons during an eclipse, shadowed by the earth's bulk, eternally confused by the earth's oceans.

It has come through me that He has changed your name, said the lieutenant. You know He does this from time to time with great insight.

The oceans tumbled. Where you were Daniel before you will now be known as Jubal, said the lieutenant.

His finger was a wand. He does this with much love, Jubal. The lieutenant paused as if to gather all his forces in his gaze.

He does this knowing you may ask yourself, who is Jubal?

It's a funny question.

If only the lieutenant would stop staring.

But then he shook off his reverie, laughing freely as he rose, Let's go spread the news to Ray and Cleary, he said, as he guided Jubal back to the kitchen.

What does Jubal mean? said Cleary. She came into focus. She couldn't help but smile. Ray lifted up a horn and saluted the lieutenant. Cleary's smile was as long as a river. She joined with the sea. She pulled them under.

What does Jubal mean, repeated the lieutenant drily.

Ray stood with his trumpet in the air, ridiculous, waiting. Jubilation?

The lieutenant coughed. Ray lowered the imaginary instrument.

The lieutenant said painstakingly, How can we know the meaning of anyone? More love for your son, Ray. Less psycho-social bondage.

Ray bowed an apology.

Your son is in the midst of a birthday. You should know this.

The Guru talked about witnessing His Own birth—He had. He had seen His mother's terrible face and the false God of the doctor. He had laughed at His Own red body. He had laughed at the beginning of the end. Now Daniel opened his throat to laughter. What else could he do? He stretched his top bones away from his bottom. Daniel was the name his parents gave him when he was almost nothing more than a dried apple, soaked in blood, when he was a star dented with ribs and kneecaps, serene and cold and unyielding to the breast (and so he was bottle-fed), when he was completely innocent of all belief, an alien. Here was a Being—for He was only incidentally "Guru"—who could wring out the old names and hear the ring of the new. Here was a Being who could take you back to the moment of your birth; and take you.

Daniel MacFarland. Died at the hand of the lieutenant and reborn: Jubal.

CHAPTER 5

EVERYONE WAS CALLING him Jubal. Everyone was taking the opportunity to speak to him, to say his new name that was the name of the Guru. He had the strange, disembodied sense— disembodied was a word in heavy rotation—that he, too, wanted to call the name Jubal—and for a long time he had difficulty answering.

He tried on his fear, he checked it. Was he still afraid of death as Jubal?

He looked in the mirror. His sister popped up behind him—he had left the bathroom door open. Even so, she should have knocked, but then again, conventions were worldly. Privacy was worldly. Handshakes and handlebar mustaches! cried the Guru. But if you weren't supposed to knock, wasn't that the same as supposed to?

What are you doing, Jubal?

Who?

Don't be egoic. She mouthed the words in the mirror. He had the feeling that if he turned around there would be no one there, no Violet.

Once again, the lieutenant held court in their kitchen. His feet were bale, pare, clawlike. As usual, he draped himself against the counter, elbows like clothespins.

Cleary, all in white, stood in her own acre of sun and her dark hair, overexposed in the light, looked silver. Such gratitude, she said softly.

Ray said, Any word on the wagon?

The lieutenant looked surprised, then affronted. I'm not here to talk mechanics.

Ray pulled an ear. Jubal knew he was bothered, embarrassed that he hadn't been able to fix their old station wagon himself, that he'd had to drop it off in town. That he was expected to pay for it.

I'm here to remind you that we're entering a Period of Leelas, said the lieutenant. Not for the first or the last time. His mouth curved.

Ray and Cleary with their lips parted—Jubal hated seeing his parents look so helpless.

The Guru is asking for you, Jubal, said the lieutenant. He let it hang. He has singled you out, you know, he finished, looking Jubal over.

Jubal went hot, cold. When he looked for his parents—weren't they going to say something?—they were just a couple of helter-skelter heartbeats in the distance.

The lieutenant was already out the door. Jubal shoved into his shoes and ran to catch up with him.

They stood on the threshold of the presbytery and the Guru held out His arms to them. From across the room, the huge beloved face beamed upon them.

The lieutenant pushed him forward and he was going.

The Guru's arms seemed to open and open, wider and wider, and Jubal felt himself sucked through space, realms and realms to get there.

When he arrived at last, he was totally disoriented. Where was light, dark, land, water? But then the Guru reached down and gathered him from the shore, and when he opened his eyes-within-his eyes, he found himself pressed against God.

How long had he already, always been there?

Years passed.

Suddenly the Guru's whisper was hot in Jubal's ear:

You are all living together
in the skull-shell of the Guru.
You are echoes of each other,
and yet it is too crowded to really echo.
I can hear everything, Jubal,
and I will listen to all you have to tell Me.

He was aware of his shoulders: the Guru was gripping him. Then he and the Guru were face to face, and he knew absolutely that the Guru could see everything, not just the weird tentacles behind his eyes and his worm-tunnel brain—

This is what I see in you, said the Guru, seeing all. Indeed, I have always seen it.

It was as if the Guru were speaking inside him—Leader of My flock, He said. My bellwether.

Let Me put the crystal ball around your neck so that I can always hear you, as you hear My devotees' hearts and voices.

Did He mean bell?

Jubal! said the Guru. If you feel disembodied now, it is just another feeling for love!

He heard the lieutenant clear his throat.

Are you dess, Jubal?

Deaf and death were the same in His Russian accent.

The Guru's voice rang the room, the room was a bell. Listen to My bell-boy! A report from My wether!

He felt the lieutenant's hand on his small.

Let's meditate, said the lieutenant.

Jubal closed his eyes. There was the throat, the heart, the navel. The elf-breath, the trickster, the triangle—he tried to remain calm. A new name and a new purpose.

What was a bell-boy?

Jubal opened his mouth but there was no sound. No ringing.

The lieutenant paused in the middle of the farmyard with an examining stare.

What is it?

Nothing! said Jubal.

Do you understand?

Nothing.

It's nothing, or you understand nothing?

Don't be coy, said the lieutenant when he failed to answer.

I don't understand, Jubal said finally.

That's more like it, sighed the lieutenant. Try this. You're a maiden at Delphi. He smirked. An oracle from the people to their King.

Sighed again, but he was already getting excited.

Spittle gathered in his corners.

Look at me when I'm talking.

Jubal flushed.

I'm trying to tell you that He has chosen you as His Own confessor. There is Eastern precedent. The sangha's confessor. Do you know what He means by that, Jubal?

Jubal stood silent.

Your Service now to listen to all Leelas. Not to make any sense of them, it doesn't matter, at your Level.

Devotees don't make sense anyway. But to bring Leelas back to Him.

The lieutenant paused. A lot of story lines, Jubal.

Lifelines getting tangled. He shook his head, he'd impressed himself.

Pigeons were edging closer without looking at their targets. A leaf with no legs—

But take a load off, said the lieutenant finally. You don't even really have to listen. We're going to set you up with a state-of-the-art tape recorder.

. . .

Praise to you, you know, Jubal, said Kai. You must have done something very much in keeping with Him when you walked the earth previously.

Walking the earth sounded like dinosaurs to Jubal, but he wouldn't comment.

Look at you, she said. She peered. Spared the shit we had to go through.

The machine clicked and startled him. Go ahead, said Kai, fumble with the machinery.

He pulled the tape recorder closer.

The First Wife would give the first recorded Leela.

He was aware that she was looking at him for a sign.

Ready, he said strangely.

She tucked a long, unwashed piece of hair behind her ear. At seventeen I discovered humankind's tendency toward Narcissism, Jubal, she started shyly.

He kept his eyes on the machine. He knew she wasn't really talking to him.

I saw how Narcissism, or just garden-variety self-importance, laid waste to love; my parents and my entire neighborhood were wasted. How could they sit there, my parents, when Joan Baez was singing protests and ballads?

The tape recorder made a ratchet sound. He was probably going to mess the whole thing up, and how would he survive the Guru's wrath? Or worse, His disappointment?

I thought I would try to live outside the box, you know, Kai was saying. As if the box were, literally, the house where I grew up—

now her look had turned inward— As if the box were recidivism to things like smile, nod, and handshake.

Everybody had run away from their parents—the meat their parents ate, their parents' customs, costumes, corsets.

You know there was that saying, reinvent the wheel, which I always took to mean a lot of unnecessary labor. But now people were going to do a wooden wheel, a mandala with a million spokes like a sunburst. People were going to make the wood by hand, visualize the trees, dig tunnels for the roots with handmade shovels. They were going to get together and do it better than thousands of years of human history. They were really open to manna from heaven. The heavenly germ. Holy crackers. Triscuit Prasad, Saltine Prasad, a little Prasad and jelly sandwich!

There was a big foreign guy with whisker-gray hair who led the free Zen meditation in Kai's neighborhood. What a strange name, King Ivanovich. (She was Kelly.) Afterward there was a question period. King Ivanovich said, You Americans always xheff questions. But grinning, flirtatious, and Kai went up to the front and waited in a small mob for an audience.

He pointed out that if Kai were living outside the box there would still be the negative space in a box shape. The box-shaped elephant in the room, He called it, the fact that Kai had brown eyes like her mother. Or is it your father? He teased her. Her attachment, He said, such stickiness, to her parents. His smile was so sudden and so complete it almost had a sound to it.

He called the cockroaches in the Zen center cocksuckers. The problem with English.

His body was all squares like moving crates stacked one way and then the other. He made His Own yogurt in plastic tubs from the back door of the university refectory, Fruit Cocktail and Tomato Ketchup. The yogurt had to stay warm under a wool blanket. He pressed His serpent against the starburst of Kai's anus when she touched herself. She found it electrifying. He called it lovemaking. Kai would have said fuck, like most people, who wanted to be less like their parents, but this was more. More godfeelings when she was with Ivanovich! More arms, she was the multiarmed Hindu god Shiva, everyone had a bronzy little statuette in their place, rioting on the skull of a demon, people had brought Shiva back from Pondicherry in South India, his octopus arms, his long curly hair in a mullet.

Jubal could see that she'd transported herself. When her eyes landed on him by accident she seemed confused for a moment. He dropped his gaze to the tape recorder. He didn't want her to know he was listening. The lieutenant had said, I don't entirely trust this piece of shit tape machine. You should pay attention, Jubal. And the Guru may say this is not our business, but He may be in the mood, you know, all of this is His move, Jubal, and He may say, Give Me your voice, your version. Yeah?

I am ready to build a chorch, Kelly-angel, said the future Avadhoot Master King Ivanovich. Leetle tiny fairm. Too much godstuff in California.

Exposure was egoic. Folks in California were overexposed.

We should go east, Kelly.

King and Kai, packed like donkeys in the time of Jesus, string bags of bread, flasks of wine and water.

They spotted the Roshi squatting against the zinc guardrail on a highway bridge near Hartford, Connecticut. Traffic loomed and snapped by in a slur of bright metal. The brown robe, begging bowl wedged between his knees and stomach. King threw off His pack in the middle of the bridge and rummaged until He found the orange Kai had caught rolling across a supermarket parking lot. He dropped it in the begging bowl and it rotated like an earth, wobbled, and halted.

The Roshi had a square hard face, unlined, although he seemed not young but ageless. His mouth was muscular, like he was shelling beans inside it. His feet, in leather straps, were pocked with grains of asphalt. They swelled up and then he had to sit down and squeeze the road out. He was from the same temple in Kyoto where King had studied.

We know all the same characters, King told Kai. Now she could discern the Berkeley bass of His English; when He spoke Japanese, His voice got higher. The Roshi's English was thrusty, right to her solar plexus.

She'd been wearing the water, but now the Roshi took it, and the little tent hung off King's belt like a pupa. There were town squares in Massachusetts, then New Hampshire, roadside farmstands with first crop apples, surplus peppers. King's hair was wild and salty and His beard—since then, clean-shaven as a baby—had scrubbed its way around His features. Kai thought she must have been down to ninety pounds, bone and gristle.

The Roshi kept his hair short with the same nail scissors he used on his calluses.

Her seven thousand dollars bought a handful of rusty nails and a kick's worth of wormy lumber. The future Guru teased her, saying she should have skimmed more money off that café she worked at in Berkeley.

The Tang Dynasty texts may have been his nursery rhymes, but it turned out the Roshi loved beer, and chocolate bars with peanuts. They lay under the stars or the clouds or the tumble of stars and clouds on the lawn outside the broken-down farmhouse and King made a basket of His hands and invited her to place her head inside it.

Winter came, they were so far from rugs or pillows. Often the three of them collapsed in such a way that some part of her touched the Roshi.

She lost herself in thought for several long moments. The tape kept turning.

Jubal looked at the machine and willed it to click off. It seemed wrong for Kai's breathing to be caught on tape. He thought of the strips of amber flypaper that hung in the pole barn, stuck with dozens of frilled, disease-carrying carcasses. Noa had ripped one down and chased him around with it . . .

King took one of her hands onto His lap. He seemed to be admiring it. Even before she knew who He was, long before she understood the profundity of His attraction, the gravity of His grace, when she came in contact with His skin, allsuffering was alleviated.

She has beautiful fingers, you think, Lyosh? The Guru had already named the Roshi after Alyosha Karamazov Brother. Roshi Lyosha smiled and looked away from the little love nest.

Then: Sit up, King commanded her.

She sat.

Does it make you happy, Kelly? To lie here among us?

Now the Roshi was looking at her amused and distant. He had to wear a parka over his robes—there was just the one woodstove in the kitchen. Kai was cold, but she thought the Roshi looked like one of those guys who tries to climb Mt. Everest.

Happy? I'm happy, she said. She gathered herself together.

Good, said King coldly. Good answer.

It was true she'd been thinking she could just lay on the floor with her parka for a pillow, happy (not unhappy), not drinking the beers with them. She had her own jug wine in the kitchen.

Does what make me happy? Kai said uncertainly.

But then King broke into a wide smile and pulled her up with Him. In her Leela she was tripping and giggling after Him like a long-ankled teenager.

He left a few candles burning on a crate in the bedroom—those old apple crates were the only furniture. In the crypt light she caught a glimpse of her own shadow on the wall. It looked like a furious insect. Then she saw the Roshi, squatting just inside the doorway.

His legs were bent and tacky inside his robe, she imagined, his hands on his knees, his head impeccably balanced. King paused for half a second, and Kai understood that King and the Roshi had arranged it.

She felt as if she and King were bugs mating. Their shadows flew around the room, trapped in the room, frantic. The Roshi's face was in the dark but Kai knew he could see that she saw him. He cocked his head, so their heads were on the same level. She came fast, crackling. When she opened her eyes, the Roshi had vanished.

CHAPTER 6

SOME PEOPLE CALLED their Leelas Disconversion; other people said the term was maladroit, awkward in English. The meaning, the lieutenant told Jubal, was to leave all conversion-behaviors behind, all hardness of principle, hardness of material like cars, clothes, houses. To disassociate, to tumble out of the worldly nest where you had forever been squawking for someone to feed you.

We were all disillusioned early, said the lieutenant. He saw it in us. Disillusioned by birth itself, as He used to say, that messy, fleshy, period drama.

They had almost reached the farmhouse. The lieutenant looked down at his hands. Did Kai say anything about me?

The Guru was waiting in the presbytery. As a form of samadhi, He was teaching Himself to juggle. Piti, the Ninth, handed Him two oranges. They looked lacquered. He levered Himself up to a sitting position. He did a neck roll. Air snapped between the joints. He smiled.

What does Kai say about Me? He said, looking around genially.

Jubal felt a surge, unexpected—he alone knew what Kai said about the Guru. He heard her voice in his head and it terrified and excited him: Tell Him how much I love Him. Please, Jubal.

I was in Berkeley, said the Guru.

Jubal was confused for a moment. It wasn't his turn to speak after all.

His soft focus on Piti. Go on, said the Guru as He began to toss the fruit around. Tell Me all about Kelly Ann Pasternak.

Was He talking to Piti?

He wasn't as good at juggling as you might expect God to be.

Piti giggled and retrieved His oranges.

He laughed good-naturedly. He dropped His fruit.

He said, Drop all forms of crankiness and greed, take on love and more love, people.

He rolled onto His other side. Silk-covered pillows rolled with him, Prasad spilled from His altar. Piti handed Him another orange.

He looked up from His pillows, from His tent of saffron satin. The air in the presbytery was starchy. The lieutenant shifted impatiently beside Jubal.

When I met Kai, people, He started, a propos of nothing, of everything, of nothing again, His mind was not divided, She was a baker at some café in Berkeley.

Jubal heard Kai laugh at herself. He looked around. No one else seemed to have heard it.

The Guru crossed His unblemished ankles and two small auras clinked together. I thought she was a boy because she cut the sleeves off her shirts to show her ropes, said the Guru, her bread muscles.

Jubal could smell bread baking and he felt queasy. He swallowed and his ears popped. He had recently learned that hunger made him seasick. When he closed his eyes, he was turning around a pole. He had learned the term axis. He opened his eyes, and there was an unmistakable thud in his ears as if he'd landed.

Whump—the heat came out like a solid bank when Kelly Pasternak—Kai—opened the bread oven.

Jubal swallowed a bubble.

"Kai" is just a name, people! said the Guru.

Realize the distinction between knowing and simply describing what is arising, dear ones! Whatever arises seems so attractive! Kai is so attractive!

The Guru looked around happily. His face was so big it could display more happiness. This café served all kinds of sprouts, He continued. He screwed up His face: radish, sunflower, onion, garlic. Everyone in California had all kinds of trace elements in their blood; probably in their semen.

There was laughter. Playing to their desire for playfulness, coaxing them out, endearing Himself to His disciples: Poor Kai was not always cold in California like here, He teased them.

So many Svengalis in California, so many Peter Pans; how do you think she recognized Me, eh people? He wiped His glistening forehead. He said, I like California. He waited for them and they waited for Him. It was mutual, He had said, like lovemaking.

But I don't like sprouts, He finished. I am very sorry.

Now the Guru really laughed with them, His fleshy palms open, His little gray eyes crinkled. If there were any who hadn't been laughing, soon they couldn't help it, His laughter was an epidemic. His laughter flooded the blood, it raptured the kidneys.

Jubal looked around. All of the devotee's lips were stretched into skeletons. Some of their teeth were as dark as dogs' teeth.

The Guru sat up and peeled the orange. He ate it section by section. Piti took His right hand to wash in a bronze bowl of warm water. Then she tiptoed behind Him to His other side so she could wash the left one.

He lay on His side again, His great head in His palm, the world sticky between His fingers. He closed His eyes. He opened them. He flicked a shred of citrus foreskin to the side. He closed His eyes again.

He roused Himself. He waved away an airy skeleton of incense smoke. Kai has long teeth, He said. He bared His.

After a while He said, That lady has long nipples.

Jubal saw Gary Messner, innermost of the Inner Circle, suppress a smile.

What are you waiting for? cried the Guru, suddenly harsh, impatient. The lieutenant placed his hand on Jubal's small, some devotees were calling it sacrum, and he did a quick prostration.

Tell Me what I have to know about Long Nipples!

Gary Messner led the laughter.

. . .

Kai ambushed him behind the giant forsythia bush by the back door of the farmhouse. The picnic table was in full sun. She gestured him toward it. Take a seat! He didn't want to. He stumbled. She sat opposite. She was always cold. For her the sun was like glass. She looked at him so intently. When she smiled at him Jubal could see the lumps underneath the gums. Even outdoors her clothes gave off the smell of rice cooking.

She started without preamble, speaking faster than she had before, her elbows drilled into the table. A few tassels of hair stuck out of her crocheted cap. She had deep lines around her mouth. Was that what made her animal?

I could say I cooked for everyone. At one time or another. The Roshi showed me how to do pickles.

She shifted impatiently and her knee exploded the underside of the table.

Where's your tape recorder?

But she didn't seem to care too much. She looked at him: You'll tell Him, Jubal.

He could only nod. His ears were ringing. Was that what the Guru meant, bell-boy? But how could he listen when his ears were ringing?

Sometimes the Beloved demanded bread, sometimes He survived on mangoes. He had really touchy intestines. If His stomach was soft I knew He'd been sneaking off to town.

Yes, she smiled, Even an enlightened being goes and picks up diarrhea.

Students stopped by to help in the kitchen. Service was really loose, you know, spaced-out devotees used to slice through their own fingernails. Then we had to sterilize the knives, we used to scald them under the faucet.

We were having these never-ending conversations, on this life, this antilife, this path toward acceptance of dying. We had conversations on who you could tell and who you couldn't. There was agreement you couldn't tell your mother you were no longer afraid of dying. The Beloved laughed pretty hard when people came up with that one. There were so many people in peoples' lives, wheels within wheels, people within people.

Disapproval, condescension, speaking sharply, He said these were the qualities I should work to purge from my personality.

I took on hissing, the way the Roshi did it, and his sour face; I took on saying the Roshi didn't want a big scene, a bunch of Westerners crushed out on robes and tablas and rice with seaweed. Did the Roshi really not want a big scene? It was my idea of him. He would hang out in the kitchen telling me that a single day on Earth was longer than a year on Venus. I always thought it was some kind of astronomy koan. He used the butt of a candy bar to pick up the crumbs of milk chocolate.

One night we built a bonfire on the bay beach to get rid of all the rat piss lumber from the farmhouse attic. It was the Beloved

Himself who had climbed up in the armpits of the roof and put wire mesh over the rat holes. There were many jugs of wine and vodka. We were all in it together. He was trying to tell us we were not separate, yet we all had these ambivalences, these identity complexes.

The Beloved had killed a pig, we were on flesh, He said we should crave for a while. We were eating God, smoke, and spirit. Meat and drink made people swear and dance, it was hedon, people were so susceptible, living on breath for long periods. Gary Messner was dancing with me, he had narrow eyes and a sick wife, Gail, whom the Beloved called an alcoholic.

The Guru's going to use me as an accountant, laughed Gary, he was so sweet in my ear, knowing his own sweetness.

There were some benches but people were mostly standing up, cooking their big fat shishkabobs. The Beloved threw the bones in the fire so everyone else did.

A lady named Susan who had just arrived, a strong and spiritual lady who had some training as a midwife, was at the Beloved's side the whole evening. She had a striking dark complexion, almost Mexican, you know; she could wear this really colorful poncho. He clapped His massive hands above His head to convene us. I was sure I could feel that clap in a way no one else could. I was between His hands, He burst every atom in me. Love was an absurd nuclear understatement.

Dear people! We all got quiet.

This is Susan Montoya's wedding, people!

The rush of the big fire. Fountain of sparks, ashy stars, open water.

Right now! laughed the Beloved, suddenly self-conscious for our benefit. He could be so innocent.

Everybody knew He and I were already married. Susan was almost as tall as He was. Her long hair like a horse's tail.

I will take as many wives as it is necessary for Me to take, He said, laughing again; were we hung-up, constricted? She who was Susan will now be Sita!

Kai stopped with a sudden shudder and closed her eyes. Jubal could see the balls tracking.

Krishna had a thousand gopis, you know Jubal?

God-girls. Some people said it was a metaphor for the vastness of His love. Some people said it was to test our conventional Western shittiness. Would we really begrudge Him anything?

She gazed across the picnic table in such a way that he felt he should make it clear there was nothing sexual between them. In Children's Talk the Guru had warned that grownups' gross feelings constantly merged with the ordeal of sexuality.

Jubal made footcircles under the table. He tried to signal that he was listening and also that he heard nothing.

She leaned toward him across the sun. He began to circle faster.

I had a real heaviness in my abdomen from the wedding food, I knew I really needed to work with it. The Beloved had said it before, jealousy was bodily, anal-expulsive. I went to sit in the farmhouse living room, leaving others to carry on around the fire. After a while I noticed that my breathing was very beautiful. I sat a long time, the blood slumped to one side or the other, before I felt His presence. I opened my eyes carefully, I felt as if my eyes had never opened before, and He was there behind me, radiant and clear, for all to see, His hair standing on end, His eyes of the world, waiting for me to open.

Eh Kai, He stage-whispered. I have been meditating on you. His eyes were really sparkling with a thousand suns in a thousand streams so clear I could drink them. My throat was open.

He said, You should go get drunk with the Roshi.

I was sitting right there on the floor of the living room but my whole being was rushing forward.

Her eyes shone now, as she finished her Leela. Then I went upstairs, Jubal, she said, and for the first but not the last time, the Roshi was waiting.

CHAPTER 7

ONCE MORE the lieutenant caught up with him. You're doing well, Jubal. He's really pleased, if you can use a word like pleased to describe a Crazy Wise Man.

Then, carefully, How do you feel?

They were on Kalma; he felt hungry. (Your intestines are just an ordeal, your hunger is in no way you, people!)

All that talk? said the lieutenant. All that listening?

He hated it when the lieutenant pried into him. He would have to figure out how to avoid him now in earnest.

Is it like walking in on your parents making love, Jubal?

Jubal stepped backward.

Do they get it on, Ray and Cleary? Did you know one of the conditions of being lieutenant is that I can't get married? Do you think that bugs me? Do you think I knew that when I signed on the dotted line? Eh Jubal? Ever think about the lieutenant's side of the story?

He wanted to turn and run, but the lieutenant caught him, then caught himself, straightened, looked off toward the forest. He said, I'm sorry. Jesus.

Time for a new Period.

Enough of the old Period.

Jubal was thirteen. He would have been a teenager if he was worldly.

The Guru sees the parents and the children, the lieutenant started up again after a moment. He sees you peeking around the door at Ray on top, Jubal. Or Cleary riding bareback.

And again the lieutenant reined it in, recovered his composure.

The Guru says time for a Children's Period. First in a series of such. The Guru says so many baby shoes now in the narthex, the smell of dirt and skin stronger than incense, children's leetle sweaters slung on hooks, when you brush past them they release garlic and nag champa. Have you noticed?

The Guru says call it the Period of the Confidante, she who attends the bodily pleasures of the child in much the same way as the traditional Jesus godparent. Swimming, eating, yoga. The Confidante relationship serves to undermine the worldly and atavistic tendencies of parent-child. So says the Remarkable Guru, said the lieutenant.

Craig R. stood watch against the wall as they filed into the Concert Barn. Jubal looked around in time to see Sita close the heavy doors behind her. He dropped his eyes. The trick was inner space. Skunk-sweat was all-pervasive, but there was no foul in the temple inside him.

Sita's hair looked like it had been burned black, coal and glossy. The Way of the Remarkable and Realized One is no banter! she called, to quiet them.

Then she called, Cleary!

There was his mother in a feather-gray wrap skirt printed from the bottom with impressionistic reeds and grasses, a third eye of ash, clods of mascara. Jubal watched her weave through disciples until she came to Zoya's daughter China. China, who the Guru said He had known when she was a servingwoman in a fine house in Kyoto: she had washed His underthings. Not this life. China comes from the domestic water-nest world to serve us, the Guru had elaborated. Cleary performed a full prostration before her.

It is the holy hour of chat! cried Sita.

It is what He has called it!

Noa was braiding Heidi's fingers, Zoya had found Jyoti's Margaritka. The hour of love talk, ghostly Confidantes shifting under white burkha hoods and long white tunics.

Jubal saw Kai moving toward his sister. People parted for her. Was the cap supposed to make her head look bigger? The Guru had said that worldly life was compensating for imperfections. Just having a self was bragging. The First Beautiful stood facing his sister like a bride. Jubal contracted.

He had seen the lieutenant lick his finger before he touched the whispery body of ashes and smudged Kai's forehead; now Kai touched her own ash bindi in order to print Violet's third eye. Violet must have been able to smell Kai's hand beneath the ash and oil. Communion hour in the Concert Barn, ruddy sunset through the stained windows, a chicken taking a dust bath in the corner.

Then Sita called, The Fifth Beautiful Wife and Jubal!

Out of the crowd Dovorh, her renunciatory balletic aspect, her aberrant thin (it was said lately), her guileless composure hiding an uncomposed heart, floated to find him. Helplessly he waited for her, her sad/happy smile. Red clouds curdled and then fell apart in darkness.

. . .

Louis Quatorze peacocks, cross-dressing roosters (their big feet gave them away, their combs also), crows liveried like limousine drivers crossed the farmyard. Craig R. had written so many bird ghazals. Jubal stood with the Fifth Wife and the lieutenant, the bird-scraped sky, the cloudy gravel, the lieutenant in his Woolrich and waders after the Guru's Old World peasant style. Hens toddled around them, babbling and toothless. Curious, but without empathy.

It pains me to start in on you, Dovorh, said the lieutenant. The hens rose as one and collapsed in an outer ring around the humans. Dovorh threw a fan of seed. The lieutenant shook his head in disapproval. Why did he have to be here? thought Jubal.

Look, sighed the lieutenant. Your repeated petitions to visit your worldly daughter, your retentive and ego-serving labor. Come on, Dovorh. Your daughter, he said, what does that mean, your daughter?

The birds must be listening, thought Jubal, trying not to listen. Otherwise why would they stick around? Why would they care that Dovorh had left her daughter when she found the Guru?

All this attachment and neurotic thinking—the lieutenant shook his head in sorrow. The Guru makes these observations with a lot of love, Dovorh. He knows you'll survive. In fact survival is very fiery and will burn up ego tendencies.

Sunken eyes like a mourning dove. Bird Wife, the Guru called her. Oldest wife, although she had the unlined face of an heiress, He accused her. The girlish body that had slept in girlish bedrooms, not the cot in the kitchen of the coldwater flat, not the empty bottle for a pillow. The Guru cough-laughed. That was His Own lifetime story.

The lieutenant sneaked a glance at Jubal. This really undermines the Confidante relationship, Dovorh. Your fixation on your daughter. You are so out of sync with Him! Consistently you are in your own world, starving yourself when He says be hedon, punishing yourself in worldly terms when He is saying release yourselves from your children, let them go, you have this dogma of finding your daughter! Let go of it!

Now Jubal and Dovorh fell in behind the lieutenant. Again, he left his shoes with the other boats in the narthex. The Guru had said that sadhana was one encounter with Him after another. As they passed the kitchen Jubal could hear the commotion of pots and Kai's metal mixing bowls, the irrefutable energy of His living quarters, unbound, unrestricted happiness.

The presbytery was warm, and the Guru had already stripped down to His navy-blue silk underpants. The altar was larded with fruit, flowers, cakes, and candies. Jubal must have blinked, because when he opened his eyes he saw that a flowerhead floated in each of the Guru's open palms. Chrysanthemums, the death flower.

They waited. So-called boredom was an opportunity to meditate. An airplane over the farmhouse, that clouds were sandbags was an opportunity to meditate.

The fact that sadness was false-emptiness was an opportunity to meditate. Happiness was true-emptiness: it was so hard to tell the difference.

The Guru shifted on His sit bones. Of its Own weather His hair changed direction. The flower poms were undisturbed. Come on, Dov-wife! Tell us why you're so damn neurotic!

Dovorh bowed more deeply and went through the breaths. Jubal went through them with her. The body within the body, the eight adornments, the fetal deer, the superb black knot.

The Guru rose and made His way toward her, He was not limited, getting stuck here or there, He changed constantly, fundamentally enlightenment was capricious. Now He blew softly at the root of Dovorh's neck. Jubal braced himself, but her skin must have quickened, inundated with love as she was for Him, her throat must have opened, joyfully and spontaneously.

Praise, Master, said Dovorh, and Jubal's own throat opened, he felt what she felt, what had been called the heartbreak of happiness.

The Guru's eyes were alight. He whispered, Food also. His eyes danced like a demon's. You can't xheff only protein in the form of cashew nut. His Russian that He enjoyed some times more than others: dismissively He said, Go to veelich and eat some bifstek.

Mischief was His prerogative, craziness was, so was love, He had said it.

His eyes fell on Jubal and He looked surprised for a moment. My bell, He said, suddenly entranced, delighted. Come on and take something from My altar.

Jubal rose unsteadily. His stomach was a hunger bone, someone else's. At least he had distracted the Guru from Dovorh, the one who saved food in a cloth napkin, who took a pear from His altar— not for herself—

He saw stars in the dry pools of his sockets.

The Guru was watching. It's so easy with Me, He said softly. He leaned forward and screwed His thumbs into Jubal's armpits.

There were medjool dates with skinless almonds tucked in their cavities, dates as big as breadloaves. It had been days since he had consumed so many calories. Smiling, the Guru uncurled his fist and filled it, and then all at once, all of his bodily juices were activated as the Guru fed him.

He called for Piti to bring a brass bowl of warm water and He washed around Jubal's mouth with His Own fingers. Pay attention, He whispered. This is My Way. Wander with Me.

Jubal regarded Ray, dysregulated, tumbling through the lobby of the hospital in Halifax. Cleary wept when she was unable to nurse the baby. His head spun slowly, the earth no longer turned in a true circle. What shape was it? Like a kidney bean, or a liver.

The Guru in His Own Godverse, devotees watched and waited.

He had nowhere else to be,
the almonds were so almondy,
why shouldn't He be self-satisfied?

It's a little bit psychological, the Guru giggled after a while. This is the psycho-scientific West, isn't it, people? He grinned, His teeth were tiny.

He had learned the term anorexic from medical journals an ex-doctor devotee brought with him. Anorexica! He called out to Dovorh, charging her with another form of attachment to the body. Sita pushed her forward. Once more Jubal felt himself contracting.

He jimmied a chrysanthemum into her hair when she got there. He enjoyed His Fifth Wife's hair. He had compared it to a cake of curly ramen noodles, only it was dark as plums, soft as a night in the middle of the summer.

Dov-Bird, davai. Stay here by Me while we discuss Narcissus. He looked around the sangha. He made loving eye contact with certain disciples. His eyes found Peter Nehud, ex-doctor. Nehud knows the human soul, eh, friend Peter? His eyes found Piti. Piti knows the German language. I hate the German language.

Dovorh sat facing Him and He put His hands on her shoulders. Don't fall into the Narcissus mirror, Dovorh. A lot of glass. A lot of cuts on your beautiful heiress face. Your attachment to your body is staggering. His hands dropped. He caressed His master bead. Jubal had oiled the beads of His mala. Dovorh had showed him how she rubbed the excess oil into her cuticles.

This is the Way that I Teach, people, said the Guru. In love, in poemform, in Open Love Letter. He looked around judiciously. Taking His time. I teach in Inspired Garbage. You don't have to make sense, stupidheads, said the Guru.

You don't analyze
and corrupt the information
you are given.
The Way is the nonway,
the Story is the nonstory.
The Master follows no rules,
no coordinates of behavior.

It is not worldly,
not sociosexual behavior.
He moves intuitively,
spontaneously,
in order to move
those around Him.
Devotees become ghosts
of themselves when
He enters them completely.

People smiled through their tears like Dovorh. Peter Nehud, dark little toewalker, large doctor hands, came from the medical world with all this terminology: Total Narcissism was another of the Guru's favorites. Come sit by Me Peter, said the Guru.

Listen.

Prince Narcissus came upon a little lake deep in his father's forest.

I won't waste time getting to the good part. The love part, grinned the Guru. He shimmied His great shoulders.

When the prince paused at the mossy edge he saw, to his great surprise, another prince, as comely as he, in the water. The two princes stared at each other admiringly for a long while. In fact, night had almost fallen before Narcissus unlocked his green-eyed gaze from the twin prince's.

You see? beamed the Guru. Green eyes, like Dovorh.

Every day Narcissus visited the pool, as sharp as a mirror, and soon he fell in love with the prince he always found waiting for him. In the gaze of the other prince Narcissus saw such understanding, such artful longing.

Narcissus could think only of his soulmate. How Narcissus desired to hold him! But if he so much as touched the surface of the water with his little finger—kneeling—ripples would obscure the face of his beloved. Narcissus would cry out in frustration and increasing anguish.

If a duck floated across his beloved, Narcissus would cast stones furiously until the bird flapped off, squawking—but the beloved image was fractured. If Narcissus came laden with gifts for his prince —fruits, sweets, clothing tailored to the perfection of the beloved body—there was no way to give such gifts without destroying the vision. Narcissus began to go mad with unfulfilled desire.

One day he shed his clothes behind a tree and approached the pool naked. His faultless body glistened, sublime with youth and beauty.

If I speak of his erection, it will make some of the men jealous.

There was laughter.

His beloved prince, too, was naked.

Do you see, people, said the Guru, how perfect they were for one another?

Here I am! cried Narcissus. He threw himself into the water.

The Guru finished and His face clouded over.

This was His nature. He did things only according to His nature. Sometimes it was difficult, He had said, for Him to be so human.

Ray raised his hand but Pritam, Inner Circle, frowned in Ray's direction. Pritam who had been Mark Lish, who would come back from New York where he sat in a traditional Rinzai zendo and say they were all gaijin, their intellectual reasoning was a loop, mind was fodder for mind, fundamentally they were fakers. The Guru would let him say this.

Master, said Pritam, bowing deeply and feelingly as if he could truly identify the softening, hemorrhoidal spot where his third eye would manifest. Help us to release our material/literal/sexual tendencies, Master, said Pritam.

Not as the Eighth Wife goes off the Sanctuary and forgets the Practice! cried the Guru. He pointed at Heidi. Humiliation is not outside the Practice. Humor, hubris, hedon, happiness. Half-assed-ness! All My h's! No h in Russian, people!

He rose and paced the width of the room. He had no ass but He had shoulders like an extra set of shoulders. His hair—they kept track of every hair of Him—had not been washed in days and it was flat and dark around His small, reddening ears. Any change in Him made Him seem vulnerable. It was Heidi's Service to wash His hair: Heidi had been given a week's leave of absence.

Come on, people! You're all implicated. Stupidheads!

Jubal saw that Ray didn't dare raise his hand again and ask some human turd of a question. Some bird turd. Canada geese all over the shorn front lawn of the farmhouse. Everyone took his or her turn—

Dovorh's turn. Once again: Sit closer, Anorexica, said the Guru. He Himself settled into His cushions. Mother of My children. He touched her cheek. Jubal felt his own cheek spangle. The Guru pulled a face and looked around, daring anyone. Pritam shook his head at his crazy Avadhoot of a Master.

Pritam thinks I am funny. I am funny. For some reason Do-vorh has not borne Me any children. Maybe because she is a Jesus anorexic?

Sita was making mudras with her thumbs, Zoya was obscured by her own cloud veil.

Dovorh. I will always call you out for monkeying with diet. He reached forward and adjusted the flower in her hair. You must gain weight through the cultivation of outgoing energy. He smiled. True-Dov. Soon you will understand that giving away all this energy you become very hungry. Very, very hungry. He grinned. You should have one hundred twenty-five pounds. A good number for you. What are you now, Dovorh?

She whispered, Ninety.

He said, Mark My words. I will always undermine righteousness.

Jubal! cried the Guru. Do you know what Dovorh's old husband tells Me? Never has she weighed that much. Not even when she was pregnant. Did you know he writes Me letters? He's in love with Me as all who know Me, even who knew Me at one time or another, love Me. Please tell my ex-wife that our daughter finishes college, writes this guy from Florida. Did the Fifth tell you she was from Florida?

He threw His head back in laughter. I don't remember what that Florida guy tells Me!

Abruptly He turned to Piti. She passed Him a mango.

Had He forgotten Dovorh? Would He leave her alone now?

Life and death are just materialistic tendencies! Your fear-stink clothing, sleepstink, I can smell it. Your limitmind is excruciating!

He stroked His mango. Did His thoughts wander? Never. It was devotees who wandered, stumbled in the dark. Let go of This and That! Metaphors for the dharma are just part of the same paraphernalia!

One of Lishy's friends from New York has sent Me a box of mangos! Did you know mangos grow in New York? What do you think this so-called friend of Lishy wants from Me, people?

Why couldn't the Guru remember to call Mark Lish Pritam?

Well come back tomorrow with another box of mangos! I like mangos! The crates would be good for hatchlings, so save the crates, yeah Pritam?

Suddenly He was wiping His eyes with laughter. Did you think, people, for one moment that I was going to share My mangoes with you?

There was the ready stir of devotional laughter.

My Dov-Bird is really hungry! I think she came here for the mangoes, eh Dov?

He really cracked Himself up sometimes.

They waited. Waiting was an opportunity to meditate.

Life, an opportunity to meditate.

They meditated.

Finally, Do My Dov, Jubal. Now I will listen.

CHAPTER 8

JUBAL WAS all voices.

Kai was the one with the long eyes.

Dovorh was the one most likely to attract the Teachings of ridicule, the one most attached to attachment.

John Hartshorn, mercenary of God from Michigan, self-taught questioner-executioner of the deep questions.

Jubal could hear him, moccasin-stealthy through Kishkindha Forest.

Lieutenant, foot-soldier—he wouldn't have been good with horses, not brawn enough to handle the cannon. His hare-haunches stiff from all that marching. He had the long nose of a hare, too, with a twitch at the tip, and a head too narrow even for the narrow body.

Jubal, the horn, all horn pipes. He turned fourteen. Dates rolled in coconut.

Jubal, the harp, its low strings reverberated like thunder.

The one who knew their stories.

They drowned out his own story.

Violet was praised in Children's Yoga, praise drowned out Jubal's story. She could sit completely flat in lotus. Noa showed off a bridge, a headstand. Violet unfolded in lotus-upon-the-water.

Cleary came home weeping from private interviews. She said that when she was with Him, she could see things as they really were. Not as she desired them to be. Not as fear dictated, either. She still came home for dinner, but she wasn't eating.

Hunger is samsaric, said Cleary.

Some devotees were donating regularly to the Red Cross blood bank. Samsara: illusion. Visions were not illusion but hunger was.

Ray said, You shouldn't donate if you're anemic, Cleary.

No need to eat, such a feast of light was her Practice. She sank to the floor, her back against the cold oven. Ray pretended to sniff around like a dog for its dinner. He said, The jikki had to tickle your mother with his bare hands to keep her awake this morning. Arthur had blue, tapered fingers.

Cleary behind the cloud wall, total serenity—

There had been talk of modifying Kalma for the children, but the Guru said He was not interested in their dietary issues. If the children were whiney the parents should read to them.

When Elizaveta Dimitrinova and I starved in winter she fed Me on philology, people. My Own mother, said the Guru.

What will it be? Cleary asked them. Her hand hung over the low pile of storybooks sanctioned by the Inner Circle. Jataka tales?

Jubal was embarrassed for her. How old did she think he was? He didn't say anything. Embarrassed by his attachment. He still remembered how she used to read at bedtime—realms and realms ago, as he'd heard her say regarding Canada.

Her hand dropped to rest on the books and it caught his eye —was it smaller than his hand? He checked discreetly. He would have been in high school.

Once, long ago in India, began Cleary, the Buddha was born as a quail. He taught all birds and they called him Sage, although his appearance, as a quail, thought Jubal, was no less ridiculous than theirs, with a bouncing crest like the radio antenna on their old station wagon.

Ah, said Ray, from the doorway. Buddhism for Western children. Jubal saw how Violet pretended she hadn't heard him. Doubt was outside the Practice. They studied the stylized illustrations. Each leaf of the forest was a spiral that contained the firmament. The stream in the foreground sparkled like granulated sugar.

A hunter could imitate any birdcall. He waited for the quail to draw near him, then threw his net over the whole quail family. So the Sage quail, who was the Buddha, taught his fellow birds how to work together to escape the tricky hunter. If they all took flight at once, they could lift the net to a thornbush, where it would become entangled, and they could escape out from underneath.

The particular plumage of the quail originated at the site of the third eye. Jubal thought this betrayed the Buddha's pride in his own comeliness. How did the Buddha choose the creature of his embodiment, anyway?

Cleary seemed too tired to protest. Buddha didn't write the story, she offered. Jubal watched his sister lean forward eagerly. What was their mother suggesting? But there was nothing else, and Cleary's privacy remained deep, and dark, like a pupil contracting. She paged ahead and sighed before she continued.

One day, caught again beneath the hunter's net, the birds began arguing. One quail had snapped another quail's crest by accident.

The picture showed the abused quail with a broken antenna. Wouldn't that part of the bird be more flexible?

The hunter, still a cunning fellow even if lately defeated, took advantage of the lapse in his prey's attention. He simply stuffed the quarreling flock into his laundry basket.

So the Sage called the remaining birds together. Who will follow me and learn to trust and regard one another? he asked them. Those quails became the Buddha's disciples.

Cleary slid the book off her lap and onto Violet's. Their mother's torso was canoed out by Kalma. I'm going to sit with Sita and

Tamsen, she said. Jubal felt his stomach squeeze with hunger. He felt it knot up for his sister.

But now Violet was looking carefully at the last picture. What were those white children doing in India? They were arranged at the Buddha's feet, interspersed with wild animals. Why was the Buddha's blue hair done up in a bun like a ballerina's? Was he wearing earrings? There were monks in voluminous robes standing on clouds and serving the Buddha at either elbow. The Western children were relaxing with their parents on the vivid slope. Were they having a picnic? The mothers and fathers had applebud faces, stylized waves of yellow hair, idealized muscular arms, thighs that bulged against the fabric of their Westernized clothing.

Were they molded plastic dummies, or images of Maitreya, the future Buddha, said to be a green-eyed Caucasian? Jubal tried to read his sister's face. How had Cleary disappeared so quickly? The front door closed, and Ray began to rustle around in the kitchen.

Jubal wanted to go after their mother, overtake her on the short stretch of blacktop between their house and the Sanctuary. You didn't finish the story! He would place himself in Cleary's path. He would jab his finger at the last picture and demand to be told what the Buddha got out of all their devotion.

. . .

Indeed, Cleary was climbing the reified ladder to where the air was pure and temperate. She had reached a high Level, Dovorh told him with shining eyes. You must be proud of your mother.

Ray was still messing around with the Guru's carpentry projects. He was constantly catching himself taking apart machinery and putting it back together in his head when he was supposed to be solving a koan. If there were rungs to enlightenment, said Ray, the Guru kept flipping the ladder. Enlightenment was when the ladder spun like a wheel.

The drafty zendo with its facing tiers of bleachers, rows of dark blue and purple zafus, would start out roasting, Ray reported. But by the end of the sitting period, weaker students began flexing their toes against frostbite. Some days the Guru allowed the ladies blankets around their shoulders, other days He barked continually, You stupid shits, spineless Westerners! You trembling fools! Even from deep in His Own meditation the Guru policed their exhaustion. He would creep stealthily behind someone and rap him on the head with a two-by-four—keisaku—from the floor of the woodshop. If a lady had long hair that covered the nape of her neck—Cleary did, so did Dovorh—He'd lift it tenderly before He stung her with a flick of His middle finger.

Be glad you're with a Russian!

Dad Ray was called back from some tractor puzzle.

This so-called Practice is nothing compared to the pain of the Tibetans!

Jubal had seen Cleary's welt and seen Cleary caress it.

He would give a dharma talk called The Breakfast of Marriage, Since you people seem to think I can help you with your excrement.

There was laughter.

Dovorh told him during Afternoon of Confidantes that he was now old enough. Mature. Developed enough, she faltered, for some of His psychosexual revelations.

To be in audience, she had corrected herself quickly.

Some people are saying that the Remarkable Master excels at tricks of psychology. It's funny, you know, said Dovorh, because He can be so thunderous, like God from On High, delivering judgment, but then, He pleads with us, He always wants the marriages to flourish. His rearranging marriages is a last resort, He is rightly our first resort and our last resort. We should know it by now, Jubal.

They all packed into the kitchen. Word spread—after the dharma talk Kai was going to serve bacon. Devotees' noses quivered like pigs' noses—moha, Dovorh whispered. No one can refuse Him, Jubal.

Shirtless, wearing only a white lungi, His hard belly beeswax-colored and bearded like a turnip, He lumbered from His make-do throne and began picking through the rows of students. Be glad you're not Naropa, whacked in the face by the dirty sandal of his teacher! He began, pausing beside Cleary.

Laughter.

Tilopa, what an asshole of a teacher, eh people?

He stopped behind Dovorh, and Jubal willed Him to keep wandering.

He leaned down and flicked the Fifth Beautiful. He stood there as if He had just landed there, as if He were bewildered.

If I speak about the marriages, people, you must understand My conception of love is not bound.

There was utterance. This was what people had come to hear. People relaxed their sawboard shoulders.

Have I told you about the Lapse from Nature?

Have I told you Heidi comes to Me because she can no longer throw pots on a wheel?

Mark My words, the earth is a flat tire!

Not a single one of you can hand milk!

Two jets of milk making two whirlpools—No one can!

Have I told you the one about Milarepa and his old house of nine levels?

Jubal saw the jikki open his owl eyes and affect a subtle listening as if he were trying out a quail antenna.

Down went the Guru like a Jacob's Ladder, one side and then the other. Without missing a beat Gary Messner slid pillows along the floor beneath Him.

Bliss everywhere, yeah people? said innermost Gary, making a quick assessment. He had such a resonant speaking voice. He should have been an actor. It really pleased the Guru that he had the classic physique of an old-time ballplayer, that he was so handsome both men and women found him handsome—

Hierarchy is a false model, the innermost continued smoothly, but it can help break down the mind. In the first four Levels we're all just meat and floss and ego. He spread his smile.

Jubal saw Ray shift, looking confused—

The insight of Master King Ivanovich is that the form of mind is ninefold. Yeah people? Gary's voice was deep and comforting. No mind, no struggle to find a metaphor for mind, either. His eyes were clear with recognition.

And then, as if the whole thing were a nonevent, the Guru stretched one of His legs out. Piti materialized to shift a pillow so that His extraordinary limb could move freely. He drew His foot in. Clouds may have trundled across the sun: I am here to disabuse you, people! He cried.

Gary smiled his even smile.

What the hell is disappointment, people?

He answered Himself: Just another bear costume. Hot and furry, with a broken zipper.

Well I'm here to monkey with your fear and disappointment!

You made God in your own image, not the other way around!

Religion is a sentimental trap! A childish desire for innocence!

Religion is exemption from pain!

Religion is self-righteousness in the face of pain!

Religion is just a reason to die, people!

The Way that I Teach is no religion!

They were awestruck, trembling. They never got what they expected. He was a total stranger. Who cared about the marriages when it was love at first sight, over and over again?

CHAPTER 9

DOVORH'S CABIN, Ozera, stood alone in a grove of ash trees close enough to the bay that you could hear the rain on the water. She had picked up a lot of smooth stones, carried them in the sling of her Punjabi tunic, arranged them to make a stone garden. It wasn't so long ago that the screen of trees had been a farm field.

I like talking to you, Jubal, Dovorh smiled. They sat on Ozeran steps, as the Guru called them: If Ozera is lake, then we're on steps of water, she smiled again. She placed her hand on his knee. The sun was hottest on his knees where the corduroy was tight and worn, minus its furrows. He could lean against her. Her daughter had.

For a grown lady, you know, said Dovorh, it's such a big relief not to have to believe in something unbelievable, like God.

She had a way of peering sadly at him, did he get what she was saying?

He wanted to confirm. He always wanted to comfort her.

You see for me the Way is love, she smiled ruefully, looking away.

He knew he should turn on the tape recorder but he hesitated. Couldn't he spare the Fifth Beautiful? He had already figured out how to put his hand over the microphone when he spoke. When he was forced to. Once when he heard his own recorded voice in the presbytery he'd jumped out of his skin, and the Guru had wiped His eyes with laughter, crying, My bell-boy is a primitive! A spooky!

The Guru didn't have the patience, anyway, to listen to their distorted, rambling voices. The lieutenant had told Jubal that He preferred to listen to the voice of a child.

It was record cold, my first winter on the Sanctuary, said Dovorh.

Cold-cabin life
was really killing people.
We're not all from Leningrad, Master!

Why are you so afraid of the cold, people? the Guru asked us innocently. Do you think death is cold?

How He loved to tease us about death! She smiled.

I was like a child, in the beginning. He could have held me in a spoon. I was a thin cold broth of sentiment He called pseudo sadness.

I was thin, very thin. She looked at him carefully. Did he judge her? He didn't want her to think he did, but he hated it when she talked about her body.

Anyway, the Guru pushed His dinner bowl toward the center of the long table, Dovorh continued. His teeth were small and angled inward. It was funny when you noticed things about His incarnation that weren't really Him but were very sweet emissaries of the material. The whitish whiskers He shaved Himself; this was before Heidi came and was asked to attend His grooming. He looked straight at me. He held my eyes in His Own and my center disintegrated.

Your love for your daughter is already encompassed by your love for Me, Dov. I will love your longing to be loved by Me.

He leaned around behind me and rubbed my shoulder blades, my small, my sit bones, as He said, the vestigial wings and tail.

Guilt? He said. What is it?

A crack in the earth,
a lie,
a letter?

It's your own love you feel sorry for, Dov-Bird.

My love for my daughter was false, He said. He said love was a phantom daughter.

It must be hard to hear some of this, she said after a pause. Then that sad half smile, Who's going to listen to your Leela, Jubal?

Silence.

It's true what He said, my ex-husband wrote letters. My Master thought it best that Sita burn them with the flowers.

I didn't want my daughter to suffer! I told Him. He softened, how could she suffer when she knows you are on your true-path, True-Dov?

Again she looked at him as if for confirmation, and he felt like there was something wedged in his windpipe. He had to breathe on the surface. He wouldn't meet her eyes.

I asked my Master after a while if my ex-husband had stopped writing.

You are so in love with your suffering, Dovorh! Mischievously, I should be jealous, eh?

My first winter Tamsen became Fourth Wife and all students were required to break Kalma in celebration of the wedding. I was required to. The Teachings said that guilt was your own sense of self-importance. Guilt involved you in a false way with suffering. I went to Him and begged to be allowed to keep Kalma.

I will force-feed you like a goose, He said merrily.

I loved to see the way the children stuffed their cushions in the hinges of their knees and attacked their food. Watching them devour, I gladly lost appetite. I passed my bowl down the long table, and I whispered for the shirtless children, riddled with vertebra, to share whatever was in there.

Then He called me out from the head of the table: You have become a yogin freak, a denier of abundance, a self-loathing mendicant! Food is merely another of your materialistic tendencies!

My face grew hot, my palms suddenly smelled foul. Even my hair was hot.

His beam of love—

She closed her eyes, she couldn't help it.

But she would start at the beginning. He was a great pelican with a peach membrane hanging from His throat and somber wings that thudded the air in time with her heartbeat. All in Leela, in document, Florida, the Gulf coast, where her Leela began. The temperature dropped, and there was a tight band of silver between the sea and the sea-colored universe. The water was the color of a martini olive.

Clever. She shook her head in self-sorrow.

Jubal looked down at the tape recorder. It seemed to turn too slowly.

She kicked at the shell chips layered in the sand and watched two old walkers with elephant skin around the knees and elbows. Hey-ho, Merry Christmas, and the old folks looked out of their folds and grimaced at her youth-and-beauty.

She was thirty-four (she would soon learn, the outside limit), she was the wife and the patroness of an artist. She told everybody the pelicans were the brainchild of Leonardo da Vinci.

Her daughter was fourteen, taller than Dovorh by several inches, so that it seemed the work of motherhood must be over; and lately her daughter seemed to lose herself in sleep like an enchantment.

By the end of December hurricane season was over. The biggest, rattiest Australian pines always came down, which seemed so obvious: Australian revenge, Dovorh's husband called it. Their little place was rather low to be hit—although other bungalows were swept into the garbage. It occurred to Dovorh it would have felt good to have such a clear sign visited upon them.

Afternoons, Dovorh's husband was out banging coconuts from

palms with Mexicans. The island of shells, folks, her husband would say, in the pompous antagonistic voice he reserved for tourism, shell collecting, and not-eating-coconuts. The word island was beneath him.

A warm wind came through the screen and a pamphlet slid along the countertop in the kitchen. Dovorh watched it skitter past the bowl of bright oranges. A tiny ancient gecko flicked up the cabinet. Her daughter was forever trying to catch them and make them into house pets.

The pamphlet was folded three times and hand-lettered. There was a line drawing of a happy fat man sitting cross-legged. His lips were curled and inky. His wild hair was blowing counterclockwise. He was making a who-cares, palms-up, laughing-shrugging gesture. Dovorh swept the pamphlet off the counter. She had a strange feeling it had actually flown in her window. She held it like a bird. She'd never held a bird before, and suddenly that very fact seemed like the strangest thing in the world.

The pamphlet was an outline for how to eat a certain raw food diet. Kalma. Some fruits were retrograde, some were alignment. Some were acid and some were base. There were yin and yang fruits and vegetables. You could laugh instead of eat. A yawn was another kind of nourishment. Almost immediately the strangest thing happened. She pictured a deep, deep hole for all her suddenly inane-seeming habits. There went salt, there went sugar. In that very moment she began to experience this wonderful liberation. She thought, so what if the gecko got in through the open window? She smiled, thinking of her daughter.

She bought a grower by mail that looked like a stack of sieves, and she began sprouting. Alfalfa, mung bean, and radish. Avocados were her source of protein. She began to reduce her intake. She had a single cashew nut before she set out on the beach for several hours. It was only a matter of weeks until she had no question she could glide over the milky sea and, like a pelican, effortlessly loop back to where she had truly started.

In this diffuseness, a plan arose seemingly without her machinations. There was an address on the back of the pamphlet.

Please tell me more about your group, wrote Dovorh. *My daughter and I*—she wrote, because she already saw how her daughter would go with her.

Your pamphlet on Kalma came into my hands, I don't know how. I walk on the beach and I watch a father trying to drill the umbrella into the sand. His children scatter and limp back. He can't convey his love of shells. He can't convey love. I watch the waves swell and crash. I don't feel any meaning, but I feel. I watch the waves mass and destroy. It seems like if I keep doing this I will just die—but I know I will die anyway, so does it matter?

I was wondering whether you allow visitors.

Miss D,

Meaning is nothing but mind. Mind is nothing but mind's own desire for itself. Send Me your photograph and I will meditate on you. It is something I can do for you.

In Love,

Avadhoot Master King Ivanovich

Suddenly beauty seemed to her like another heavy body. Her body was lighter than thought and sometimes the sand squeaked beneath her. She was now Level Two, King Ivanovich had written, marked at the onset by susceptibility to material transcendence. Indeed, she was wearing only a bathing suit. Her hips were hollows. Her body was a curtain, she could not tell the difference when the wind blew it. Her skin was all she needed. She was all body, now, and no body. A stick cross, going this way for arms and that way for legs and torso. It was this pure light thing—what made her think her body was hers in the first place? It was just the remnants of some soft, junked sea animal. She could already feel that her Master held it.

Jubal? said Dovorh gently.

He came to, apologized.

Again he said he was sorry, but she looked nervous. Had she spoken out of line? It was true, he didn't want to listen.

Dad Ray had raised his hand in dharma talk and asked for just some simple, some basic, clarification on his son's role listening to Leelas.

Jubal saw Messner shake his head, poor MacFarland.

The Guru stood up with the lieutenant at His elbow.

Has there been some misunderstanding? I don't try to hide what I do. His lungi was stuck between His thighs.

I have to know the truth, people, not the grownup subjective. You all call yourselves adults.

The lieutenant tucked his smooth chin and smiled. Messner began to laugh and those in the front of the zendo joined him. Soon the whole sangha was laughing.

Jubal stole a glance at Ray. His eyes were closed. Two naked eyelids. But he too was laughing.

Dovorh's husband came home early one day saying he had knocked a nest of coral snakes out of a palm tree, and the Mexicans had all run off. A good excuse for running off, anyway, he grumbled. Dovorh and her husband stood in the kitchen at odds, in silence, when they heard someone crunching up the pathway. Grinding calcium, her husband was fond of saying. The front door was closed in the heat of the day, a black-coffee carved door her artist husband had found at an auction. The inside of the bungalow was dark, and the outside, then, when her husband opened the door to the visitor, was a shock of brilliance.

Dovorh stayed where she was.

She was very, very quiet.

There He was, King Ivanovich.

She looked at Jubal with the same shock of pleasure she had looked, that first time, upon the Guru.

She rushed back to it so easily. His broad face full of mirth— nothing ethereal or angelic. He stood in the doorway but He filled the whole house. He stood there beaming at Dovorh's husband. She looked from one to the other. King Ivanovich had come to Florida at her husband's invitation?

May I present the girl who wrote you, goofed her husband. The girl who's on your diet. He dipped into the fridge and pulled a beer out. He handed it to King Ivanovich. He took the bottle back and opened it barehanded on the lip of the counter.

I'm off work, he said. I'll show you the island. King Ivanovich followed him outside and the house fell into darkness.

From the yard, Dovorh could hear her husband start in about the coral snakes and she plunged in a great isolating disappointment.

For four whole days King did not say a word to her. He and her husband went around to the bars and the beach, hiking in the Preservation. He's a great guy, her husband reported.

On the morning of the fifth day Dovorh went down to the beach. The clouds were brown and disheveled, scrunched up like old blankets. The sun was somewhere else. She said to herself that she would walk until she no longer felt disappointed. Felt foolish. She could hear her husband say that religious guys were just regular guys who had some initial emotional talent with women.

Well, at least she was glad for her husband to have some companionship. They'd been so bored all winter.

The sand was littered with crimson sea sponges like fingers, brains, and branches. There were open-mouthed scallops, shells in fans, funereal, ancient cormorants. She was a mile past their path when she saw King coming toward her. It was still early; He must have started out in total darkness. There was no one else on the beach, and she thought it would be awkward to turn back, as if she were avoiding an encounter. She tried to think what she would say: Hey, like her husband, or, Out early! She told herself she didn't really care if she sounded like she was tired of making up the guest bed.

The early morning pelicans out over the water looked like pterodactyls—or shooting stars—as if it should have been a very rare thing to see one. The way they climbed, stalled, and plummeted, bodies slack, big dark feet distended: every single time was a death drop. She slowed to watch them. Still, she was thirty feet, twenty, only ten feet away from King Ivanovich. She was about to call out. It would be impolite, after all, very strange if she didn't.

But when they were as close to each other as they would have been in a very small bedroom, Dovorh saw that King Ivanovich wasn't looking at her at all. The sand all around them was the color of the water all around them was the color of His eyes. So that His eyes were the water, His eyes were the cosmos.

She had the sensation of dropping out of her body. A vision of her body left behind: sheer curtains (again, curtains) caught in a thermal, a window with no glass, birds rushing through it. Then she was saturated with pure light and, as light, she could be with Him.

She understood that her incidental shell was the barest startle upon His retina. A brief tangle of skinmatter, a star that had died ages ago. She had no preconception of a realization such as this.

No notion at all of communion with a Divine Being. She had never bowed in her life. But now she laid herself—"herself!"—down in the sand before Him.

All this time she'd been keeping track of such garbage! The dried skin of seaweed and the egg pods of unknowable translucent creatures. Eyes, nose, mouth in the sand at His feet when ever so gently . . . Miss D, said King Ivanovich. Look at Me. The purest most exquisite invitation. At long last, her heart addressed directly.

He squinted into the sky that was same color as the sand and the water. His hair was the white-gray of the sand and the water and the sky and it stood up from His head in feathers.

She looked at Him and He pointed. A pelican in free fall.

Then, just as He and her husband had laughed at her husband's Level, now she and King began laughing. She could not get up from where she had fallen. King laughed harder, huge rolling waves, and lowered Himself beside her. He was a giant! He pulled her against Him. She couldn't think. Did He invite her to lay her head in His lap or did she just follow her instinct?

You are right about your unhappiness, said her Master.

Dovorh found herself weeping. Again, "herself." She joined the weeping-for-joy of the world. They were together at last. The true, blessed, God-merged moment. From now on there would be only this moment.

CHAPTER 10

My Own lazy Westerners,

You are dear to Me
but you are incompetent.
I have shined for you
but you will not receive it.
You soup noodles, shudras,
hangers-on to falsity
and feeble,
you have to be happy
to be happy.
Do you hear Me?

Well listen.

Now is the time for Me to step in,
wade in your mired ideas
of right and wrongdoing,
your ideas of being parents.
Do not claim your children
to the breast of your own stupidity.
You must release them,
surrender them to God-consciousness,
to realms of sacrifice that are
not substitutionary, as Jesus,
for you I died,
instead of you,

Me, people.
No. This is not a complicated
Judeo-Christian drama, people.
This is not soldiers,
cross, and weeping.
There are no nails here,
no garlands. No whore
come back to haunt them.
You pour yourselves out for Me
like water. From this time on,
I shall separate the boys
from the girls as a reminder to you
that you cannot do this.
You have necessitated
the Period of the Schism,
as you dictate all Periods.
For I have seen
that the girls are very incarnated,
while the boys are spiritual beings.
Sometimes I Teach in Levels.
Now I will Teach in separation.
You must abide by this purdah,
you must know that there are precedents
in Buddhist tradition,
but I Am A-traditional!
I Am Not That,
I Am Boy and Girl,
I Am Uniquely Everything!

If the Second Level was characterized by an overawe of devotional trappings and miracles that seemed to penetrate the material; if there were holy hobos in India, atrophied ancients with bowed legs and bloodshot eyes who acted like magicians; if cement statues of the Virgin Mary wept real tears, never mind getting off your ass and going to Asia!

If a monk or a nun, rabbi, reverend, mullah, might attain fluency in prayer characteristic of the Third Level, an understanding that meditation was a lot more than an inner monologue, then the Period of the Schism would come down bodily.

People looked around at other people. Was this a provocation of their moha, vain befuddlement? What was He saying?

Ray raised his hand but the lieutenant intercepted: You're fond of your own questions, MacFarland!

There was charged laughter.

There's been a lot of talk about Leelas lately, the lieutenant continued.

Gary bowed his head, taking good care of his little smile.

A lot of woolgathering by the bellwether.

Jubal felt his edges curl like paper on fire.

The lieutenant dammed the corner of his mouth with his forefinger. Allow Gary and me to do our little act here, sangha. He paused. Laughter would be productive.

There was laughter.

Just where do our Leelas fit in, here, Gary?

Once again: Gary's smile was so warm and steady. His heart radiated and so he put his hands there and some ladies in the front did also.

People wanted to put their faces against his chest. His heart was not a metaphor for a certain Level; Gary's heart was real. Ladies, but men also. Their hands and their faces.

Ray raised his hand again and now the innermost nodded as if he were unperturbed, endlessly patient—his little act, for sure. His good-cop-bad-cop with the lieutenant.

Was the Guru playing into peoples' chronic interest in sex and the genders? asked Ray. Was it because He knew sex got people to really pay attention?

The innermost leaned forward off his sit bones. Those little knobs got achy. He grinned in the style of the Guru. You need some good sex, MacFarland?

Everyone knew Cleary had been sent to the cabin Lupine for a while. Everyone knew the Guru would stop by when He happened to be wandering through His holy forest.

Gary waited for the laughter to subside. The Guru has said that He alone understands child development. He is not a missionary or a movement. He is not out to convert vast numbers. One person, for Him, is as good as many. One is many, Ray. He is not a government. That one person could be a child.

The silence in the zendo was hefty. Smoke unfurled in the air above them. It smelled like tea, dawn, cedar. The jikki struck the gong and Sita led chanting. Jubal heard his voice out in front of all the other voices.

Gracious mind is Dharmakaya,
(Gracious mind is Dharmakaya),
refuge from expectations,
free from attributes and accomplishments,
our organ-forms shelter nine diseases,
may disorders and devils aid our worship,
abnegation unbind our egos,
mark His words,
His Pith-Instructions,
resolve our habits,
our form-and-merit-clinging nature—

The Guru was just sitting there before them like a regular guy who happened to possess flexible hip joints. He stroked Mukti's small, His Own son Mukti who had crawled up to be stroked by

Him. Understanding is overrated, He said as if He were talking to Mukti.

And if He feels us turning away,
(And if He feels us turning away),
He will not die of grief
as at the death of a lover—

Families are a reminder of death, you know, people, said the Guru at long last. The same thing as the Mystery before birth. Mark My words, the same thing as the puniness of the human condition.

Amina's Lyet wandered over and He lifted her up with His other arm and she settled against Him.

Quit acting like you're scared of being strangers to your present selves! cried the Guru.

Lyet, alarmed, pressed herself into His armpit.

Do you really think the old self and the new self are sworn enemies?

Do you really think the old self is the mother and the new self is the child?

Children shouldn't be allowed to leap around and dramatize self-involvement! What is this, cried the Guru. Girls trying to out-girl their mothers?

What use are the mothers? What use was I to My mother, sewed into My mother's coat, Moika Embankment?

Elizaveta Dimitrinova, said the Guru, soothing Himself now, spreading Himself out in a smile.

Biblical Adam is nothing more,
not less than the limit
of human imagination.
Not the first human-monkey on earth,
just the semantics of typical hermetic thought, people.

Human imagination can't bring forth childhood.
So go touch them then,
feel what they feel,
their feelbodies,
the cushion-crowns of their fat-heads,
those children who never knew the Garden of Eden,
well they didn't fall from it either.

Look, said innermost Messner, rising. Despite the name, Schism, there is no violence to its form or function. You must trust Him, it is very simple. All forms of distrust undermine your own Practice. Yeah people?

Children should be out in the open. Children should be radiant, out in the open, caught up in it, samadhi, children are spiritual sponges.

The Guru has seen the sexual tensions, the chronic undermining, He does not like to come down so hard, people, but He's sick of hand and foot, sick of handmaiden.

People apologized for needing it spelled out for them. People apologized for their morbid, low-Level feelings for their daughters.

Don't apologize. This is the form the Teaching takes when Kaliyuga is imminent. He only wants you to pay attention. Pay attention to the way you cling to each other, yeah people?

Was Jubal still clinging to his parents? Wasn't their mother proof of their very existence?

Their mother was love before love was defined—and divided. If God was inside them, they had also been inside God. In the form Cleary.

He watched Violet now, sitting on the ladies', thin-fingered and spiritual. She had been praised for spontaneously weeping, and mascara ran down her face in pale, polluted rivers. Noa sat dry-eyed beside her.

He closed his eyes. He would not activate. He thought of his Confidante, still clinging to her daughter. All in Leela, her beautiful jewel-eyed daughter—who said the beach was a moonscape after a hurricane—who asked, What's the closest star to earth? And made it a trick question—

Do you know the answer, Jubal? Dovorh asked quietly.

The answer was the sun, which had no business calling itself a star, said Dovorh's daughter.

CHAPTER 11

SANCTUARY CHILDREN ran in a pack in scaling laughter or quick flares of acrimony. Jubal wasn't part of it. He liked the solitary, thinking sadness when he walked alone on the bay beach. Even though Gary Messner had imitated him, making his legs go soft and pigeon-toed. Now he wondered, being alone wasn't a sign of ego, was it?

The pebbles on the beach looked like hermit crabs; the crabs looked like pebbles. The bigger rocks trailed membranes of seaweed. Beyond the bay the sea was silver. His homeschool course had poetry. Under the surface the sea was digesting and dreaming. The sea was night and land was day, thought Jubal, in the voice of the coursework poems.

Noa poked around their lessons at the kitchen table for the sole purpose of dysregulating Violet. If he tried to bring her into line she laughed at him wildly. Or she'd climb up and ride a chair, pushing her tongue through her puckered lips like an anus.

Dovorh had said the Schism was just as an experiment. People didn't have to be so psychological and serious. So allsuffering and neurotic. We all know families are a profound source of suffering, Jubal. He hadn't asked her to explain anything. That family life promotes attachment. It was unlike the Fifth to carry on. He wants people to remember, Dovorh's voice was really rising, He's studied the sacred texts, He's here to help, you know.

People were saying it constantly: Attachment is hindrance!

There was a horseshoe crab as big as a salad bowl.

He looked down in time to spot a shard of cobalt. The Guru

collected seaglass. You were supposed to offer it to Him. Jubal picked the chip out of the gravel and hurled it into the pigment-rich water.

. . .

He bowed to the Fourth, Tamsen, and Tamsen handed him a whisk broom. There were three separate braids of pathways from the Sanctuary to the zendo, nine paths altogether. He followed Violet at a distance.

Noa's father built the zendo. Roshi Alyosha. The Guru liked to joke that Walt Disney should have adapted Dostoevsky. All devotees had struggled through *The Brothers Karamazov*.

Up ahead, Violet pulled her sweater tighter. All the girls in the same navy cotton sweater since the Schism, rubbery buttons down the front like a cat's long row of nipples. When she bent to pick needles and bird gunk out of the gravel the corner of her sweater brushed the ground and made a soft cursive. The peacocks eavesdropped on everything. Ants smaller than seeds pedaled frantically through space when she swept the tree trunks.

Jubal paused when she paused at the edge of the clearing. Midmorning, and the cedar sides of the zendo would be warm and scented from the eastern sunlight. Who was inside, in absence of thought, budding up the ladder of enlightenment?

It was as if the zendo breathed of its own accord, like an iron lung. It didn't give a hoot, Ray liked to say, about human devotion. The sand around the base would still be night-cold between her toes and fingers.

Then Jubal saw the Roshi, sitting on the edge of the deck that skirted the zendo. He was wearing Western clothes—a jogging suit and sneakers. His legs were wide apart, and his strong square knees were tables where he rested his elbows. He was smoking: a cigarette had just stopped and materialized between his lips for a visit. He coughed; later Jubal would hear the lieutenant say that anyone could pick up a bug on an airplane. The sun was on his face, but it didn't light his face up. His skin was as drab as the gravel on the bay beach—a dead-star face.

A pinecone dropped and Jubal started. Was the Roshi aware that Kishkindhan cones dropped one single one every half hour?

Tamsen, who had renounced competitive swimming—all in Leela—surrendered a PhD in religion, her hair pulled stringently into a topknot, had reminded the children that in terms of spiritual scale, they were not even the fiber of a feather. But now Jubal couldn't help thinking: What if the Roshi gave him a koan, right then and there, and he solved it? He imagined enlightenment—satori, mukti, nirvana—as an aerial view. If the Roshi could see the lines of haiku on the floor of the oceans, wouldn't he be able to see the steeple point of Lupine, where Cleary awaited the Guru? The shiny thread of the stream, Cleary's heart bending for water?

The Roshi didn't smile. He didn't not smile. He puffed the cigarette. He didn't care, he didn't not care. Whatever you thought, it was the opposite, then the opposite again, the logic of the universe accordion-folded.

Jubal remembered how Noa had strutted around for days, after the Roshi's last visit, showing off handfuls of butterfly hair clips and grapey kimonos from Kyoto. Everything Noa did was excused, deflected, by the Roshi. Noa could be a regular despot, as Ray said dangerously. Noa's carelessness tested care, her arrogance tested humility. Jubal had seen her give his sister a hard push into the handles of the wheelbarrow after Tamsen praised Violet for her crawl stroke.

I have to call you out on that, Violet, said Noa haughtily. You let Tamsen praise you constantly. Tamsen was silent.

Up ahead, Tamsen and Noa appeared deep in contemplation as they watered the plush velour mossbeds. He watched Violet pause and drop her sweater behind a bush. Tamsen would not like it over her arm where she could break twigs by her clumsy breadth, by accident. Sita didn't like to see anything over the arm or around the waist like a worldly tourist. Sita would mime snapping a camera.

Tamsen looked up to greet Violet, but Noa recoiled and charged off abruptly. She indulged in moods everyone else tried to steer clear of. Indulged in her father, thought Jubal.

Devotees were gathered on the lawn that sloped from the farm-house to a gate of old maples. The Eighth, Heidi, had recently had a magnificent vision in which she was a bright cord from the Guru's navel: all in dharma talk, poemform, Open Letter. Now she entertained the smaller children by picking up forks and spoons with the rectos muscles and blubber of her stomach.

Craig R. paced, fastidious and freckled, making sure people sat where they should be sitting. "Self" was a story they told themselves, just a vanity of survival.

The girls imitated the wives and pulled their sweaters around their shoulders. Summer was behind them. Violet alone was bare shouldered.

Jubal found his place. There was Cleary, her face streaked with shadows. It came down that the ladies should continue to use mascara. When they cried, their eyes looked like caves in their faces. There was Dovorh—she caught Jubal's eye and smiled. The lieutenant turned to see who she was smiling at.

The sky was open, the woodshop quiet, and suddenly people were turning to see the Guru as He came up the aisle on Messner's arm. People were bowing and yearning toward Him, breathing the air He breathed, He and Messner thick as thieves, flanked by the Inner Circle. Jubal saw the lieutenant hoist up a smile to mask his envy of Messner.

The Guru settled before them in lotus on a pure white zafu on a sky-blue blanket. He made soft mudras in the air above the offerings.

Moments passed in His grace.

Compared to Him, time was nothing.

All fundamental existence should be converted to the yoga of communion, dear ones, He spoke finally. Will you live with Me?

There was a gentle burr of sound, a hundred notes merged in love for the Guru.

I abide in human form to suffer you, people. You see, the laughter comes out of My ears, and My bellybutton. He pulled His kimono open. His bellybutton looked like lips, pouting.

Om, nama, shiva
God, I saw You naked

The Ninth Beautiful bore trays of raw fruits and vegetables. Jubal anticipated the bile-sting of carrot on an empty stomach. Ray said Piti had a look of Germanic, stoic misunderstanding. The Guru made a flicking motion to dismiss her. She didn't go, and He scrabbled at her, on the ground, where she had performed a full prostration. Jubal hoped she would get up in time to pass the trays of food. Dovorh had a trick of snatching something extra, folding it in her Punjabi to give him later. He never wanted her to go hungry, but neither could he refuse her offerings.

The Guru looked out over the crowns of His disciples. What I say first is for the children, He started. He blinked slowly, like a reptile. Go and tell the so-called grownups, surrender the Mortal Recoil. He touched the air before Him as if He were feeling the fontanels of His babies. Tell them death is the human coincidence. Should they happen to coincide with their own lives, they might taste the salt of death, the natural state we call the Mystery.

If the sangha had a collective breath it was up in the shallow pan, the collective jaw of the sangha had lockjaw, the group lungs were airless.

The Guru was fearless.

All fear was fear of death.

Dess, in His Russian.

The Teachings were simple: they weren't supposed to be afraid of it. They weren't, until they imagined someone they loved dying.

He called out, Jubal!

Love and fear and shock were indistinguishable in His presence. Jubal thought fleetingly, fear was also the stupid thing that kept you from death, wasn't it?

This is your Schism, Jubal! Who would you rather die, Ray or Cleary?

Death was at the center of sadhana, the Practice.

My bell-boy! Who would you rather?

He turned His gaze toward the girls and He beckoned Violet. The lotus was a floating flower, she floated. The Guru paddled the air and the current drew her closer. She was a tiny fish in His ear, she shone like a ripple. The Guru looked out over His students.

Have I made Myself clear in My love for you, loved ones?

The sonorous group murmur. He was the King of Happiness, the baby who smiled. He shined for them and all they had to do was smile.

Violet smiled, smiling was a ribbon of bliss that pulled through her body.

They were shining. Their mouths, eyes, noses. Protein and shining. Their eyes rolled back. They gasped because the whole world loved Him. They felt the brunt of proof of His love, the whole world loved them.

Listen, said the Guru. They were listening. You don't understand your own creation. Even in His reprimand He loved them.

You can't solve its Mystery. What is this Western construct? That the Mystery has some solution? Am I making Myself clear to you in semantics? Do you see what I mean, people? The Mystery of which I speak defies solution-salvation. Your limitminds, I suffer them, your literalminds, I bear them.

He smiled.

Out of your unknowing you assign God to your lifetime. This is the way it is with you. God is the answer to any question, do you hear Me? You're so practical. You made tools in caves and scratched your pictures.

He was tickled by their human. It was only human to invent God, to breach the Mystery. They only had to be what they were—He would take care of the rest of it.

There was a scuffle where the girls were sitting, and Craig R. sprang to attention. As Jubal shifted to see, there was a piercing bird shriek. Jubal had heard Noa practice that shriek on his sister. He shifted again, and he could see Noa wrestling herself away from Jyoti, trying to dive under the Sixth Wife's tunic. What was Noa thinking?

Now people were distracted, looking around to see what was happening. Noa hung her head, then shook it fiercely. She let her face shake too, her lips and her eyeballs. Her black hair went out like a flying saucer.

I want to go up, she said. I want to go up with King!

He will call you, said Jyoti, looking around for help from Sita.

What is wrong with you? hissed Sita, leaning forward. Her teeth looked frozen. She took Noa by the shoulder without taking her eyes off the Guru.

Noa flung herself forward. Sita pulled her back by the other shoulder. People were watching.

You're acting egoic, said Sita furiously. Turn to the Divine, Noa!

Noa worked herself into a squatting position. Sita: Sit down!

Jubal saw that the Guru, oblivious, rested His love-eyes upon Violet.

Sita grabbed Noa's wrist and pinched between the tendons.

The Guru rose, lifting Violet with Him. He caressed her head, He had called it a seashell, and once again He looked out over His students. Noa paused her drama. The whole invention of time waited as devotees waited.

It is all of your tantrum!

They should never underestimate His understanding. It is your mess! Do you hear Me? Mark My words, it is yours!

You all rage against your unhappiness, well get the hell over it!

Get the hell over your unhappiness, people! Your chronic failure to love Me as I love!

He noticed Amina beside Him. She tipped her head forward so that her straight blond hair closed before her. He pulled one half of it open. He let it go again. He cried, Get the hell over the merits and demerits of turning off the light switch when you leave the bathroom!

Jubal saw Sita signal and Jyoti yanked Noa out of the crowd and across the grass toward the farmhouse. Noa struggled, but more for show. They disappeared into the farmhouse kitchen.

The sangha seemed to resettle. Messner rose and continued for the Guru, his voice velvet but unconsoling, Now we will sit in silence.

People loved to say the domes of their heads were the dome of the heavens.

People loved to say there was vibrato in the silence of the Guru.

But there seemed to be some low-Level restlessness of the sangha that preceded the sound. A huge sound, like the air itself breathing.

For half a second it could have been the noise of the powersaw starting up in the woodshop.

It happened so quickly.

Later, people said He must have sucked time out of the air, as if it were oxygen.

Before people even smelled anything, the sound became the whoosh and roar of fire.

Heidi and Piti held on to Kai. (Kai could smell His musky sandalwood on them—she must have been able to.) Kai kicked the junior wives' shins and thighs, and she got her shoulder underneath Heidi's jaw and—this came out later—knocked out two of Heidi's molars.

Was this the sonic boom of God's presence? Was this, finally, the Beginning, which opened its mouth to swallow the Ending?

Fire poured out the farmhouse windows. The smoke seemed solid. The lieutenant was there, and he held Kai against him. Smoke mushroomed over the farmhouse as if smoke were earth. Afterward, people would say it was like being buried.

CHAPTER 12

SO HE WENT TO SEE what was happening back in California. Pritam spirited Him off to the airport. He would speak to another community of disciples. Five hundred people in San Rafael, longing for the Bright Beam of Him, avowal of enlightenment. Privately Ray said five hundred was an exaggeration. Five hundred was banter, Ray muttered. Jubal stayed quiet. Banter like bantam, a rooster. Or badminton. One whole summer He played against Gary. The two of them naked behind the pole barn. Before it was a lot of dead cars and rotten machinery. That was the summer He invited people to become aficionados in the history and psychology of all rackets.

He would tell disciples in San Rafael what He always told us, said Pritam. People use God to wrangle power. Beware of god-heads. Beware of language and the manipulation of true understanding. Disciples' power and veracity is all tied up in God's power and veracity. Pritam said, He is more than God, if your Western minds need quantification, people.

He was not punishing them by leaving, said Sita. The Second Wife was unadulterated and rational. She had never been pregnant. Heidi staggered around the Sanctuary with her God-belly. Ray said it was probably Messner's. She had pulled up her tunic and showed Jubal how her skin was flowered and itchy.

He was nonpunishing, Sita insisted, but still, two people left, people who were easily shocked, inconstant. Penny del Deo, their sponsor from Halifax, and a lady who had at one time been the wife of a famous cultural anthropologist who had, in worldly terms, to the press, endorsed the Guru. The names of these two ladies were now associated with the Fire. They had been burned off, they were the signifiers of purification, they had left their ash to fill the coffers.

Every afternoon Ray drove Violet in the Sanctuary station wagon to visit Noa in the hospital. It came through Messner that the visit should be no longer than fifteen minutes. Dad Ray should sit in the lobby. He should work on his koan or count the beads of his mala. He didn't need to speak to anyone. Temperamentally your dad is merry, affectless, Jubal, said Messner. He never tries to get a rise out of worldly people, does he. He turned back to Ray: If there are newspaper people there, for instance—Good man, Ray, said innermost Messner.

There was talk of Noa's transformation. Some of her willfulness and morbid attraction to power had discarnated, she had become gaunt in the hospital, almost as thin as Kai now, and as aloof and sober as Sita. All this was attributed to Him, He always knew what He was doing, they were like hens scratching up the dirt-cake, their rusty little beaks, their thrust-out breastmeat of self-regard, their fundamentally ludicrous questions.

They were already in the car when Dovorh hurried out of the farmhouse. Ray stopped and rolled down his window. Jubal climbed through the crotch of the seats into the back. Ray honked at a peacock.

Ponked a heacock, thought Jubal. Dovorh looked around at him. The sorrow in her eyes—how could she smile?

The peacock picked his way across the gravel. His thoughts were the size of a raspberry. A planet.

Have you seen her? asked Dovorh. Ray shook his head. He raised his eyes to the mirror to make contact with Violet.

Jubal attached himself to the flickering forest. To the road like a belt, cars slammed by and vanished. His sister closed her eyes, she got carsick. The car hurt. Jubal could see Dovorh's string wrists, her tips pressing the dashboard. Ray was a choppy driver.

Dovorh took Jubal's arm in the hospital lobby as if she would take him with her to see Noa. He tried to pull away but she was suddenly strong and elastic. He looked for Ray but Ray avoided the confrontation.

A nurse stared them up and down before leading them busily down corridors; doctors' and nurses' work spilled out from behind curtains where patients were lurking. He tried to fall behind them, but his Confidante pushed him forward. The nurse came to a halt and pointed them into one of the broom closets. There was Noa, propped on an elevated cot underneath a cold window, her head shaved like monk, her dark eyes in heavy shadow. It wasn't a broom closet. He told himself to breathe, his fear was overtaking him, when would he ever master it?

Noa turned her head away from them almost regally. The twin of her cot was unmade and empty.

Where is King? said Noa to the wall.

What are you saying? pleaded Dovorh, drawing closer.

Don't come near me, Dovorh!

Dovorh stopped and bowed her head.

You are so mundane, Violet! said Noa.

Jubal thought she didn't know what the word meant. It was getting a lot of grownup use lately. He looked at his sister and he could tell she knew Noa had misused it.

Noa, Dovorh tried soothingly.

They waited. Noa, said Dovorh again. Jubal is here to listen.

They waited. To listen to your Leela.

Now Noa turned to look at them and her eyes narrowed, reconsidering.

Kai never comes, she said witheringly. Dovorh was already making her way closer.

Noa, be peaceful.

The television hung from the ceiling, dark and mirrored. Who was inside, thought Jubal, Narcissus? Dovorh sat carefully on the edge of the cot. Jubal was aware of a dried urine smell. He didn't have his tape recorder.

Jyoti locked me in, said Noa. They're always plotting against me! Her voice was hoarse already. Later he would learn it was from the breathing tube.

He loves to watch Disney with me above all others. He told me I was Sixth, make no mistake, said Noa, He told me!

Jubal noticed food on a tray on the metal windowsill. Had Noa rejected it? He was hungry. He was so hungry he was queasy. A plastic trough of macaroni, a white cup of pudding. He couldn't take his eyes off it. He was sick and hungry at the same time, it was unbearable. The room was too warm. He closed his eyes. He opened them and caught sight of Noa's hand bandaged like a mitten.

I made Him so happy when I gave Him my bowl of ice cream, He put His whole face inside it. I called Him Bowl Face! cried Noa.

Violet was also staring at the tray of dinner.

I saw rice balls and prunes in honey, said Noa. For my father the Roshi. No one told me! she cried in anguish. No one told me that my father was coming! She turned away again. They all waited in silence. Finally it seemed as if she might be sleeping, and Dovorh gave a sign that they should leave her.

Kai met the station wagon in the farmyard and immediately sent Jubal to the presbytery to change the flowers. He was like a houseboy, Zoya had teased him.

He opened the door and votives fluttered. Their flames were

always sinking into their molten wells, it was China and Meenakshi's Service and the girls were not reliable. He bowed at the threshold. Pillows and mats and zafus made human shapes even in the dark—soft things, the Guru had said, that people had tied to the tops of their station wagons when they arrived to give up soft things altogether.

I want this place cleaned out! the Guru would roar periodically. We'll live like monks and then you'll see what I've been through! Worldly men and ladies are out there grinding their unhappiness day after day in the mills of their own invention! You are chosen! Every single day is an opportunity to divulge yourselves of that same shit you call unhappiness, people!

He could really pelt them if He wanted to, said Ray. If He needed to. They understood the contract. The innermost would say, You think anything He does or doesn't do is not meant to test us?

Jubal went through the inventory of offerings at the altar. Icicles of rose quartz.

A dried four-leaf clover.

A sandalwood incense holder like a sleigh.

A couple of tumorous papayas. His eyes adjusted to the dark, and he reached for a clutch of chrysanthemums. He knew their stems would be slimy and he shivered.

He hadn't thought, somehow, that Noa would be alone in the hospital. After all, she and Kai still shared a bedroom in the farmhouse.

Her burns kept burning. That's what Dovorh said, that the progress of burns was to turn flesh-eating. Dovorh said it was their nature.

Just then he caught movement in a far corner. He froze, but it was too late. Jubal, said the lieutenant.

Jubal laid the dead chrysanthemums on the floor beside him. They would make a puddle.

Did you know He came back last night? The lieutenant's voice was dry, as if he hadn't spoken for hours.

Jubal shook his head.

He's tan, said the lieutenant. We're not tan, eh Jubal?

Jubal began to fidget with the pills on his socks. He stopped himself. He was still trying to train his little toe, although he hadn't practiced in a while.

Five o'clock this morning He was banging around my cabin in His diaper, said the lieutenant.

You got a lot of rest in My absence, Gartshorn!

Quit playing with your feet, Jubal, said the lieutenant in his normal voice. Were you at the hospital?

Jubal nodded.

I can't hear you.

Yes.

How does she look?

He couldn't really answer.

The lieutenant cleared his throat, switched back to the Guru: Let's take a walk down to the woodshop. How are My enterprises? You let this place go to hell in My absence. I come back and you're all sphincters. Kai comes to Me complaining about her daughter. Kai is engaged in cunt behavior. What I mean by that is literal, sexual, and derogatory. Look into that, Gartshorn.

The lieutenant gave a harsh laugh. My poor feelings, you know, Jubal, all stuffed down there at the bottom of the basket.

If he took too long Kai would call him out for being distracted, thought Jubal. Just like China and Meenakshi. Of its own accord his hand made its way to his sock again.

Quit playing footsie, said the lieutenant.

If others have suffering—now the lieutenant imitated the Guru imitating His disciples—then I am not entitled to anything. If others have suffering, I am excrement. I might as well starve.

Eh Shorngart? Do you remember when you were always hanging around Kai in the kitchen? You were this overgrown rabbit, humpy-jumpy Hartshorn, peering into her bread bowls, salad bowls, not looking into her eyes, afraid to, but telling her what she thought, this gentle mindfuck.

He laughed in my face, said the lieutenant. I could smell the onion.

You revolve around suffering, you define yourself in terms of quantity and proximity to suffering, you are enslaved to suffering. Does that surprise you? Are you going to tell Me you're suffering for Kai? Do you think I don't know My First Wife suffers for the Roshi's daughter? Are you going to remind Me you love My wife, lieutenant?

The lieutenant stopped.

Almost to himself: You know a Divine Being doesn't have the same social skills as a bourgeoisie, a shudra. It's just a role we're playing. Life is a role we're all playing.

But we saw Noa, didn't we, Jubal? Wrapped up like a mummy? Grafted like—he cast about—an orchard? You know the doctors had to take some of the skin and tissue from her thighs? Did you know that, Jubal?

He didn't know that.

I told Him I'd just been to the hospital. I told Him I went with Kai, Kai was going, and He wiped His eyes, you know how He does that. We were getting closer to the woodshop and I could hardly keep talking over the noise. I can feel her pain, I shouted. Noa's. I can feel her terror when those kitchen towels caught fire. The door was locked, Master.

The lieutenant paused. Her back is the worst. She was on her stomach on the floor, where the air was. She passed out quickly. Jyoti told me.

I blurted out, I don't understand why You don't end it! Why You don't heal Noa!

And the Guru said, I cannot alter the course you people have chosen. If I healed the burns I would be called a freak and they would throw Me out of the hospital. You know that. If I healed everyone's pain I would be a healing machine instead of a Teacher. You people would get your fix, as you say, and forget the Practice. Bow to Me and feel My love, John.

Jubal was aware of the thrill the lieutenant took from taking on the voice of the Guru. The darkness of the presbytery seemed to disperse from the excitement. The lieutenant turned to Jubal again, and now his look was a challenge. Jubal wanted to use his sleeve to dry the floor where the dripping stems of the flowers had made more of a lake than he'd expected.

Get your hands out of your socks. It looks like you're doing hanky-panky in there, Jubal. A short laugh. Did He send you here to get my confession? All in Leela? Is it my turn, Jubal?

As quickly as he could, Jubal swiped the wet floor with his forearm.

CHAPTER 13

THERE WAS THE Period of No Seen Thing. Nothing came of it. Jubal turned fifteen. Daterolls, Dad Ray with a screwball, vodka was a way for some of the men to laugh at their screwy screwy selves again, said the Guru. Or was it screwdriver?

His hair had gotten darker. Closer to black, now. His eyebrows were suddenly coarser, so that his eyes seemed shy.

Jesus, Jubal, said the lieutenant. You're growing a mustache.

He touched his lip, but it wasn't true, and the lieutenant laughed at him. He wasn't Narcissus.

The lieutenant had invited him to walk down to the bay, and now Jubal hung a half step behind him. If he was protecting the self in a low-Level way he apologized silently to the Guru, the self, the nonself, the universe, whomever it was who took apologies.

Was he supposed to have a mustache? There were no other fifteen-year-olds on the Sanctuary.

The bay was as clear as maple sap in the early spring, none of that scum brown around the edges, no fish corpses on the beach as pale as balloons. The lieutenant gave him a hand up to the top of the seawall. Nimble Jubal, he said. There were the humped backs of three islands, dollops of earth all covered with the same tough little spruce forest. Jubal felt unsure of his balance. His hands on the cement to steady himself were that bleached-out barnacle color. The lieutenant jumped off the wall and made a half turn to relieve himself in the pine needles.

He sprang up again, hare haunches. You ready? he said, eyeing the tape recorder.

It's broken, said Jubal.

The lieutenant placed the machine on the flat of his hand as if it had stump legs. He shook it, shrugged, gave it back to Jubal.

We came of age in the Age of Experimentation, the lieutenant started. We were under the impression that experimentation loosened the soul.

He sounded as if he were quoting himself, thought Jubal.

Well newsflash, said the lieutenant, the soul was never angelic. In fact the soul was voyeuristic, the soul was prurient in its impulse to host the body. It snooped in the body's bedroom, it had no shame rifling through the body's medicine cabinet.

He narrowed his eyes at the nonworking cassette recorder.

Sure, I was always in the kitchen. I used to try it out on the First Beautiful: You think the soul's an angel? Kai protesting, me waving her into silence. You could say the soul was like a teenage girl enthralled with a pack of angels. It did whatever they did. Smoked in the stalls, flushed the butts down the toilet. Kai smiled, I took a step closer.

The lieutenant stopped. He looked curiously at Jubal. What sense do you make of this?

Jubal didn't know if he meant the Leela or the two of them perched on the wall together. The blue spring sun riding the blue water. Now the islands looked as if they were jostling one another.

The lieutenant picked up his thread again.

All I'd ever been was another aspiring shithead. Jesus. I was twenty-four, teaching two sections of freshman expos and two sections of the Victorians; the big thing was I'd landed my own apartment in Slummerville, not wholly unrelated to Boston. I'd tracked the listings in the separate local papers, I'd made shit-eating bows to slumlords and bottom-rung real estate agents, what I'd done was wag my university contract under their noses. See? Four classes. Nobody knew the difference between sections and classes.

The lieutenant shook his head in appreciation of the stupidity of others.

I was self-serious. I had no roommate with whom I could toke away another weekend. I liked to think of myself as being as lonely as the bottom of the giant lake I'd grown up on.

Already Jubal heard his voice in the lieutenant's voice. He heard himself in the presbytery, the throne room, speaking for the lieutenant. The Guru liked to keep the tapes, to turn them into Prasad along with the jumbled barricade of fruits and flowers, forbidden cakes and fancy chocolates. But He never much liked to play them, His musician's ear offended by the hissy, drugstore sound quality.

Lonely and giant: Would a girl appreciate John's understatement? Hopefully she would never have stood on the shores, looking into the depths of Lake Michigan. The lieutenant felt he should have a corner on contemplation of the fathoms.

Jubal tried unsticking his palms from the seawall. The cement would have perforated them. The water was an arresting patch-work of textures.

The lieutenant wanted a girl to see his barren refrigerator, his handwriting on student papers. He wanted her to pad across his tacky lino floor, her eyes raccoon-ringed from waiting into the night for him to finish marking up student papers.

Winters he maneuvered his moped through eight inches of in-dustrial slush like saliva, until he was forced down the burrow with the rest of the rabbits. Rats. No choice but to let himself be rumbled through fetid tunnels, inched along gray trestles that flexed above neighborhoods in grayscale.

One morning he found himself on the crowded platform of a rank and humid T station, the seams of the cement walls dark with sweat stains. Girls must have been hot in those Inca ponchos they were all wearing. The nearest light was buzzing, and he broke out in fresh sweat along his hairline.

He cut rudely in front of a couple. No protest, no pause in their conversation, their bodies accommodated him as if they were all in this herd together. He hated couples, and yet the crowd pressed in from all sides as if he were destined for them. His agitation grew. He looked down at his feet—crowds could lift people off their feet like a force of nature. He was alarmed by how easily he could imagine it happening.

The Guru would famously say He wasn't above working in revelations—in clichés and aphorisms, algorithms, baby talk, pillow talk, paradox. But what were the chances: the couple was talking about someone John knew. Knew *of*, rather—a celebrity professor in Cultural Anthropology—and John leered to himself in perverse appreciation of the hours he'd spent stoned with various lowly roommates wondering whether they could get famous and girls and famous girls if they changed their names to Professor Pablo Amanguarda.

The gist of the conversation seemed to be that Amanguarda had a guru. What was it that struck John out of nowhere? It was as if, when he heard the name of this guru, the name was amplified. As if his skull became a great echoing cathedral. He had the sensation of sudden space around him. In fact he could move his limbs as if through light, freely. He must have lost himself for some long moment in this new sense of freedom, an expanse that transcended the tight crowd, because when he came to, as it were, when he looked around for the couple, they had vanished.

The announcer gave the warning, and the train married the platform.

Looking back, it seemed to John that in one single blink of some great eye he arrived at the Guru's doorstep.

Late afternoon, raw spring, a half-junked farmstead, a new world order. The place seemed deserted. He didn't know enough about life to figure domesticated birds and animals meant recent humans. The cows were fat and, more important, although John didn't notice, their udders emptied. He rolled the bike into some bushes. Eight hours was plenty for a TA who skippered a moped because he couldn't afford four wheels. The bushes were packed with yellow flowers. He knew even less about plants than animals. But it smelled good all the way up the country. Springtime, and he'd ridden away his hangover.

He knocked on the door of the farmhouse. No answer. He thought they'd all be really stoned, pursuing happiness, necessarily happy in pursuit of it, so he decided to go inside uninvited. After the ride, he needed a long drink of water. He needed a long drink after all the bullshit. The whole flimsy mind game. Life barely concealing the deep dark hole of existence.

The kitchen was clean and simple. He found a glass easily. Without knowing it, he drank the wellwater of the Guru.

He let himself back out and wandered around among the animals. They looked at him or they didn't; he found he liked their shit smells layered in the brine of seaweed.

He drifted down to the bay. It was thick and purple. The sun was already setting. He thought he could sleep in the bushes by his bike, not quite a Goldilocks, and see what happened in the morning. It felt good, curling into himself against the cold, which wasn't sharp or threatening but purifying, mentholated.

He must have slept for several hours. He woke up to noise:

whooping and song from the direction of the farmhouse. When he opened his eyes he could see flickering lights through the bushes. He propped himself up on an elbow—he was wonderfully rested. He got up and walked with great certainty and gladness in the direction of the farmhouse.

A girl opened the door, a vision. She was as tall as John was, a bump in her nose, and long, Virgin Mary-Modigliani eyelids.

Come on in, she said, in the middle of some other laughter. Perfectly natural. Perfect. The first person John ever saw touched by Him, made beautiful by her love for Him, and by her first straightforward smile. Kai. He didn't know her name yet.

In he came. A beer? she asked him. Her legs were so long they started at her breasts, which were boyish.

He saw a couple of bottles of vodka, a platter of darkly roasted fowl, a rich feast smell of cornbread and garlic. Another girl was dancing in a corner, her long hair piled on top of her head like a turban. There was an ambient joking, laughing feeling, and John saw someone grab the turban-girl and kiss her deeply, thoroughly, at once public and private. He smiled at Kai when she handed him the cold bottle. It was just what he wanted. A drink had never tasted so clean, his thirst had never been so completely pegged to the universe.

A girl with short spun hair and a small reddish nose winked at John so he turned to follow her. From behind she was eye-poppingly curvaceous. In the kitchen she handed him a plate and a fork that clattered. She bent over and opened the oven. The heat went straight to his heart. He could feel his heart muscles opening. He could never figure out who she was, later—the weird thing about first impressions.

He didn't ask any questions for fear the dream would end, but it was easy to find out everything. Nothing was hidden. Love was out there in the open. The Guru was radiating robust love, drinking beer that turned to vodka. John loved the way the Guru looked, like a grizzly, with enormous loafy hands and split knuckles.

At dawn folks started peeling off toward the bedrooms. John was filled with love for everyone in the farmhouse. He and the Guru were still talking. Kai came over and sat at their feet—the Guru stroked her head and John could feel everything.

Come with Me to see the sunrise, said the Guru. He rose and lumbered out of the farmhouse. Kai held still. Was she waiting for John to say something?

Me? said John.

She tipped her face up and nodded, smiling. He fell in love with her right then and there, and he leaned down over his whole life and kissed her. Her mouth was soaking wet, and salty. Then he went out after the Guru.

The sky was now a lampshade. One rooster, then another, and another. Effortlessly John could tell they had different messages. He wanted to sound off with them. The Guru said, Come back to this place we're making, John. As My lieutenant.

John was under the impression that they stood there irresistible to each other, laughing about nothing, laughing about empirical-existential-inexhaustable nothing.

He handed over his moped, sold his books to a secondhand shop in Cambridge, presented the Guru with two twenties. The Guru whooped, The lieutenant doesn't worry about money! The lieutenant wasn't sure if it was a joke or a fundamental truth of the new Buddha.

That first winter, harshing out of the cold cabin behind Gary Messner, snow stinging the side of his face, having shaved with the side of a scissors, the Guru would provoke him: What is it with you, John? Some full-time love affair with suffering?

The Guru pulled a face, then reached around and pinched the skin of his waist with His fingernails. He kept His nails long like a lady's. As if suffering was never the fault of cold-cabin-life, the woodstove with acrid smoke that gave you red eyes like a devil and chronic sinusitis.

Allsuffering isn't stubbing your big toe against the threshold of the outhouse! cried the Guru. Allsuffering is samsara, said the Guru. Samsara, illusion.

The illusion of Kai falling for him. She said you hate the people you love more than the people you hate. Sometimes he hated the Guru, but which hate was it?

No running water in his and Gary's cabin, no illusion of running water, just his nemesis-roommate Gary, great-looking accountant, known back then as the guy with the glasses, with the face behind the glasses that devastated both men and women. Even the teeth, which were really white, like a boy's teeth. They were ancient bachelor brothers. They shat in a bucket in front of the tin-can woodstove when it was too cold to sit in the outhouse. The milky plastic window tore at its nails like a trapped animal.

Kai lived under the eaves, in the farmhouse.

Summer came around with scourges of black flies and mosquitoes. He had Service to scout firewood, and he threw it under the tarp on the side of the cabin. He had Service to clear brush barehanded; he and Craig Reich, the Guru called him redfox, horny poet from Rhode Island. Get the roots out, warned the Guru. Craig R.'s head bobbing in the undergrowth, head too big for his body, even before he starved himself down to poet size, 130. Once he tripped and split his chin open. Poor poet. They worked under a vow of silence. Abhisheka, hard initiation: sunburn and sweat welts, horseflies that stung through blue jeans. Deerflies like B-52s, said Craig R., later. He was interested in martial imagery for his poems.

Their backs were bare too, and the sun shuttered through the forest. The sun clattered through a million open sockets in the woods to fill the clearing. There was so much salt in their eyes it was hard to see anything.

Once, at dusk, they got into a nest of porcupines. The porcupines must have thought the men were dogs—no tools, not talking.

Jesus! cried the lieutenant. So much for the vow of silence. The animals lowered their prehistoric heads and swung toward the humans. Later Gary practically had to strap them down to pull the quills out. Soused and doused with vodka. The long barbs shredded their flesh in the name of the Guru.

It made a good story.

The Guru had a tendency to use the word lifetime when John was pretty sure He meant story.

He stopped abruptly.

You still listening, Jubal? He tousled Jubal's hair and Jubal shrank.

Am I boring you? said the lieutenant.

He understands that you can't just tell your Leela to a wall, though, doesn't He, Jubal. You're a quiet guy, but it helps to have you sitting beside me.

One stipulation of being full-time-student-lieutenant of Avadhoot Master King Ivanovich was that he couldn't marry. The Guru said marriage was just a code for dealing with another human's unhappiness. Or, later, He would crow that He had enough wives for everyone. All in tradition: Krishna had to multiply himself to satisfy his thousand gopis. The lieutenant loved Kai and the Guru called that abhisheka also. Initiation was not some initial hoop you had to jump through. It was constant. Sometimes the Guru teased him:

She was asking about you, lieutenant. As if love were the junior prom, it killed him.

People slept three or four hours. Sleep was mind, said the Guru. Mind control. He would grin: better for Him to control them. People were sitting at three-thirty, four in the morning. The sun wouldn't have breached the bay, not even in summer. Dinner was at ten or eleven, Kai in the kitchen, a bottle of white wine tucked somewhere, getting warm, she drank from a mug, never a glass, he'd drink from hers to keep things simple. And taste the garlic, if they were on garlic, she left on the rim of it. Her loose tank tops that showed the sides of her breasts and her damp armpits. The Guru made the material holy, and the holy—material.

One day he and Gary took a hike through the ferns and blueberries and up into the scaly pine trees that had to crack rocks to get their roots in.

A day off for us shudras, said Gary. Stupidheads.

They had been told to clear out: Go knot your feet elsewhere, said the Guru. Quit crawling all over the Sanctuary like ants on a corpse, you shudras. Gary pointed out he'd rather be an ant than a maggot.

The lieutenant went ahead, he always did in those days, but he could hear innermost Gary steady behind him. It was late summer, and Gary, vintage Gary, called up to him, You can eat the blueberries! Two skinny Zenheads, a whole selvedge of lowbush blueberries.

They grazed companionably, even though the Guru had lately been playing them all off each other. Divide and conquer. The Guru prodding him about Gary: Does that guy have homosexual tendencies? One of His favorite lines of questioning.

When the lieutenant didn't answer immediately the Guru laughed, Protecting your guy's shitty Practice, eh lieutenant?

They hiked along in silence. They came to another patch of berries. It occurred to the lieutenant he assumed Gary was a rational person. After all, they lived together. They lived in a goddamn one-room cabin. Gary straightened his sleeping bag on the cot in the morning so it didn't look like a disemboweled cocoon, just like the lieutenant did. Gary threw wood in the stove—he didn't like to be cold any more than the lieutenant did. They put their few clothes together, sure, even the soiled underwear, to be washed by one of the ladies in the farmhouse. One or the other of them dropped the dirty socks outside the kitchen. Neither of them wanted to be alone with death; both probably had the same idea he could pass death off on the other at the last possible moment.

The lieutenant cut himself off with sudden intensity. You know what, Jubal? We all want to be absolved from fear of death. Isn't that the point of life? When it comes right down to it? He didn't wait for confirmation.

There we were, he continued, rummaging like bears, like devastated March bears, fur on our ribs, and it came to me that all we did, we did in the name of the Guru. Our own names meant nothing. It might have been the first time I felt it—felt it, and accepted it gladly.

At that same moment Gary looked up at me. Gary's glasses had big square frames back then, I'll never forget those glasses, and his brown eyes, all magnified, seemed unfathomably innocent.

Hey lieutenant, said true friend Gary. You know Kai's pregnant?

I was sucked way past quiet. Way back to the origin of things, silent and frozen. I looked down and I had purple stains on my fingers.

Up to now I'd consoled myself with the idea that when we got through some of the low-Level stuff, when we'd established our

Practice, we'd leave together. Me and Kai. I'd find some means of courting her—I told myself it was only natural. We couldn't stay with the Guru forever, like children. However much we loved Him. Just sharing a mattress on the floor of some Zen-simple apartment, in Boston, wherever, it didn't seem like a lot to ask for.

The lieutenant looked at Jubal pleadingly. He caught himself and turned a sneer on the ocean.

I didn't know what I was doing, my own strength, until I'd already stepped up to Gary and swept the glasses clear off the harmonious visage. I caught Gary's nose and it went white, just bleached, before it started bleeding. I was so quiet about the whole thing that both of us heard the glasses landing far off in other bushes.

Those brown eyes were lighter and shallower without the glasses. Gary covered his nose with his hand. The blood was already getting sticky. I walked off from the fucking innermost down the mountain.

When I hit the road I kept walking. Cars blurred like spinning tops. I thought about bus stations, pay phones, the old world. I pulled out my wallet. The old wallet of animal leather. Jesus. Two dollars. No idea how I'd come into two dollars. The Guru knew I loved her.

The Crazy Guy knew everything.

So she shared her wine in the kitchen. Once, when she reached up to a high shelf, I got a glimpse of her pinprick of a bellybutton. Then she said, John—and I poked my hand up to the top to retrieve her raisins. A big jar of them with mouse shit stuck to the bottom.

I allowed myself to slow for a moment. I leaned over the stone bridge on the main street and looked into the dimly lit river. Waterfall above. "Loved her."

Meant nothing. Buddhism was the joker in a deck of cards,

wearing a stupid pointed hat. Pointed toes, tights, at the will and the wit and the wisdom of the player. The Guru was the player.

I turned away from the waterfall, it even had a white sound, you know, Jubal?

Although it's decidedly yellow.

I kept walking through the town until I came out the ass end of it. Pines and cedars didn't mind the gravelly edges. Moss padded the bases of the tree trunks.

Jubal imagined himself looking back at the lieutenant from one of those islands.

The lieutenant was just a guy with his legs dangling down the seawall. Jubal could raise his hand and wave from that island—he chose the one in the middle, protected by the others—and the lieutenant wouldn't even see him.

But in that same moment the lieutenant made a side grab for his shoulders. I have nothing to hide, Jubal.

Jubal could see the pulse like a twig in his temple.

There is this adversarial attitude of flushing me out, but—he spread his hands in his lap– what you see is what you get, said the lieutenant. He looked away as if to bare himself, to allow Jubal to look at him.

CHAPTER 14

ALL IN LEELA: The Guru called the lieutenant to Him. The lieutenant was in loose pants and his body, after a long sitting period, was mush inside them. He felt he could hardly get up and walk to the Guru where He sat on His King's cushions in the throne room. And yet when the lieutenant took the first shaky step, it wasn't shaky. He was suddenly enlivened, new legs were hardening inside the old ones.

The Guru was watching, smiling, knowing everything. Come to me, John, He said again, in His immense kindness. That was a good session.

It had felt as difficult as ever. Although the lieutenant had been fully engaged, not thinking about Kai, not thinking about something Gary had said to him, fuck Gary, not thinking, Is this a good session? But with the second step toward the Guru the lieutenant's body was strong and ready. He was Paul Bunyan, why the hell not, he'd go out after zazen and do ten hours of brush clearing and it would feel like ten minutes. In one fell swoop, He reached the Guru's side and knelt to receive Him.

The Guru leaned deeply forward. Go catch Me a chicken. The Guru was grinning ear-to-ear like a Fu dog. I am very serious!

The lieutenant rose and stumbled through the farmhouse with the Guru on his heels, His long strides, farmer-yogi, swinging His loose arms like a strapping peasant.

Right away a bird with muddy wings and a growth around its ankle caught the lieutenant's eye. Old and weak, easier to snatch up in a smelly bundle. Still, he knew he would be forced to lunge this way and that, the chicken dance, ridiculous.

The lieutenant stood toeing BB's of gravel at the chicken. The Guru put His huge head back and roared with laughter.

You really look like you're suffering, lieutenant!

So maybe the chicken was Rama, Krishna, Vishnu, Buddha, all pure heart underneath the feathers. How was the lieutenant supposed to know God if God kept trading places with a chicken? It was hardly even a winged creature. The moment the lieutenant took his attention off it, the bird had already forgotten the lieutenant's existence. It was off under a bush like a nest of sticks, nothing had leafed yet.

Abruptly the Guru emptied His face of humor. He could do that. Neither was He bound to the physiology of conventions.

The lieutenant was ready to be lacerated for his failure to catch a chicken. But then, from behind His back, very, very calmly, the Guru handed John a flower.

A fresh, white crocus. The stem was warm from His love-touch. When had He picked it? Where?

The air itself drew back in wonder.

Go to Ozera, said the Guru simply.

The lieutenant stood there with his heart building to a crescendo.

Go on, Gartshorn. This flower is for Dovka.

The Guru gazed at him expectantly. The lieutenant was swamped in His love, astounded.

Are you going? said the Guru. His yellow teeth and His gold ones. Bemused, melancholic, tragic in His human. Because I want to look for peacock eggs now, lieutenant.

Kishkindha was really open, and spare. The lieutenant felt himself to be on another silly, ardent errand. The leaves weren't out yet, and the hemlocks and cedars seemed still diminished with winter. The sun poured through, the tree trunks were warm, and there were no blackflies yet, either. The Guru's purpose was the lieutenant's purpose. Messner had defined purpose: When He takes a shit you have to go also. The lieutenant laughed now, true friend Gary, it was true. Crocus in hand, he fairly bounded. He felt a weight had been lifted, the ground was slightly springy, why not spend the day snorting around the fallen logs and glacial boulders?

He caught sight of a strange pattern of light up ahead, some sort of bright hump in the middle of the pathway.

Was it an animal? He stopped and tried to squint it into being.

He was almost upon it before it suddenly took shape: Jesus, all of that openness — now he contracted.

He put it together in slow motion. There, bundled before him, was Kai's baby daughter, all in a white sheet, caught in a halo of sunlight.

His mind went blank. He could make no sense of it. He took a step closer as if to solve something. He had no idea if she was a beautiful thing — he had never believed in babies — not that he was against them — but there was no doubt now that this baby was in harm's way, and frightened. The eyes were wide in alarm. The tiny blunt arms and hands punched the air as he cast a shadow.

The lieutenant knelt and put his fingertips on her forehead. The skin was deep and warm. Too warm, her cheeks too rosy. He saw the dusty fur on her neck, the little lips were chapped and flattened. Her breathing sounded dangerously rapid.

What was going on here? Was he supposed to be the woodcutter in a Disney fairy tale? Kishkindha was so quiet he could hear a fly purring. It wasn't warm enough for flies, he realized. But it seemed warmer in this spot. Above her. Around her. Why was he implicated? He had not, in the end, protested when the Guru took

Kai away from him. He never said anything. Never showed any ill-will toward the Roshi. He had accepted everything. Why did he get continually hounded? He only wanted love to triumph. Love of Kai.

He hadn't held the baby before. Or any other baby. When he picked her up now the underside of her bundle was hot and soaking.

The Guru was in the farmyard where the lieutenant had left Him, throwing corn for the same chickens. It looked like they'd scratched all around a good-sized maple, picked every last nit out of the bark, every last ant-of-life from the dust.

The Guru aimed a fistful of corn at the tree and the kernels shattered against it. Chickens rabble-roused, wing-slapping each other—He stood blinking at the universe. The universe contained a stupidhead bearing a really overheated baby.

Have you been to Ozera, My lieutenant?

The inside of the lieutenant's elbow was drenched from the baby's sweaty fever. No, Master. No, I found—

I asked you to deliver a tiny flower to Ozera, but you could not do it?

The lieutenant was astonished.

Still quiet: What is this, John?

The lieutenant watched himself feel astonished.

What are you doing with this baby? Still the Guru spoke calmly, And where have you lost My flower?

The lieutenant found he could not recall parting ways with the crocus.

The Guru leaned over the bundle. He poked her. She didn't move. He shrugged. So now you will bring the baby, He said with exaggerated resignation. It's so simple. Because of you, John, Kai will lose a baby, and I will manifest the desire-guilt of Dovorh. He shrugged again. You see the Way I work.

What was the Guru's act here?

In place of a white flower, Dovka will have a white-wrapped baby. The Guru shook His head. Kai is getting mixed up in her conception of her own Level, you see John? She is under the impression that because her child was once a part of her, she is now a part of her child. This is bullshit, said the Guru.

Too much mother-daughter, He said, disgusted.

The lieutenant bowed his head over the baby when he thought the Guru had finished.

Stop bowing, you shudra! Neffer you lees'n! The Guru switched into it, the over-Russian, according to His Own unknown logic.

The lieutenant bowed again, before he could stop himself.

Stop looking for righteousness, John! The Avadhoot's stories have no morals!

Listen, Jubal, said the lieutenant.

He leaned so far forward Jubal thought for a moment he was going to fold onto his own lap.

In His name I marched through the woods carrying the baby; in His name I took no path but wove through the fucking wilderness. Dovorh's cabin was cold and empty. I left the baby there exactly as the Guru had told me to.

Kai came to me the next morning. I could see she'd been awake all night crying. She performed a full. Her hair was rubbed and stiff on the back of her scalp. She lay there for three or four breath cycles till I thought she might be sleeping. I understood that I was now higher, and you know what? I hated her for it. Even more, I hated the baby. I understood fully that if we ever loved each other again, me and Kai, it would not be equal.

Get up, Kai, I said.

She did. I couldn't bring myself to ask her to look at me. She didn't.

I have to thank you for your guidance with my attachment to my Noa, she said finally.

I knew the Guru had meant to put us together, unequal. The Guru was laughing. The Guru had no purpose that couldn't be served. His purpose was proved in the ashes of our misdeeds. The same ash He rubs on our foreheads, Jubal.

. . .

Afternoon of Confidantes: they made their way to the end of the rocky crescent beach to the cove below the turnout, Jubal behind Dovorh. There were some worldly people in the lot above, congregated around the picnic table Ray and Craig R. had hauled up there, but Dovorh didn't seem to be concerned about them. The wind was skating across the glass bay, and it carried worldly words away with it.

It was cold, and they burrowed inside their jackets. Farm Life jackets, He had called them. They came in bales from the Salvation Army. Pritam had figured out how to get nine wives and all the Sanctuary Children on public assistance.

They sat in silence, muted by their jackets. Protected from worldly neighbors by their jackets, Jubal taunted himself, his fear, he hated his fear, only he held onto it like he loved it, he knew that.

He never gives up on me, said Dovorh after a while.

Jubal told himself he wasn't listening.

He felt his jaw solidify. An ache was spreading.

She was picking up where she'd left off, but he didn't want to listen.

It was pitch dark outside, Dovorh continued, and I had to feel for the smooth wood block on the door of my cabin. She looked at Jubal searchingly. I gave it a half turn on its nail. It took me a moment to light a candle.

There on my bed, curled in a mammal ball, was a baby daughter.

At first I thought it was a hallucination. Fasting as I was, grieving for my daughter, my recidivism— But I held my breath and moved closer. I thought she had a teacup skull, beautiful words, images came to me, her elbows were plum points.

My Beloved could be so forceful. Dovorh spoke calmly through tears, as if they fell like ordinary rain. Many of the ladies had practiced this. You know, she smiled. He can be ornery. He has better things to do than loom up there before us. The sitting period I was coming from He'd really let me have it: You never stop crying for your old daughter! And so on. I'd backed out of the zendo as if I'd been banished, not understanding, so unable to give up my own unhappiness.

The cabin was really freezing. Before I touched her I hurried to light the woodstove. I didn't think I could stand it if she was cold. I used more kindling than I had to. I made up a little pallet on the floor, even though I knew I was going to hold her. I felt all of my movements to be really quick and quiet. I was buoyant with love, animated by love, in love with Him, in love with the baby.

When my Beloved appeared several hours later, what could I do but fall before Him? He blessed me. There was nothing to eat or drink in the cabin, I felt my own empty stomach in His, I had nothing to offer. He seemed to read my thoughts, and He said, You think I came here for refreshments? Of course I blushed. He had not visited like this since He delivered me from my old life, my nonlife before Him.

Noa woke and He took her on His lap. He was so gentle with her.

Does she have a fever? I said to my Beloved.

He looked at me so forgivingly. His great benevolent bright-shadow filled the cabin. It was only my imagination that was fevered. He slid His hand across the table. A plate of tea biscuits appeared and He took one, smiling almost apologetically, then shrugging it off, and popped it in His mouth like any worldly husband.

He took another. He praised me for the biscuits and placed His finger under my chin to make me smile. How could I resist Him? I carried the baby to the little pallet. My Beloved and I relaxed in each other's arms. Once more I was inundated with love for Him. Flooded with gratitude for His unending love for me, and He held my face between His giant hands and I was completely for Him.

Your old daughter doesn't benefit from your attachment, He said gently.

Mercy—or pity—or sentiment has no place in the realms of love in which He dwells, but still, He relented. Noa will stay here with you for a while, said my Master.

He is always out to remind me that "daughter" isn't limited! That attachment is so limiting! That hunger is materialistic. He has given me these things to work with. "Why" is such a neurotic question. When He put His hands on the skin of my back I felt myself dissolve in His presence. I felt my attachment dissolve. All-suffering was simply eliminated. I was sat-chit-ananda, Happiness Spreading. I opened to Him then, and it had been so long He held me afterward as if I were a trembling virgin.

She fingered her mala, falling silent.

He knew her Leela by heart, but did she know he felt he knew her? Not just Dovorh, all of them—did they understand that he didn't want to, but he couldn't help it; that he was always listening?

He heard the Guru: Life is a one-sided clamor for Me, eh people?

One-sided Leelas. He wanted to comfort Dovorh but it wasn't appropriate. What if he could find her daughter? Pride was false, ego-swelling, ego-contaminated.

When they walked back to the Sanctuary he noticed that Dovorh's beads hung to her navel as if she were shrinking.

CHAPTER 15

RAY SAID with false wonder, You're taller than ever, Violet.

Like everyone else, she was thinner. They sat with bowls of rice and tahini.

Tahini is really wonderful, said Ray.

It gummed his beard.

Then they ate in silence.

Jubal was sixteen now.

Violet cleared their bowls. There was a bowl-song from the kitchen—devotees were adding song to everything lately. They had received word that they shouldn't drink any liquid with meals.

She returned to the table. Not even water. Ray coughed dryly. He had recently called it feedback.

What are you calling? said the Guru. Some people had already suggested static.

Are you calling fear, MacFarland?

And before he could stop himself, Ray had heard his own remarkable voice: Yes indeed I am, Master!

Beyond that line of fritzy surf,
beyond playwords and the shallows of language,
stiff yellow froth left behind,
past feedback was mind like ocean.

Cleary opened her eyes and closed them again where she sat sewing burkhas in Lupine. Kishkindha opened and closed around her.

Ray said, Believe it or not there's a group of Buddhists in Halifax. Different Halifax than when we lived there. His wondering was close to vanity.

They were doctors and lawyers and teachers. They raised money for Tibetan refugees, and they laughed easily and indulgently about the foibles of their own teacher, who was Tibetan. Actually Tibetan. They hadn't monkeyed with an ancient religion. They pretty much just followed it.

That my life be beneficial to all sentient beings, said Ray. It doesn't get any simpler, he said. Phew. Did you hear the one about the Sikhs, Violet?

She shook her head.

Ah. Ray leaned back expansively. His Salvation Army sweater rode up, and for a second Jubal imagined his torso was inside-out, the ribs were so obvious.

So the wise old Sikh calls his two best students, Ray started. He gives each of them a goose, a couple of fatted-up gray geese, ugly and innocent. I'm really hungry for meat, confides the wise old Sikh, whose physical body is nothing more than a crooked walking stick.

I told you this one, yeah Jubal?

No answer.

Go kill the goose where no one can see you, says the wise old Sikh, lowering his voice, to his students.

Let's call him the first student, said Ray. Well the first student scurries off with the big bird under his arm. He comes to an alley. Down the alley he goes, breathing hard, the bird crushed into his stinky armpit. He crouches behind some vegetable crates and takes a quick look around him. No windows onto the alley, no one coming. He takes the goose across his knees and crack! Breaks the bird's neck like a piece of kindling. Then he goes trotting back to his teacher.

The second student gets his goose under his arm and heads out in the other direction. This alley, that doorway, high and low, but he can't find a spot that is truly hidden. Finally he returns to his teacher.

Pardon me, says the second student. But everywhere I went the goose could always see me.

Triumphantly Ray looked from one to the other. Was that a good one, Violet? Since your brother has taken a vow of silence?

But Jubal could see that his sister wasn't really listening to the story.

She was listening to the Guru. When I say surrender to "Me" I don't mean surrender to this person you see sitting up here on this pillow! Don't get caught surrendering to someone! Spiritual Life is not a repetition of little superstitions, ablutions, pujas, and koans! There is only surrender in this lifetime, people!

. . .

But now Jubal began to hear people saying that this was the kind of Practice that led you into yourself instead of outward in service or relationship. God is within—well some people, said some other people, were taking it literally. It could lead to depression, said Peter Nehud, former doctor; psychic isolation mimicked the grief-state, said Nehud quietly. Jubal saw Ray in the little group around Nehud.

Some people were saying that God is without—as in Western tradition, which was natural and correct for Westerners. People were getting dizzy with disconnects and contradictions. With oxymoron and with the sham of metaphor. The only path was the nonpath and so on. In dharma talk innermost Messner reminded them that gurus weren't saints and that they were Occidentals venturing into oriental tradition. We're on shaky ground here, yeah people?

Jubal heard people say He was self-aggrandizing. And heard other people argue that His power-mongering or egoic display was spiritual theater on His part, designed absolutely to test them.

Doubt is a form of ego, said innermost Gary. Of self-love, and self-protection. If ever you feel challenged by His apparent display of ego, please know it is your own ego that is challenged, people.

So you have them, the Guru had said huskily in dharma talk. Egos.

Egos like opposing thumbs, He had said, and He held out His Own like a couple of hitchhikers.

They had earlobes and penises.

That was Ray's line. Dad Ray the jester.

Ray's second line: There was a chance He had four earlobes, two penises. Jubal saw Gary suppress a smile.

The Guru asked Heidi to join Him on the bay beach for swimming. Tamsen was the swimmer. Then He asked Ray and Craig R. too. He cried, Bring My bell-boy!

It was said that the indigo water was forty degrees; gravel-colored starfish spiked the gravel. There had been snow like soft salt, cold could burn your skin like salt and you'd better have had a tetanus shot if you stepped on a frozen starfish.

The Guru and Heidi proceeded to the bay at the appointed hour. The Guru picked up a stick and threw it. Vash came out of no-where, and the Guru laughed openly when the dog ran over himself and rolled chasing after it. Otherwise the Guru was not really a dog person. There was a holy site where His first cat Bobcat was buried. Recently He had asked Pritam for two Tibetan temple cats, eighteen lives altogether.

Heidi's long hair was loose, and it rattled in the cold like a beaded curtain. Ray and Craig R. were already shivering, finding it inconceivable they would take off their shirts, their shoes and socks, finding it almost hilarious, finding Heidi's naked breasts un-believable torpedoes of milk and shiver. Jubal caught Ray looking sideways at him. Cover your eyes! blurted Ray, embarrassed, laughing. Jubal raised his arm and looked out underneath it. The sky had separated into two skies, one pushing huge boulders into the silken belly of the other. He watched Heidi wrap her naked arms around her naked middle.

The Guru was very, very calm, and He was beatific. Beatific was a word in heavy use lately. He reached His hand out toward a con-trail of white feathers. His encounters with birds were famously childlike. He was famous for loving to watch ducks mating. Jubal had been among those He'd gathered to observe the emerald-head mallards tiptail and splash down their quarry.

Ray said soberly, He really is crazy.

Craig R., lightly: He never said He wasn't.

Madman walks into icy water, Eighth Wife feeds multitudes of children with her mountain ranges. Jubal tried it out silently.

It's not doubt, though, Ray persisted. He forced a laugh. Forty degrees, that water! It's self-preservation, you know, when you're born with a body.

Craig R. looked away, distancing himself from Ray's low-Level morbidity.

Jubal watched the Guru dismantle Himself of robe and zoris. His flesh was stacked in giant blocks, yellow-white to rosy, the human hair growing sideways across His back and His buffaloes. Jubal thought Ray cringed like a little kid watching a grownup clown around for his benefit. Jubal understood that He was swimming for them, that swimming was like dying, which He would also do, in the same way that He was living for them, had chosen them, and Jesus Christ had hung it up at thirty-three, but Avadhoot Master King Ivanovich was an old man in a gross, American century and He was plunging with great joy into deathly frigid water.

The Eighth Beautiful followed the Guru. She held her arms in tight triangle wings against the sides of her giant bosom. She put a toe in.

But then, before their very eyes, Heidi relaxed into a bodily smile. Her shoulders came undone, her arms tumbled down her sides. Playfully she kicked at the water. She took a generous step deeper. What was going on here? Craig R., forgetting his coolness, leaned toward the spectacle alongside MacFarland.

A soft cry, a bubble of delight, and then Heidi pushed off and sunk to her shoulders. She didn't bother looking back at them, but Jubal could hear her cooing.

Fools! the Guru called up the beach. Children! He sent great warm splashes in their direction. Why do you insist on all this suffering?

He dunked and came up with a mouthful. Playfully He turned and spit at Heidi. When she tried to go under, her breasts buoyed to the surface.

Jubal! He called.

He wouldn't be forced to take his shirt off, would he?

Go tell everyone! Plainly where I am concerned there are miracles! I deal in water and I command fire! That is how you should say it, bellwether!

. . .

I am the Patron Buddha, said the Guru. Venerate Me. It is time for a new Period, marked by a Celebration lavish with cashews and dried apricots, marked by butter, made into ghee. No milk, we can't have milk. But we can have butter! Hedon is the Way of the Patron Buddha! Go tell everyone I said it, Jubal!

Ray plowed the sloshbarrow down to the bay, Milk Bay, Amygdala Bay, swirled with milk, gray as gray matter. The old yoke had broken, but still no dairy. The new Period of the Amygdala would be recognized by the first formalization of the Guru's supernatural powers. Devotees knew that He had strolled Moika Embankment materializing confections and tchotchkes, but that was the fantastical drip-castle city He called Peterborg, as if the Guru had come from a different time as well as a different continent.

Now He turned His palms up and there—an apricot. Go ahead, Jubal, He said. Take it, eat it. It's not the Snow White apple from Disney.

Jubal hesitated.

Devotees laughed openly. Still so small for his age, slender, and blushing like an apple, he took the apricot.

The Guru hadn't taken His eyes off him. Are you working on your spiritual libido, Jubal?

There was more devotional laughter. There was so much love of His high forehead like a precocious child.

You people are so out of touch with your own desires! You are Westerners in the raiment of traditional oriental embarrassment! You think you have to subvert desire!

Self-knowing/self-forgiving Guru-loving laughter.

You are so amusing, people!

Your Level Two shame is neurosis, not the coming of Level Three. And yet you persist in thinking I am going to deliver enlightenment! I am your husband, eh? Your big provider? This is expressly not the Practice, people! Sadhana is not sitting around waiting for a handout!

He could be bombastic.

He could be coy, like Zen was coy.

Like Zen, He was funny.

He could be tender. The Sanctuary was the extension of His material body. Walk all over Me, people. Walk gently, though, and use your hands sometimes.

Touch Me, people. Attend Me, said the Guru. Let's do desire!

Enough of this austerity, bullshit, asceticism, let us reveal to one another our scatological material natures!

Some people said it was to test the real commitment of Pritam, who would provide full funding during the new Period: Pritam's karma was all tied up with money. With commercial zoning, with waterfront. But how was He to know if they wanted fur coats or blenders or watermelons or any other kinds of melon? He was a many-melon-headed monster of melons. Of individual births like lights coming on at night in a valley.

Jubal found his sister and Noa in the crabgrass behind the wood-shop, their backs against the raspy skin of the outbuilding, pinching jewelweed pods between pointers and thumbs until the little green rockets exploded. The Guru's love was there, with them, and His love was with the lieutenant watching Kai chase rolling onions from a fifty-pound sack across the kitchen; watching Kai face down a monkey tree's worth of coffee-colored bananas. The peels were thin and flaccid.

His love was with Dovorh, He winked at her, she flooded.

His love is with you, Jubal, claimed the lieutenant, when He reminds you that attachment to family is divisive in sangha. His love is with you when He is troubled by your affiliation with your sister. He sees that you think you're her, Jubal. This is a kind of greed of possibilities. He calls it worldly empathy, false empathy, the desire to escape yourself through association with others. His love is with you in this reprimand, Jubal.

The Fifth started forward as if to protest, but the lieutenant raised his hand and she diminished. Your Confidante is not aided by your false fidelity, Jubal, said the lieutenant. As you are not your sister, neither are you Dovorh's daughter. The Guru feels the stickiness between the sheets of air, Jubal, Dovorh's sticky side, always attracting particles.

He wants you to take on more responsibility, Jubal, the lieutenant continued. More love, more responsibility. He is in a Period of Periods. You should know that. New forms of love are constantly arising. He feels you know something of forms, Jubal, shapeshifting as you are through your adolescence, small as you are, He sees in you all Leelas. He sees all your possibilities.

As form arises from the void-mind of all Creators, from Kaliyuga, twelve thousand years of subhuman vulgarity, another new Period, hard on the heels of the old Period.

He was the Creator

Avi

The Hoot

The Fully Realized Being

The Living God

The Live Wire

Patron Buddha

Lamb, Lion

The Uprooted Center of the Cosmos.

Violet and Noa in the doorway of Sita's bedroom, His love was with them, where He kept the state-of-the-art television set Pritam had received from a wealthy admirer. There had been a lot of crazy hooting in gratitude, Pritam getting Messner to help him unload the huge box from the passenger seat, Messner patting it like it was a passenger.

The Guru and Gary, sacked on Sita's bed watching Walt Disney's *Sleeping Beauty*, they'd watched it so many times the tape ratcheted with daylight. Through days and nights of Disney I have been meditating, Jubal! Tell him, Gary!

The Guru heaved Himself from the bed like a bear.

Hit that button for me, will you Jubal? said Gary.

Jubal turned the TV off.

The innermost tossed him one of Sita's pillows.

Don't cover your lap like a girl! The innermost burst out laughing.

Are you listening? said Messner.

Jubal tried to tune in again.

Until the Sixth, form needs name in order to be perceived as such. The innermost gave him a crooked smile. Who gave you that haircut? Jubal ducked instinctively. If you're going to take a role in the Loving Monkey—he shimmied his shoulders like the Guru—let's get you a haircut.

Yeah?

Yeah, Jubal?

There was a lot of issue, though, a lot of people wanted an Indian name, or a Japanese name. People said there were a lot of hard edges in the world now that couldn't be washed away by taking baths together. The Loving Monkey sounded like sponging each other's pimply shoulders and sharing towels in the seventies.

Since when did monkeys signify anything other than back-scratching and fornication? People had been to India. Seen the real thing in Madurai, Madras, Pondicherry, traveled second class, where sleeping accommodations were slat benches. Not the India other Westerners bragged about. People had felt the whole Hindu, life-death, people had striven to act in ways that were culturally appropriate. The shitty curry, they had stomached it.

There was a lot of heavy grief leaving the Period of Amygdala. There was no transition whatsoever. A lot of talk about whether the Monkey was a joke, whether devotees were being gratuitously made fun of.

The Loving Monkey had many arms and legs.

Maybe it should have been called the Loving Octopus, said the Guru.

Grab on to your smelly parts! said the Guru.

Had anyone seen an octopus? The lieutenant said it was all tissue and movement. It had three hearts in its head and everything else it owned too. In its head, said the lieutenant.

There was a lot of talk about it. The Guru said, A lot of octopus. Pritam said, Open. Open to the Guru.

The Guru laughed. Pritam is telling you to open!

Across the aisle, Ray sat with his legs closed and his mouth small as the head of a nail.

You people have all grown cold and jealous in your striving, said the Guru. Tribe of Narcissus, and everyone groaned, everyone was so damn tired of hearing about Narcissus. His water kiss, his wavering reflection and the ripples of his gorgeous body.

Listen! said the Guru. Instead of loving your sprouting eyebrows, ninny necks, and thumbheads, you have begun to hate your bodies!

His gaze fell on Jubal. Jubal thought a few people snickered. He'd managed so far to avoid the haircut. The place where the third eye would be was blemished, sore, and hidden. His back was so ugly he called himself disfigured. The truth was always in the dark. This was a hard test. It was ugly. But the Teachings said there was dark and light and when they canceled each other out, beyond words, there was the limitlessness of enlightenment.

Enlightenment isn't just light, you people! Don't pay so much attention to the word for it!

You are caught, He said, like birds in a basket!

Poor birds, this fence of life, this sticky net and cruel hunter.

The Guru said people had become totally disturbed from their animal selves. From their monkey selves, from their bananas.

Stop warping the whole thing! All I ever ask you to do is open! You think it is an accident we have a farm? You think I like to play in a barn when I have played in Alice Tully? Jordan, Carnegie, I have played in places in Mosko you have never heard of. You think I do this for Myself? Oh, you think a lot of Me, I know. You think I am your Hoot, eh. Your Big Teacher.

Monkeys were like squirrels in India. Devotees had breathed the burning corpses on the water, Benares-Varanasi, had eaten the world's sweetest pineapple, had laid down in lice-infested corridors of cold-water hostels hating themselves for being soft, Western, for not lying down with the corpses.

If you ate off the street in India, and Ray had a stomach like a vise, Ray was lucky, then you could expect to share with monkeys. Their flat eyes. Ray said you had to have a stomach like a vise to kick them.

Ray MacFarland, said the Guru.

Master.

Why are you holding onto your son?

I know that I can't hold onto him, Master.

Then what Pritam said wasn't true, MacFarland?

Jubal could see Ray lean forward into the smog of incense, a dense, salty-sweet rose, trying to understand better.

If the hearing isn't true I get targeted immediately? said the Guru. His enormous face was filled with disappointment and sorrow. It was unbearable to look at Him. Yet love continued to pour through Him. Jubal could see that Ray's heart was a barnacle, but He swept the sea over it. Ray's heart opened and devoured a filmy strand of plankton.

The Loving Monkey would start with the children. Children were little monkeys. Snuffly little beasties.

Now people were saying it came at the right time. People were getting frustrated with abstraction. There should be some psychology. Some carrot, some stick, too, keisaku, because punishment shouldn't be entirely outside the contract. The human contract, the stigmata. After all, He was dealing with a bunch of Westerners, all props and material. Reward and punishment.

The grownups are fossilized in their unhappiness, said the lieutenant. Let us turn now to the children, both those whom He has spiritually Fathered and those who have come to Him via their fathers—and the mothers.

We can't forget the sobby mothers.

Jubal saw that his sister, up in front on the ladies' side, sat like a girl guarding a basket.

The sun was in the lieutenant's eyes. He was squinting, facing them on the lawn of the farmhouse. He had misbuttoned his shirt. It hung crooked on his funnel chest. He had the muscular face of a monkey. The tiny ears. His eyebrows and his hair matched perfectly as if his face were vain despite his profound level of humility.

Messner put his hand on the lieutenant's small crossing the farmyard.

The lieutenant said, Don't do that.

Messner: Want to go for a walk? He snaked his fingers up under his glasses and rubbed his eyes. Do you need anything in town? As if the whole thing were spur-of-the-moment. As if it were casual: Join us, Jubal.

The shoulder was a crust of desiccated tar crumbled and mixed with gravel. They kept having to adjust for who would lead when a car passed them. Not Jubal. He could see how the lieutenant felt like an idiot leading or following Messner. Jubal kicked a nest of stones. The woods were shabby the whole stretch to town, and overgrown driveways would pop up out of nowhere. Suddenly you'd be in someone's yard, with the peeled trees left over from when the lot was carved out of the forest.

How's your Practice? the innermost called back to the lieutenant.
Chop-wood-carry-water!

Messner laughed but he didn't turn around.

He has identified you for Jubal's sister, eh Jubal? said the innermost. He wants to know if you can recognize Sixth Level. He says she may or may not be. He leaves it up to you, Hartshorn.

You know what, Messner, I'd just as soon hear it from the Guru.

Now the innermost turned and halted their little procession. The human condition is breaking the human back to dig a hole to shit in and then breaking the human back to fill it, yeah Hartshorn?

So?

So nothing.

They walked the rest of the way to town in silence.

. . .

The lieutenant's cabin was Morye Odeyal, Sea of Blankets. It had no foundation, just wood sponge against the sponge of the forest. No crawlspace for porcupines, but you could taste the termites. The threshold was paved with the small heels of beach stones. Knocking was condemned as a worldly gesture, but Violet would not want to surprise the lieutenant. Not far off a woodpecker was knocking.

For a moment she imagined Hansel and Gretel from Disney. She should have dropped a trail of crumbs. They weren't on baking.

The forest swayed one way and then the other.

How long had she been standing there? The lieutenant stood staring at her from his open doorway.

She looked around the Sea of Blankets like a worldly visitor, fearful and dissonant. There was the lieutenant's altar, swimmy yellow silk over a crate, candle, incense, ash, and murti.

She said, It's different from Ozera. Dovorh's bed is over there —she showed him. She had never been inside Lupine. Cleary said it was inappropriate, too much mother-child.

Ah, said the lieutenant.

They were going to start at the beginning of the Loving Monkey, said the lieutenant. The whole thing would take them through the summer. Wasn't she glad she had been chosen?

He had already laid a couple of blankets on the floor between the bed and the table. The Guru had said clearly that it was not appropriate to practice on a bed. You people in your culture think that it is not appropriate on a bed, said the Guru. Here I am in the West. What can I do about your hang-ups?

This is a spiritual game, said the lieutenant. First we'll sit together on the blanket. Master King Ivanovich is quite a Teacher. We are all so lucky. You are really lucky to have escaped the junk of worldly existence, Violet.

They sat across from each other. Now look in my eyes, said the lieutenant. These are just eyes, jelly, glass, making the rounds, picking you out of all this light and shadow, ah, here's a bookshelf, go the eyes, that's good, here's a bowl of fruit on the table.

She laughed a little.

Now, he said, just fall.

She straightened.

No, no, he laughed at her having done the opposite. We can fall into each other. He leaned forward. Violet did the same, she had to. They bumped heads. Foreheads—he still hadn't taken his eyes out of her eyes. Tears came. His eyes were swimming in her eyes. His breathing was loud, too loud, as if he had some physical ailment.

He sat up again and so did Violet.

You should just open and breathe, said the lieutenant. He breathed, showing her. You should feel fear exit from all the holes in your body.

He went down his own body with the side of his hand. He said, The Life Force will fill you. It's so simple. He smiled.

Now put your hand at the base of your spine. Like this. He

reached his hand around back as if he were wiping himself in the bathroom.

Your tailbone, he said. Rub it with your thumb, your finger. It feels good, the root of bodily energy. You can feel the bright and the surge, can't you?

She could feel the tingling. It went from her tail all the way up to where they'd just touched foreheads.

Now put your hands on my belly, said the lieutenant. He wore a thin Western shirt with pearl snaps and pointed pockets. She felt nothing at first. Just a cottony slab, not really soft or hard, not really there in fact. Maybe she wasn't really. That floating feeling like after she'd given blood, the blood bank wasn't supposed to allow children—

Tingling again: fear, or kundalini? Suddenly, the lieutenant's belly hardened. It filled upward, outward, like a balloon, and it was moving toward her, moving her hand, she could see her hand moving. Then he hissed out sharply.

He put his hands on her belly. His fingers were all spread out. Her heart was in fingers, all separated and ugly. His hands were opening her up from her tailbone to her sternum. Inside her.

Her eyes had closed involuntarily. She imagined her eyes had been closed forever. His breathing had always been whooshy, insistent, too loud, as if it were a shell pressed against her earvalve. She could almost feel the shell. She wanted to twist away. She really wanted to grab the shell from her ear and smash it.

Don't strain, said the lieutenant.

All the way down to your navel. This is a good and happy feeling. Your belly is full. Doesn't it feel good? Down to your hands and feet, Violet.

She wound out of the holy forest.

She must have wanted to run. But she would avoid attracting

attention. She had a vision that the fiery pain was the feeling of a tree's bark being peeled. The cool, pale woodskin was the first layer of fire.

Tamsen was working around a small boulder. Violet bowed and Tamsen looked up and nodded.

She'd taken the path that came out behind the Concert Barn. She heard the first few notes on the piano. She stopped to listen. Soon the notes adhered, added up to melody. Music was the materialism of God, the Guru had said it. She stood against the silvery clapboard. Fish-scale silver—how did wood? It was Beethoven. It made her heart shoot up to the surface. She had been chosen for the Loving! Was it possible that He was playing, now, because she had opened to the lieutenant?

The Guru stopped and started over.

Are you coming to Morye Odeyal? said the lieutenant. Violet was clearing lunch dishes. She hadn't felt him approach her.

This afternoon would be a good time, said the lieutenant.

She had the sense that the bowls and cups, the chopsticks, would go twirling off without her. She was nonmaterial. She was a column of smoke, of nothing. She nodded—"she"—and the lieutenant made a little bow to her.

She stood again at the heavy handmade door that made a sinking sound when it was opened or shut, and again he answered without her knocking.

A large rice bowl of pale yellow ice cream on the small, scarred table. One spoon, she noticed.

Objects, said the lieutenant. This is a part of the Practice that has been neglected. The Guru says sociosensual. Eating ice cream in the sun, sun outside warming rocks— The lieutenant smiled. He wasn't looking at her, though. He waved his arms as if to spread his smile.

What are the objects? A bowl imprinted with grains of rice, mass-produced in—he checked—Taiwan, shipped to New York City. A spoon. A spoon—this too he picked up—of virgin origin. Cheap enough to bend. He bent it. He still hadn't looked at her. Ice cream, he said. Ice cream from Kai. Would you believe Kai knows how to make ice cream? He put his hands around the bowl as if it were soup and he were warming them.

The spoon bit off a chunk of ice cream. The cheap spoon levitated. It didn't really. He opened his mouth. The lieutenant's teeth were the same egg cream color as the ice cream. He opened his mouth for her to open her mouth. She had to open.

Lie on your back, Violet. Did you find a feather?

That was the assignment.

Jubal: I was there.

I was ready to drop down onto the lieutenant's shoulders.

The Guru played the same tricks. Over and over.

I was in the rafters, the bookshelf was a ladder, Eastern Religion, back-to-the-land, Dostoevsky.

I was ready to monkey the lieutenant, tear his back, my stomach like a vise, this time I was ready.

There I was / there I wasn't.

Didn't find a feather?

Shook her head.

There I was!

Her nipples looked like matching scabs on a washboard torso. Her front might as well have been her back, from the rafters. The bookshelf.

It's cold, Violet, said the lieutenant quietly. He handed back her undershirt. He turned and took a feather from a jar on the bookshelf. Crow—all obsidian, no silk. He ran his finger along its blade. He said, You can imagine how they invented airplanes.

He knelt down and held out the feather. This is simply an exercise for the skin, Violet.

Drop the feather, shithead!

I could imitate the lieutenant's voice but I could not command him. Savant of all voices, of imitation.

The lieutenant was kneeling. Not just the tempo but the sound of his breathing accelerated. He said, Open to it.

I was there, and I could have jumped screeching.

The lieutenant wore loose meditation pants and a paper-thin T-shirt with sweat stains like ancient charts of islands. Every tiny hair stood up on Violet's body, her coat of skin looked like it had been pelted with rice, naked wedding.

The hairs on the lieutenant's arms stood up first—like her hairs. Then it surged, that power, just as the Guru had predicted. Magnificent. It drew all his love. He sat back on his heels and he closed his eyes and took a deep breath as the Guru had instructed.

The sun slanted through the high window of the cabin as if through a cloud. The window was covered with murky plastic, the same plastic that was used to cover woodpiles and outhouse doors, the same plastic rocked down upon the vegetable garden, ogorod, the Guru called it, in winter, the same plastic tented over the roof tree of the former chicken coop, up the road, behind MacFarland's, the roof of which had long since blown off and been forgotten. Through the plastic lens the sun was gray and bright, rectangular.

Her eyes had been closed for Kaliyuga. Or was it the generative dark the Guru talked about?

The lieutenant put his fingers between her toes. Did monkeys have toes? They had bare feet, Dad Ray said you could see the corduroy bottoms, all the monkeys scrabbling in the tangled tangka of the great banyan where the Buddha came up with Buddhism.

Time to jump! I was barefoot. How else would I have climbed to the rafters? I was known as nimble. Jimble Nubal, I was known—
    Memory is an alter ego. The wet sun and dark green drooping trees and the clouds blowing beneath other clouds and the sun like a cloud through the window.
    Time to go.

BOOK TWO

Jubal

CHAPTER 1

FORTY DAYS' DRIVE to reach the high desert. Maine to New Mexico in His rattrap farmtruck, the only eye I caught in the rearview mirror was my own, but there were many voices. Leelas.

Somewhere in the middle, I saw a tractor rise up as big as God's tractor and I thought of Ray. He would have shaken his head slowly, the world never ceased to dog him with its wonders.

I was like a second sun. At least the sun's chariot. The distance was a sheet of hammered silver. My thoughts clattered. A milk jug of gas station water at my feet evaporated faster than I could drink it. I changed the oil in a field of wheat, dead fox in the ditch stiff as a seahorse.

Finally the faded highway curved and banked and swept through an underpass. Mounds of loose earth covered by a drum skin, piñon trees like fists, roots like talons—

I pulled over at the city limits.

Wherever I raised my eyes there were mountains—it took me a while to figure out how they fit together.

No one who knew me knew where I was. No one else knew me.

Nights I spent counting stars.

I followed a wrinkled streambed down the centerfold of an arroyo. Even my hair got sunburned.

Finally I found my way to the center alongside the fortress walls of a salt-encrusted mission. The sky gleamed like metal: inner ore, a melting pot of rainbows.

There was a cast iron bell as big as a bull in the churchyard, wind sculptures in the parking lots of galleries.

The bowl of a public park was willow-green. I knew the therapist the moment I saw her, as if she'd just landed against the willow tree the same day I wandered into Santa Fe.

There were the high strains and squalls of worldly children, and a couple of young men with loose hair flinging a Frisbee.

I thought her eyes cast a lampy glow even in sunlight. Her dry, rosewood curls, arched nostrils like a camel's; a cool dew beaded her narrow nose.

I circled around the swings. A family dog the color of woodchips was tied to a lightpole. His rear half jerked when he felt my steps in the ground beneath him.

My second pass she looked up from her lunch and smiled. I saw that she had packed the food from home in various containers. Her feet were bare and lively.

"Ruth!" a friend called out, skipping toward her.

My timing was perfect.

Ruth the therapist. The gleaner, good listener. I had never seen her before but I knew her.

My chart says, Intake. Eighteen-year-old male, no current address. That's all, before she slides it out of view. Eighteen, wiry as a mountain goat, having bathed and shaved my fuzz in my very own mountain stream before my appointment. No former address either. I don't undress to bathe. I don't need to see my own pink naked.

We sit facing each other, but I watch her face like that same wheatfield I drove through to get here.

Peripherally.

The dog hairs on the back of my neck get stimulated. It's not her it's the air conditioning.

Not to be creeping around, crumbling bread for her to follow—

Not to be cult-exiting in a dark watchcap, but I've seen through the window of her casita. A blouse on the bed, a hairbrush—

A bearded white fellow in a truck like mine with homemade wooden rails drives around town honking for peace.

He's not me.

Neither is the girl with windy blond hair trying to secure a bellowing sign to the chainlink. I've slowed on the overpass to watch her. I've hiked above Tesuque, picked up honeycombed mesquite antlers, snake bones, stumbled on cholo homes, a cross rises at dusk, white against the sky like asphalt—

I've watched people tend to themselves as if they were whole countries with capital cities and agricultural regions and a couple of mountain peaks as purple as erections. Watched them tend to their lives with deaths attached like pricetags—

Looked ahead and seen the next two traffic lights, the next two days' worth of sunsets.

Some leggy clouds in the distance. The cars wash up and then disperse, the warehouses on Cerillos with their loading docks and dumpsters and employee picnic tables, the sky sears the town and the cars shoot off their belief systems.

I hate belief but I want her to believe me.

Inbreath. I start over.

My name was Daniel.

I pause, cooperative to her cause, and watch her put the old name down in her records. She crosses her legs the other way.

Not to be casual with suspense, not to pull a fast one, but I lived to tell the tale. I enjoy saying it. Evenings I sit on the hood of my little farmtruck with my feet on the fender. My narrow cowboy boots remind me of mahogany bean pods. I keep them spit-polished. There are many little inroads where no one seems to mind a boy and his stolen vehicle.

Anyone could drive this day away, I tell her. Dusty blue day with keys left dangling in the keyhole. Warm hills and cool lines of mountains, fiesta-striped wind serapes . . .

She touches her fingertips to her bare arms, cuts a quick look at the air-conditioning unit. I pause and visualize the watercooler in the hallway, I hope she feels free to rise and seek refreshment. She returns looking chastened, as if she should have had the foresight, before the session started. She shields her face with her teacup, but her profession prevents her from rejecting my story. Her history prevents her from being impartial.

She leans over the notebook in her lap, and I can feel the shadow. Looks up, "Sorry. Is it distracting?"

Life is a distraction until death, said the Guru. Sometimes He hooted when He said it.

"Whenever you're ready, Jubal."

The patient patient.

"We generally use the term client?"

There's a little client on the desk behind her, Buddha-toad squatting by the tissues. She follows my gaze to the marble trinket.

"Would you like me to move it?"

I'd like to smash it.

Her eyes widen, glisten with inner ore, retained moisture. Not what she expected. Should talking to a therapist be the same as talking to yourself? I ask her.

She stops at the top of her breath, bristles for a breach in the relationship—she mustn't bristle. A therapist must keep her hair to herself, must not leave personal items lying around, visible to creeps like me through her bathroom window.

But I'm not really interested in her armpits.

We sit in silence.

Silence is the hard void of meditation, the Guru sending His lieutenant around the hall to inspect posture.

Isn't she supposed to do the asking?

I never said I wouldn't answer.

"It seems that you've been living out of your truck, Jubal?"

As I said, Ruth the gleaner. She drops her eyes to her papers, giving me privacy to bed down on the bench seat of my buggy. She pictures me frying eggs on the hood, flipping hood pancakes, swami-savant of the highway as my sweat sizzles—

I've gathered that part of her job is to decide if I have any grounds to be homeless. I'm too old for a "placement." Too poor for a motel room. The agency has let me know she's my advocate. We were all so sick of avocados.

A quizzical smile, "Let's stay on track for just a minute."

Trail of breadcrumbs.

As you know, I say, eyeing her records, I've been not exactly arrested but dis-encouraged from different establishments in whose so-called public toilets I've made my encampments. The smell of the bathroom in my hair, in my doughy T-shirt.

I learned that it's not against the law to be without an address, but you can't rely on the endless hospitality of local businesses. You can't endlessly use their toilets. A number of complaints were received and I was "opened"—

"Your case was, Jubal," she corrects me.

—and "processed." When they detained me I fell to my knees and then my belly. I was officially granted some sessions, to make up for sacking the city, for drinking from my hands, dribbling in the basins. They returned my backpack. I was to pull myself together and report back on a specific date for therapy.

But when I showed up, a male counselor stood before me. He was hardly older than I was. His bushy hair was still moist, his narrow shoulders still cocked from squeezing through the bony pelvis.

It came to me without thinking. You and I could be brothers, I said. Suddenly it was as if someone had accused him, not me, of taking a two-hour shit in the bookstore bathroom. I told him I'd prefer a female provider.

She holds up her hand, refers to the chart, puzzled, "You told them you'd wait for me."

I must have passed your office.

She tips her head. Am I convincing?

While I waited I got started on college.

It seemed to interest people that I was homeless. A castaway, a runoff, a nonconforming performist.

"So you identify with itinerancy?" they said.

Silence.

"With protest?"

I sat in on some classes in Great Books and experiential psychology.

A kindly professor offered me a bed in his basement for the winter. His wife did the laundry on the other side of the partition.

Now she nods, it tracks with my chart, her work folder, we're on firm ground, my gaze falls on her leather soles—nothing rubber about them.

Nothing irreligious.

She wears a leotard and a long skirt, she's a dancerly thirty.

A bell on her desk—

Silence.

"Would you like to continue?"

I was a bell.

How do I tell her?

CHAPTER 2

I HEAD UP Atalaya before dawn, somebody's blue-eyed sheepdog already cartwheeling down the trail. I claim a tray of rock at the summit and watch light wash the sky like dairy. Then the sky splits overhead and the sun shoots through the cracks we call sunrise.

I jog all the way down the mountain with the dust like a dog at my heels.

Across her courtyard, past the pool without looking for my reflection, no counting coins crabbing along the black bottom, down the half stairs, the hallway, to her half basement office. She meets me at the door, reaches her slender hand out.

"You look hot!" she chides me.

"Are you alright?"

I hesitate.

"Come on in."

Even though I've made myself uncivic, uncivilized, without God, as crazy as a bandy-legged old Guru? His pink skull beneath the aureole—

"Would you like the air conditioning?" she says doubtfully, dropping her sweater over her shoulders.

There's a dental buzz from the fluorescent.

A pink-tinted landscape in oil, requisite adobe dwelling in the foreground; a rock garden on the windowsill below the air conditioner.

She positions herself in front of her desk, one knee in the elbow of the other. She's beautiful—"Jubal!"—but I don't love her. It's necessary to make that clear with a therapist.

Once again she casts her shadow over the notebook in her lap
—the way she used to shadow the wading birds of her childhood.
Virginal-looking ibises and egrets whose stillness was premeditated.

Pencil poised—"Do you mind? Just to see if we can find some
patterns as we go along here?"

Patterns! Shouldn't therapy be as simple as the light at the end
of the tunnel? The mirror?

I imagine she leads me down a hall of mirrors. What do *you*
think you're thinking, Jubal? I let her lead me. Let her think she's
leading.

Why is there a mirror at the end of your hallway?

It takes her a second. "Maybe someone wanted the hall to look
longer?" A decoy laugh—

You can't really laugh at your patient.

"Did I say we use the term client?"

Silence.

She looks at me carefully.

"Are you still hot?"

It's cool at night. Days can be problematic.

My T-shirt smells like freshwater fish, like the hot rock where I
laid it out to dry after bathing.

She shuffles her papers, covering my silence. "Maybe we could
talk about how you chose Santa Fe," she tries when the silence gets
autistic.

It was one of His heatfields, I say. It was one of the Huru's
gotspots.

"He's been here?"

Nest of the phoenix, the burning three-fold crown—He would
have thought it was hot, already He was so heated.

"Alright," she says. "Is there any chance of starting at the
beginning?"

Why does she have to be so literal-minded?

What have I told her already?

Life is an elaborate ruse for God, I answer myself. I ask myself, When will this heat break? When will it really shatter?

I start over, but I'm silent.

Silence is a void, a vortex, give Me your v words, people!

He could be literary. He could be pornographic.

Violet! He cried. Who named you?

He lunged for her, got into the v's of her armpits where mist had collected— Kishkindha was visited by morning fog, noon depression.

The poet called attention to His speech forms and there was always a period of emulation: for example, Disconversion was the name the Guru gave to the story of how you found Him. The story of your true shit was your Leela, your beginning.

She touches the hide of her face, a mark in her notebook.

Unconversion, contraversion, another version of the same old lifetime. It's not true but it could be. It is true but it couldn't be, me finding you here in the high desert.

She looks up sharply. "I'm not sure I understand where you're going."

Where my tale is going.

One minute I'm wagging, the next minute I'm skulking around the backs of buildings, my plume pressed against my asshole, a fundamentalist of myself, an ass-and-tale worshiper.

I'm overexposed, uncovered.

I urinate against the backs of buildings.

If my story were going nowhere, like the Practice, I wouldn't be here. I wouldn't have gotten away, the night was dark, in the little white farmtruck. Have I said it?

I would still be with Him, going crazy with the Guru. I would still be with my sister—she used to wander around with sunflower seeds for the birds in her tunic. I had shown her where they were kept in a garbage can, the lid secured with a bungee cord, in a cool corner of the summer kitchen.

She jumped in fear when Kai caught her: Hunger is samsaric, Violet! When the Guru thundered, You are not with Me to learn fearlessness, but to forget that fear ever existed!

Violet was singled out constantly.

All devotees were.

Then they were tossed back in the basket, dark and crowded, spackled with light, a laundry basket like a hair shirt, a hair basket.

I start over.

As Daniel I was stubbornly small for my age. The lieutenant cornered me. Sable eyes though.

The therapist checks my eyes.

My sister was tall and stemmy. Her silver-blond hair was parted on the side and you could see her seam. My hair is dark like my mother's—

I've adopted sideburns here in the high desert, my Western boots were waiting like dogs beside a dumpster.

My hands are cracked and spiderwebbed with cinnamon.

Ray slowed the station wagon past the Sanctuary, philosophically credulous but too shy to pull over, Cleary stared out the window, trying to see through the forest . . .

All in Leela.

In conversion—

"In psychiatry," the therapist interrupts me, "conversion syndrome is real bodily pain with no bodily explanation.

Not covered by my college courses.

I can tell she's proud of her professional development, diplomas on the wall—"It's often related to trauma in your history."

I encountered belief in man as God at an early age. A ghost in the machine, I say, a glitch of the soul, a guru in childhood.

CHAPTER 3

WE FACE EACH OTHER in her subterranean office, as chilly as a bat cave, captives in the act of captivating one another.

Whatever I say she bats carefully back to me.

I can't see her playing baseball. She's not an extravert, although in the not-so-secret clusters of her heart she believes in the helping profession.

My arms make a diamond over the body of my backpack. Otherwise there would be nothing between us.

Is nothingness the same as darkness? Since we're in the dark here, there are as many starting places as diamonds in the sky, I tell her.

I've counted.

Professionally her aim is to show she knows when to listen and when to course-correct, I've read up on it, when to demonstrate she's full of stars like bright ideas.

As many false starts as there are bats like bunches of dark fruit in the corners. As there were oranges, tossed around like meteors if He felt like it. He was cosmological, He was at home in the Mystery, He was out to enjoy a curious crazy time as a mortal.

The air conditioning cycles on. It smells like pickles. The therapist creases her nose, crosses and uncrosses her legs like a folkdance. We're facing each other like dance partners.

"I'm not a dancer," she informs me.

I start over.

Ray and Cleary had identified a guy, a guru, a contemporary thinker who was outsmarting misery. He was talking circles around pain, laughing in the face of the fear of death, possibly the only living human for whom unconditional love was constant, a state as natural and irrepressible as breathing.

The main road made a tight curve around the farmhouse. I pictured our worldly neighbors rubbernecking. Kai said they had glassy eyes. They wanted to see, without believing. Impossible. Have I told her this already?

It came down that there should be some kind of sex education. The canon of life, declared the Guru, lounging on His flying carpet, surrounded by pillows, tassels, candles, the wiggle lines of incense.

Tell them how they cannoned out of the mother's liver parts, tell them how papa cut the twine and wrapped them up like little Jesuses. You all persist in thinking I am so antilife, renunciatory. Well this is your big projection, people.

What is the spermcount around here, what is so antisexual about you? He laughed like grinding rocks, a rock fall in an echoey canyon.

Ray raised his hand and said he had seen Violet coming out in her slimy coating, blue like Krishna.

Yeah MacFarland? laughed the lieutenant from his zafu beside the Guru.

Her birth was a miracle. Dad Ray asked the nurse if she'd ever seen anything like it, and she gave him an elbow to remind him who had swaddled ten thousand babies.

Far out, said the lieutenant, wiping his mouth between his thumb and forefinger.

Ray tripped backward and upset the pail of ice chips—frozen stars with the germ of apocalypse. Cleary was a white tent. Ray stumbled again, into the doctor, who'd been just in time to see the baby swerve out of Cleary's nether region. The doctor held Violet out like a used, drenched bullet.

The nurse was going down too, and the elevator dropped them to the lobby. There were the folks close to death that night, not their own but a loved one's, and Ray thought they looked like shepherds in a Christmas play, baffled. The lobby chairs were donkey gray, bolted into the gray stubble of carpet.

Ray's fear of death was sharpened. He tried to nod to a man with pores filled in with ashy stubble, a man with a face like the carpet. Where was the exit?

He tumbled through the lobby. His neck hairs prickled as the shepherds closed ranks behind him.

Babies were born every day. Men became fathers. Being out in the summer night was better. There was a sheen to the warm air. Look at that. A thousand snails had inscribed the asphalt. Ray staggered across parking lots like craters, somewhere he'd left the car in another epoch. He'd half supported, half dragged Cleary toward admitting; she'd bucked against him each time she had a contraction.

Or the contraction had her, in its teeth, under its wheels. Glad he didn't have to be a lady!

The parking lots spread out in a dark, deserted patchwork. Ray had chosen a spot, it turned out, at the outer edges of civilization.

Then it came.

The UFO bellied down before him in absolute silence. It seemed, in fact, to siphon up all the sound around it, and Ray lost his breath in a silent spasm. No engine, no breath, no wings whirring. No fenestration, no flight deck like in the movies.

Not even the sound of time passing.

Finally the lieutenant snorted.

Ray hung his head.

It was no bigger than a small car but made of another element, and Ray felt like he was peering at it under water. Suddenly he noticed a glossy darkness spreading on the pavement. There was ammonia in his sinuses, the back of his throat, his tongue thickened.

How long had he stood there gaping before he noticed the UFO was leaking?

Jesus, he thought, it had probably landed on broken glass, a hypodermic needle. Indeed, its walls seemed to be getting thinner, as the doctors said, effacing. He could see movement behind them, shifting between dark and light, varying concentrations of matter.

Just then an ambulance screeched out of the emergency bay and instinctively, protectively, Ray lunged toward the jellyfish. The oystery body thinned upward. In a matter of seconds it appeared to Ray as a long strand of shining mucous, vibrating, stretching higher and higher. Then it broke, and vanished.

Ray found himself shaking, not just his teeth but his bones were chattering. Inordinate relief: the same relief he'd just experienced, without knowing it, when what unplugged Cleary's body was his daughter—and not the gelatinous, tobacco-colored body of an alien.

I bow to gather up my backpack. Ray's Leela was Violet's—my Leela is my back hurts: I wish it were a frontpack.

The window of her basement is too high to see out of.

No—it's counterintuitive—from down here, there's the sky, sand clouds like mesas. I can't remember, for a moment, whether we face the parking lot or the shopping street or the alley.

We're tilting.

The air conditioning turns over and I evanesce, just like an alien.

. . .

Out of her office and into the daylight, hotlight, even the sky here is made of adobe. Too much sky, too much sunlight for the tourists:

Texans with their needle-nosed boots up in air-conditioned hotel rooms. Even the Indians selling tourist jewelry under the long shed roof facing the plaza seem limp in the heat, and there are conspicuous spaces between their blankets.

Ray would really like having the town to himself, Ray would simply blot his forehead with his bandana. Dad Ray, unreconciled loner-joiner. Also at odds in his nature were pessimism and optimism: they canceled each other out, they emptied the chamber.

I walk down the jewelry row in the shade making these kinds of calculations, but no Indians call out to me. I'm not a good enough human to make friends with them. The Guru didn't teach goodness.

I turn up toward the Scottish church and Fort Marcy. Is this how hot it is on other planets? If I disembarked from the spaceship?

I picture Ray's crumb-dropping aliens.

If Ivanovichian Buddhism was breadless and loopholes, therapy is even loopier.

But am I the only one crazy enough to climb the municipal stairs in the noonday sun to the viewpoint? There's a giant white cross up there like a tiller.

I reach the flight deck of the fort and the air is so dry it cracks like a platter.

A faint wind lifts my fur, transmits a shiver. A hardluck rabbit has its eye on me from the camouflage of a thornbush. My eyes are the horizon, my shoulders are the mountains Sun, Moon, and Atalaya.

There's a lot of broken glass, bottle caps like upholstery buttons. I can see how the quantum story tells the big story. Not to be a godhead about it, but when I look down, my tale is draped over the swells and slack in the arroyos.

The Guru wouldn't like climbing the stairs but He'd be pleased when He got up here. I imagine Him at my age, anointed in the Himalayas. Was He slim like me, only slightly bent beneath a backpack?

Captured on cassette tape: You ask Me where I am from and the answer is the Mystery.

He was from behind His eyeballs. From the subtle body that predates bodies of muscle and bone, bodies of knowledge.

He was once a baby boy, and He was born to worldly parents. At least His mother was present; His father had walked off in the most profane manner.

Even as a baby he was full of the knowledge of human suffering. His mother was an old gray horse at twenty-six, and His father's curses were drowned out on the factory floor in a different city.

His fresh baby tissue was made of old letters. Bleary lead, clogged ink, brittle paper.

There was no star over His cot, no herbal fug of cow breath moistening His blankets. Stars were brass and valor in Soviet Russia, stars were because there were so few streetlamps. Cows were starved and slaughtered. Why weren't they slaughtered before they starved? the baby boy already wondered. But He wasn't to be an expert on world hunger.

There were no nurses in the provincial hospital. (His mother had traveled south to her mother to have Him.) Only shuffling babushkas who quit chewing their lips to stare at Him.

But the baby boy wasn't born to save the class of kerchiefs, He wasn't born to light dead streetlamps. The baby boy had the knowledge of a billion stars already. He knew a billion souls of suffering.

Hospitals then you brought your own soap and your own towel. You brought the chicken leg in a jar of broth. Do you hear Me? said the Guru. You squit to shit—squot? said the Guru—like falling down a well, that's how close the walls of the shitter.

Do you hear Me? Nobody told you when you were finished giving birth. Not the babushkas. The trees outside were black spires.

My own mother hoped to die, said the Guru. Even so, My baby urine did not trickle but splashed like a baptismal fountain.

It came down through Dovorh, I imagine telling the therapist.

The nativity of the Guru came down through the Fifth Beautiful Wife of the Guru.

Lay your subhuman at My feet, people, said the Guru. My feet are just feet, formed from a baby's pudding. The little bobs and yellow crystals. My feet can take it, people.

There was a lot of weeping. A lot of laughter after sorrow.

A boy from the baby. It was clear He was different. When they went to the "uncle's" dacha in summer, the boy dreamed the figs on the table. Cucumbers came to be as a result of His dreaming. His body was golden in the farm pond. The drunkard farmer saw an angel and quit drinking. There were a thousand other drunkard farmers, pensioners, everybody, but the boy did not want to attract attention. He already had with His gift for piano. The uncle was all accordion and bluster. When the boy was eighteen. He went to Altai in the Himalayas. He went to Kyoto. At some point He showed up in Berkeley, California.

Then He made His hermitage-sanctuary in the shell of an old farm behind the Atlantic.

I imagine starting over and over: we found Him where He had built His lair against that dour seascape.

Plenty of people had come before us.

Devotion was free. Practice would cost you everything.

An aromatic deck made a fan around the low waist of the zendo. We sat on the soft cedar skirt with Dovorh. We learned how He had curled His hand inside His mother's and transmitted the Great Happiness of His being.

Dovorh wept long gray tears when she told us. Dark eyes were gopi-girl, were Hindu goddess. If we closed our eyes we could see into the kohl-dark corners of temples slicked with clay-tasting waters, the crown of a red tower redder than sunset.

My sister, kneeling, walked her knees closer to the Fifth Beautiful, the one who had left her own daughter to join Him, who still couldn't get over her daughter.

What I want you to know is so simple, said Dovorh.

The pale hairs rose, pulling the flesh of my sister's forearm into starpoints.

He doesn't have to be here, said Dovorh. The smoky tears were for her daughter. But it is you He chooses.

I start over, from the end.

I was seventeen when I left Him. If your Western brain needs a timeline, lifetime, if your head needs a heads-up . . .

The therapist drops her human head, her neck is animal.

I left Him but I still loved Him.

Mark My words, My personality is for you!

My human condition is a lighthearted experiment in suffering!

My body is a teleological metaphor for My love for you humans!

Would you love Me if I were formless?
As formless and lightless as death?
If I forwent language would you be able to hear Me?
There is no dilemma.
If you leave Me I will still love you.

CHAPTER 4

OTHER DAYS downtown Santa Fe has a trading-post hustle. The old counterculture Willie Nelsons, one of my professors called them; those Indians in Wranglers and boots and blanket coats selling turquoise. I watch a group of teenagers cross the plaza, all black and silver.

I take a side street to the post office, follow a curved wall of adobe. Low-beamed sandcast tourist shops with tile floors as smooth as leather. Dried blood ristras, kiva fireplaces in deep corners.

I check my PO box for fortification from Old Dad MacFarland. Salt fish, words to the wise, Canadian dollars. I can see him spotting his own lower back with his own two hands, hear him grouse, Our backs from that life the bane of our existence. I can hear him laughing in wonder at himself, telling his new girlfriend he's burned out on searching. He's home in the cosmic sense, he tells her, hanging out with her toddler in the upset kitchen where he spends most of his time now, flies dried on the sills, the toddler pressing poop into a diaper, my dad tee-hees at the puckered toddler face and asshole.

I nod to the old man posted in the post office. He surveys everyone with the same suspicion.

"You from Canada?"

He's told me before he's from Sea Island, Georgia, and when he retires he's going back there. "You turn to dust before you're dead, in the desert," he informs me. His wife is half Navajo and she works for the BIA. Again he looks at me suspiciously. "Half means a quarter." He presses his lips together. "Half means anything but whole." He meets my eyes now.

The vestibule door opens and I can't help but whip around. Heat is a body.

I am Ray, checking my post office box in Nova Scotia.

Nothing.

I am the lieutenant, still waking up with the slope of the farmhouse lawn to the bay in my body.

The farmbirds wander off in stupidity. Follow Me! cracks Gautama the parrot. Nighthawks, dayowls, undercover foxes. More likely our worldly neighbors. Smash the altar! A crane crosses the road at the elbow. Peacocks with their skirts lowered in blueberry bushes. The Sanctuary like a ghost town, holy ash covers everything.

I imagine devotees absorbed by the spongy substance of worldliness: Pritam, real estate magnate-tattletale, his short forearms like a marsupial; Peter Nehud, slight, nervy, doctor-parrot; Craig R., the poet, pointy freckled sternum. Messner Beautiful Messner, the Guru had taken on teasing him about being bisexual. You're a Greek god, Gary! He was the right color, as if he lay in the sun in lanes of olive trees on an isle, waiting for a wandering youth of any persuasion. Is it true, Gary? the Guru goaded.

Mark My words, Spiritual Life is neither refuge nor circus! No giants like Hercules, speaking of the Greeks, Gary, no minotaurs in the bullpen!

I see them gathered in the courtyard of her office building in Santa Fe, New Mexico—I could do all of them. Hanging out around the pool, getting parched, waiting to get in here where there's air conditioning. Hey, Jubal!

Out of the corner of my eye the therapist waves her hand in front of her face as if to wave them away, she gets omnipressed. The Guru claimed He was omniprescient.

"Sorry, but all those faces, the clamoring voices—how can we help you tune them out? At least quiet them down a little?"

Her courtyard is a town square in a rounded city. I don't want to see myself creeping around, as I've said, but I remind myself that it serves my purpose if she thinks I'm crazy; it serves my purpose if she thinks she serves me.

A sash of clouds, the statue of a jet towed across the sky above me. An old shade tree with gray leaves, an ambient dribble, a water shortage, adobe dust blows up into the rainclouds.

I watch her slip into the courtyard from the direction of the parking lot, her eyes on the cobbles. She has a couple of cloth bags hanging off her arm, the lunch she packs must be in one of them. She stops short when she sees me, curls her toes against the halter of her sandals.

"Do we have an appointment?"

I gesture toward the pool. There's the lieutenant, thumbing the surface of the water; Gary Messner always referred to Penny Del Deo as the catalogue model; Craig R., fidgeting in his foxbeard; I spoke for all of them.

I follow her inside unappointed. My dried sweat feels like a second skin, like plastic. My hair was always crinkly and filmy to the touch after swimming in salt water.

"We're a thousand miles from the sea," she laughs. But her hands leap to her curls: suddenly she looks uncomfortable with the way she's tried to pin her hair back. I've heard her complain to her boyfriend that it's still too short: it makes her feel impotent, like Samson. One of the Guru's favorite stories.

Or like she's fourteen and she doesn't know her own hair yet. Doesn't know she's going to grow up and be a therapist.

"I just happened to see the temperature on the bank clock." She looks at me curiously. "It's really cooled down, Jubal."

A great deal of life is spent on the weather.

"Would you rather spend it on yourself?"

On substantiating my claim to be crazy enough to be here; my very own heatwave; on covering my tracks, my Western boots with their dainty heels, I don't want her to know I'm leading.

Leading her on. I don't want her to have to think she's a follower. The air conditioning is quiet as a cat—quiet, I say, as a Buddha, the statuette on her desk by the tissues. An idol idling, waiting to be waited on—

"Oh!" she cries, sweeping it into a metal drawer, covering her ears at the clatter.

I'm just joking.

She looks amazed that I would tease her, as if a dog teased a person.

I've seen her on the shady side, leaning out of the way for a golden retriever ambitiously shouldering its owner.

I've seen how she can't quite bring herself to step on the hump of landscaping that borders the parking lot, like scar tissue, the only liquid it gets is dog piss, out here in the high desert.

I imagine her strolling the historic streets quaint with acequias and adobe walls overflowing apricots, stopping by the bookstore café whose bathroom I frequent, whose front is cluttered with little sidewalk tables of singletons and deuces contemplating foreign newspapers and miniature teacups of that creamy-headed espresso. I imagine her casting her gaze over art magazines, manifestos on hemp and Castro, the smell of the rich coffee, eyeing a mother in pigtails with babies like strawberries. A boy wearing eyeliner and jackboots. Poetry too. A vesty old guy with a wrinkled Dalmatian—

"I know him!" she says with some relief. She stares at me for a half breath longer than she has to.

I get angry when I see those Hare Krishnas in melon dresses outside the bookstore.

It takes her a moment.

The gray-stubbled murti of Ram Dass propped up amid invoices and junk on the desk at the back by the bookstore bathroom also makes me angry. A million tons of paper, a cultivated forest, the co-owner of the living-wage enterprise in a soft bulky sweater, following my arrest from the safety of the cookbook aisle, the other co-owner sharp-eyed as a docent.

The same pious golden retriever watching my apprehension from the shady sidewalk, the same old glassblower from the extinct Rio Chia commune up the mountain, rag wool socks and wire rim glasses, and those Hare Krishnas. Watching. Milling around in cantaloupe tunics.

I stand up between walls of pinkfake adobe, cross the room to graze my hand over the rock garden on the high windowsill, daggers of purple amethyst, all atmosphere and no sunlight.

"Would you like to sit?" she asks after several long moments.

And what if I say I wouldn't?

Second thoughts about inviting me inside disappointed? Unanointed? Caste out. Here in Santa Fe I'm an outcast of society. I picture myself squatting in the wilderness, tweezing piñon nuts in my teeth, scratching underneath my loincloth.

I take my seat. I try to read her mind: How does she know whether to believe me?

"Belief is a starting point!" she protests.

Innocent until proven guilty?

She looks flustered. "This isn't a courtroom." With an edge. "We have to start somewhere, Jubal."

. . .

The poet and I sat in the sun on Holy Cat Rock, the rock where the Guru's first cat, Bob, had sat, the holy site where Bob was buried.

Life is no better now than it was before, said the poet.

Life was no better before than it is now.

But that's not the angle, eh Jubal?

The slab side of his red-and-white neck was irritated. He tested the skin, grimacing.

He pressed a little harder and the blood rushed to the surface.

At one point I fled out west, he said, his fingers in his beard now, Sita had pointed out he couldn't keep his hands out of it, yet still the Guru said, Keep the beard, Red Craig, R. Poet...

There was another teacher, but no chemistry between us.

How do you figure that, Jubal?

He shook his head, spooling his beard again.

Arthur, His roseblush, His jikki, all in Leela: The Guru's Zen mystique, His Pentecostal call and response, how He takes you to the edge with His crazy-Avadhoot-stuff, and you think He's going to push you over!

You will live in this cabin called Sava, said the Guru, and you will be My jikki jitsu.

But at first I didn't know how not to be adversarial. All my relationships to that point had been ugly. Without going into it. I had opposition-to-authority syndrome, I had weak-or-silent-father syndrome, I had a mortal fear of locking eyes with another human being, as if I'd get locked out of my own suspicious heart. Although why would I want to be there in the first place? Jubal. You have His ear right now. Could you tell Him something for me? How much I love Him?

The truth is always hypocritical, grinned Gary. Get used to it, Jubal.

The truth is that there is no truth.

The Guru always said the innermost had a movie star smile.

Gary continued: I thought I was too street-smart for a bunch of hippies. Earthworms in the compost, tapeworms in the shit. I had heard accounts come back from devotees who'd been to town with Him, folks who had seen with their own eyes how worldly people coming into accidental contact with Him found their hearts spilled out through their bowels, nonbelieving folks puddled at His feet in the dairy aisle. And I thought, Yeah? There seemed to be an awful lot of Anandas this guy, this guru, you know, had trained under. The whole pedigree of the East, I thought, come on. Everybody knows those guys drive Lamborghinis back in their Third World countries.

The innermost stared at me. He kept staring. He said, The Guru knows there's the you of you that doesn't love Him completely, Jubal.

I realize I'm staring at the therapist.

She hasn't flinched, though.

Is that her breathing?

I digress, I say. Divulge, divest—one side of her mouth lifts to smile.

No discernable order.

Not one of the four directions.

I'm going where my memory goes, between light and shadow.

"It's okay. There's no right or wrong, here, Jubal."

You sound like the Guru.

She claps her hand over her mouth. Then, "That's not quite fair, is it?"

Craig R. had a couple of poems published, laughed Ray, absently beating around the kitchen. And the Guru confiscated them and burned them with the trash behind the pole barn.

No explanation, said Ray, banging the doors of the Kalma'd-out cupboards.

Again, where was Cleary? What was this bullshit association of truth and inwardness? he wanted to ask her.

He can really assault the ego, said Ray, the ego flare, fire consuming fire. He opened the silverware drawer, peered in, kicked it closed with his knee. He paced the gangplank of the slanted floorboards.

Sometimes the Teachings seem bizarre, outrageous, occult, malicious, perverted, I know, Jubal, said Ray, reopening all the cupboards.

Actually, said Ray, when don't they? He paused midsearch. There's nothing to eat, he noted.

Curiously, Are you actually writing stuff down, Jubal? From the recordings? Is anyone? Will we go down in Avadhootian history? He laughed at himself.

One more look in one more cupboard.

Ray: Do you remember the spring we came? What were you, Jubal, ten? Eleven? Right off the bat, things were looser then. I was blessed to watch a sunset over the bay with some of the Fourth Levels. Did you know that Messner's wife Gail died later that year from drinking? Phew. The Guru pastored us through that one.

I remember there was a cloud that looked just like a great big blue-veined liver. We all wanted to gesture toward it. It was this grotesque thing, all deep and bloody. We all wanted it to mean something. Then Messner started laughing. There is no meaning, absolutely, he said, through his laughter. And I felt it, for a fleeting instant, that the Guru was truly, as He has called Himself, our Liberator from Meaning.

Put that down, eh Jubal?

Listen all you people, He cried, everyone is inside you!

I looked toward Violet on the ladies'. Grownups were saying she was going to outgrow me. Tall like Ray. Her back was very straight; I flexed my small to fix my posture.

You have to stop resisting one another! cried the Guru.

You are all God!

You are all Me!

Do you see Me resisting Myself?

Wonderfully He kept laughing, feeling up His bare stomach, one hand noodling down His loose drawstring.

The lieutenant paced the rows of students. I saw Violet stiffen when he paused behind her, her breath stuck in her ear—

My breath stuck in my ear—

It wasn't hard to find you, Jubal. What's that stink? The lieutenant's nose twitching, he could strangle a rabbit with his bare hands along the side of the warpath if he had to. Are you constipated, Jubal? What's this business about living out of the Guru's farmtruck?

His hips in lotus were killing him but he wouldn't kneel.

Messner: No one blames you, Hartshorn. Kai doesn't.

His rabbity hips—

Well-oiled Messner: It's an option. To kneel is an option.

Through his teeth, Goddamnit, Gary.

The kind of pain that drowned out his conscience. The kind of pain that made him feel so punished he couldn't conceive of himself as the punisher. The lieutenant simply wasn't meant to sit in lotus. He lifted a lid. Painfully. His eyelid seemed related to his hip socket. Messner, damn him, was smiling in his sitting-slumber.

The lieutenant opened both eyes and the zendo was like a larger eye and the Guru was the iris. The jikki crouched beside Him.

You never knew who was the eyes and the ears of the Guru, said the lieutenant. Sometimes I thought I was. He shook his head, looked at me without seeing.

He closed his eyes again. Things welled up, but he didn't react. The world ended, he did not activate. He was full of the appropriateness of enlightenment. It's appropriation.

Forty-one practitioners in the zendo. The lieutenant's Service to count them. Afterward they would take some cooked rice, wash their bowls with tea, drink the tea, stand around on the deck of the zendo trying not to let on how much their backs were knotting. All the bones in their necks and shoulders fused, a single throbbing epoxy of bonematter.

Then it would be time to head back in for the mirror of the sitting period they'd just sat through. The Guru would call somebody out for lousy posture. Maybe the devotee who thought he was the eyes of the Guru. Who thought she was the ears. Whose Service was attending His trenches of earwax. Whose Service was counting the hairs on His head. It had been attempted. The Guru let it be known that it wasn't any more or less stupid than the mantle of any other Service.

Than life, lieutenant.

I don't hate the lieutenant.

Hate was worldly.

So was love, I tell her. At least I mean to tell her.

The fact that everybody was born from a spore and unspiraled like the leaf of a fern. The therapist, me, John Hartshorn.

Ding-dong, Ju-bell, said the lieutenant. When would I learn how to evade him?

Did you give Him my Leela?

No answer.

No room to scoot around him on one side or the other.

Silence. A damper on my bell.

Did you tell Him the part where I still find Kai attractive?

He stood there chewing his smile.

Well? What did He have to say?

The lieutenant's voice rises again: Did He appreciate the fact that I toned down the part where He ripped the baby out of Kai's arms? Did He, Jubal?

I closed my eyes but I couldn't close out the lieutenant. My eyes flew open. He took me in, disgusted. You smell, boy-bell, he says matter-of-factly. You have body odor. You can't just head into the throne room with body odor.

Jesus. Did you think you weren't old enough yet to have armpits? Yeah?

He reached for his bald spot. The feel of his skull was both intolerable and seductive.

The lieutenant: Turn on your little machine.

It's already broken?

We were in love with a man who was born as a man because He loved us. Before He was born He was God, if your Western brain needed a timeline. When He died He would still be God, if your Western brain still needed a goddamn timeline.

Shall I tell you a story?

Yeah, Jubal? drilled the lieutenant.

We were creepos. Cultists. The piano tuner wouldn't come again. I couldn't locate another tuner. In the meantime the Guru couldn't play, and I thought He was going to have me out on my ass any day now. Kai was all over Him, offering baked things to console Him, playing handmaiden, really unbecoming for a First Wife—

Froth in the corners of his mouth. He had to use his finger.

Well I finally found somebody, happened to be a woman, and you can imagine how I congratulated myself.

I'd already told them to quit down at the woodshop, and the Sanctuary was really quiet. When I heard her car I ran out and, Jesus, I had the feeling of running out to meet an old-fashioned doctor. She had her black case of tools, she wore a pair of men's dark flannels, and her big round glasses were tinted to suppress her other senses.

I deployed my throwback worldly style. The Fellow, I said, all rushed with mention of the Guru, who made magic on this particular instrument—I was so lovestruck, I really loved myself for loving the Guru—the Guy who was hidden away here in the boondocks, well you should hear Him play, I was saying to the tuner. Or rather you should have, in Carnegie Hall, 1950-something, a young prodigy in a borrowed tuxedo. I was smacking my lips with self-importance.

Vash the dog joined us with feathers in his beard and the doctor bent to pat him. In that moment I was even stoned on the beard of the dog. That dog I hated.

I led the lady to the farmhouse. The Guru was waiting. Very human, He looked her over.

A she-tuner, He said, finally. I thought He smiled. I began to smile. I was so used to smiling when He smiled. And then out of nowhere, it seemed to me, He was blasting, Get out! Get your she-ear away from My piano!

I see them all.

Their senses of themselves, struck-senseless devotees all had senses.

They're getting agitated out there in the hotplate courtyard.
Courtiers without a court.
Where's their King?
Hey, Jubal!

The Guru would tease them during extended periods of meditation. He would list alcoholic drinks and rich foods in alliteration,
He would sing the names of psychotropic drugs, He would impro-
vise more orgiastic kama sutras. They had to keep meditating.

It was so simple: they had to show Him their true natures or He
couldn't help them! He was always the practical Guru, why did they
forget it? Human terms and farmwork, He kept repeating Himself,
He kept forgetting they didn't know their true natures. Shudras.
Jubal. Are you the only one living on this shitpile of a farm who
knows your true nature?

You are all life, house,
car, bloodbank!
Survival is the root of all neuroses!
You have to imitate saints,
not just wheat-head housewives!

He signaled and they laughed their asses off, He brought them to
their knees, to the intersection of mind and body. Five hours later
the zafu was proctologic. Their intestines were scoured by rice and
tamari. Their minds were clean. Stoned on air, the wives swayed
at the head of the zendo.

It's fucking hot in this courtyard, mutters the lieutenant.
The shade is practically transparent.
They're sweating their salt out, they're getting skinnier and
skinnier.

He waylaid me in the farmyard. I didn't see you last night at Children's Talk. Squared his shoulders.

Each pellet of gravel had shrunk in the cold of November.

What's going on, Jubal?

I could tell he thought he sounded important.

The light was dull, one plane, one stunted palette. Observe the mind, divvying up thinking. Observe the butterflies of the mind, observe the hornets. The mind was in birds. Suddenly the lieutenant picked up his foot and sure enough there was egg and eggshell in his boot tread. He shook his head. Eggs were rare in November. He said, Grab me that stick, would you?

A sharp piece of maple. The opportunity to present it to the lieutenant. He grunted in the style of the Guru. He gutted his boot tread. A stick was not really the implement. I need the hose, said the lieutenant. He dropped the stick with the dripping yellow and stubbed his boot in the gravel topping. Loose dirt on top of the frozen dirt that would be frozen till April. The morning was lined with shadows. The reluctant light did its best with surfaces. There was still a whole month before the pinhole of solstice. The trees were the sound of their gray branches scraping together. Maples. My stomach was oatmeal. I was loose and scared; my heart was down there in my stomach.

Hey, Jubal. Go find me the hose.

All the hoses were put away for the winter.

The lieutenant scuffed and checked and scuffed again. We'll take a walk, he said. He couldn't resist picking up his boot one last time to check the bottom.

What was worse was time slowing down so that the lieutenant's breathing took over, harsh and snuffling and deliberate.

The sun was so cold it felt wet. The seasons repeated themselves. The earth never finished anything.

I have to feed the geese or else they'll leave us for some worldly neighbors. Yeah, geese? the lieutenant scolded.

Narcissus geese. Gazing at their soulmates in the cold muddy water.

We walked around the pole barn and the bird sheds. The lieutenant in his plaid Woolrich, yogin farmer like the Guru, the kind of heavy workboots that would have drowned him.

Your parents have a lot of recidivism with your sister, you know, the lieutenant started. It's been too much gaijin behavior. The whole conventional parent-child. Its shittiness. We've left the Schism behind but still. He's not saying let's go back to attachment. He's hoping we've learned something. He always wants to move us up a Level.

Was she a sickly child? the lieutenant continued. Did she bring them back together in a rough period of their marriage?

I thought the lieutenant's querying was false. These are the kinds of things the Guru doesn't ask but He needs to know, right Jubal?

The lieutenant slapped the cows on their hips just like the Guru slapped them. A chicken, a rainbow of browns, kept weaving back and forth before the humans.

I am about to talk to you about the Fire, said the lieutenant.

You couldn't handle it before, could you?

The lieutenant seemed to have heard himself ring false again, and he stopped as if to take stock of me. I contracted. The hardness of tears in my throat—emotion was material.

What is the heartfeeling when you're in His presence, Jubal?

My blood was bathwater. My palms smarted at the point of the stigmata.

There is something the Guru wants you to know about the Fire, the lieutenant was saying. Wants to know more about, you know, Jubal?

Flesh-eating stigmata.

This world was always fire. We are here to work with fire.

Vash tiptoed from behind the Concert Barn. It was as if all the animals were listening. A crow, loping sideways, its arms inside its jacket. Where there was one crow there was always another.

The lieutenant stretched his hands inside his pockets. Cleary was His new seamstress. She fashioned loose meditation pants with big rounded pockets for the Inner Circle. I could see the lieutenant's fingers. I held my hand out for the dog. Vash came over, pretending not to, pretending not to notice the neckless crows, the lieutenant with his turned-up collar.

The lieutenant said, Noa has chosen her own Kaliyuga. For example, she chooses emotions for her father. As if her father would have come to lay eyes on her burned body. What a drama.

Why is this dog everywhere it's not supposed to be? said the lieutenant, spraying the dog's knees with gravel. Vash wound himself into himself and vanished.

Listen. The lieutenant's voice was steady but his eyes betrayed the flagrance of his message. We know that your sister produced burns on her own body.

We passed the banya. It was formal; men and boys, ladies and girls bathed separately. Except that the Beautifuls bathed the Guru.

How did she do it?

Some of us feel we need to know what the Guru is up to. The lieutenant forced a short laugh to cover up the impotence of not knowing.

What's the matter, Jubal?

Silence.

Nehud says it's a kind of conversion. Converting psychic wounds to the physical.

Now the lieutenant's eyes hurtled forward in excitement, train lights racketing through the darkness. Where the burns were seen on your sister, Noa's seem to have healed. Disappeared altogether. Your sister transferred pain and injury from Noa's body to her own body. Do you understand what I am saying?

I nodded to deflect him.

If it's true, she must be protected. From your parents. The truth of your soul is your sister, Jubal. Its tenderness and its shame. Its fire. Your sister has moved far beyond your parents. This happens. There is Eastern precedent for it.

The lieutenant began to speak faster. Was he suddenly nervous? We need to know if you've seen the burns, Jubal. Your sister must have been in a great deal of pain. Could still be. It seems she will absorb this world with her own body.

The lieutenant was rushing headlong. Ray is such an idiot-aspirant. It's hard not to like him. But you should be very, very careful.

Abruptly: Ray doesn't know, does he?

Again he tried to cover up his ignorance. Kids are basically just replicating the neuroses of their parents, yeah Jubal?

We stood in front of the Concert Barn now, the piano was in the farmhouse for the winter. Crows galloped along the roofline.

I still hadn't said anything.

The Guru has said it: It's hard now with all these families, said the lieutenant. A family, of course, becomes its own community. This undermines the real sangha.

Whenever I passed the Concert Barn I could hear music. The Guru said that the piano only captured the music that was already there. The Guru said that magic was the materialism of God. My sister—

Does this whole thing ring any bells with you, bell-boy?

He picked up again without waiting for an answer. Your parents shouldn't find out about it. The Guru assumes our maturity. Not hype, Jubal. If we're not mature then He'll have to dismantle the whole thing. He doesn't always know what's happening at that Level. So it's complicated, because we think we're complicated. Do you see what I'm saying?

He was wild-eyed. Again, almost hectically, Do you see what I'm saying?

CHAPTER 5

YOU LET THE GURU praise you constantly, said Noa.

It was true, I got a lot of laughs. My renditions of various devotees were famous. I had a good ear. He would wipe His eyes.

Give Me a Leela for Dorothy, said the Guru. My leetle Dara, the one who licks her finger to turn My pages.

Happiness is just an adventure, Dara, He said, finding her in the crowd. Those other adventures: Meaning, Power, Sex, Breakfast—

I want a Zoyan Leela! He cried.

Slyly: Davai.

We didn't know Princess Di at the time, nobody knew anything in the newspapers except the occasional local slander against us. But that's who Zoya looked like, with her Grecian nose and dentist's smile.

Princess Di with hippie hair.

Zoya and I had set up in the kitchen, the tape recorder on the worktable between us. A votive candle flickered before the murti in daylight.

I could smell the wooden spoons and tangy dishrags. There was a batch of pickles on the counter and bread—we were on bread, we were on baking—we were rising like bread under towels, we were like islands being born—

A drum of soybean oil, the silver dashboard of knives.

There were footsteps overhead, the old floorboards were an organ.

Zoya pressed the pedal on the broken tape recorder.

It doesn't matter, I said.

You'll remember everything I say?

One afternoon my love Master called me, began Zoya. Tamsen was there and she said I was to fan Him. She handed me the beautiful frond. Soon my arm was tired and I switched arms. Then my other arm, and very shortly I could not seem to stop switching. I hoped not to annoy Him. He had teased me before about doing pushups: once during Walking Meditation He dropped to the forest floor and accomplished one hundred. People said that His form was flawless. His asana, like a marine, said people. Afterward the men understood that it was okay to use brute strength in their Practice and they all did pushups. There was a Period when the men gathered in the farmyard for morning calisthenics—it was one of my Master's lifestyle experiments.

He called Himself the Allperfected Being of Jumping Jacks! The Jack of Crazy Wisdom, Zoya giggled.

I would bring a tray of screwdrivers for them to toast when they were finished. Za nasha zdarova! He used to say, We have to imitate Olympics! Not just punk housewives!

We never knew if He was talking about gods or athletes.

Listen, said my Master.

I was trying to listen, switching the frond, the mosquitoes were terrible.

Too bad you have carried your anger to the Fourth, Zoya, but somehow we will deal with it.

I was Fourth! That's how He announced it!

We will now be able to make love through the air together, He said. He has the soul of a poet!

Now, He said. He paused. Do you feel Me?

My insides were all in a rush, we were rushing together, my cervix!

And He pointed to the dried palm frond to indicate I should resume fanning.

My inner ears are open. The whoosh of Zoyan fanning is the air conditioner in the therapist's office

"Jubal?"

I open my eyes and ears.

"They spoke through you. I understand. They told you what they wanted the Guru to hear."

Yes. Through me.

"And let's just try—let's say I'm not interested in hearing any more from them."

She crosses her arms over her chest. She notices she's crossed and she uncrosses.

"I'm just wondering how I can help you steer back to yourself, to your own story."

The self was merely semantic, a little knoll of words for the ego to mount egoically.

"Myself" meant nothing, I remind her.

When He said surrender to "Me" He didn't mean the person we saw sitting before us.

What is Me?

An affair of ego! A construct of consolation!

"It doesn't mean nothing to me," she counters. She sips from her teacup which I suspect is a prop; she covers her face with her empty teacup.

"I" was Zoya who was Zoe, gathering up China and Meenakshi in Dovorh's presence, she made an exhibition of kissing them in front of the Fifth Beautiful.

The motif of living is life, Dov! cried the Guru.

I was Dovorh: Did He mean motive?

The Way to enlightenment is lighten up, you xheffy lady!

Heavy.

Let go, Dovorh! Why the hell can't you do it? He reamed her.

Jubal! He cried. All My wives are crazybirds! Give Me their chatter, chatterboy! Bell-boy! I am neffer so xhigh to xhear it!

Tamsen: That time He went behind Zoya's back—

Kai: He laughed, that laugh, people used to say it broke their hearts because it was so evident He was trying, for our benefit, to sound human—

Zoya: He removed my daughters to my mother—

Tamsen: Zoya came from this estate outside Boston—

Zoya: My mother who was bare as a tree in winter, scraping the dead skin from the sky—

Kai: The Teachings say Open to the Guru to the point that His choices flow through you. His choices in sexual partners, dietary, exercise regimen, childrearing, personal hygiene—

Piti: The first time we are kissing He had a cold. Sita said bronchitis. She said don't let Him kiss you, Piti! But she is laughing, and I know I can take on His illness—

Kai: We can't keep You a secret! You Who embody the intersection of East and West, You Who are the vector of the spiritual and the phenomenal!

The therapist throws up her hands.

Have I overdone it? Too many characters? Too much babble?

"Whose head are we in now? What does all this have to do with you, Jubal?"

She lets it settle.

"Where are you, in all this?"

Where was I?

She's wearing a skirt with tiers of ruffles, a prairie dancing skirt, or maybe Western. Those flat sandals, as if the earth were still flat, a penny of a planet—

Bare ankles—

Once, in the dim throne room, I saw the Guru playfully grab Piti and bite her ankle.

Then He got His mouth around her calf and Dovorh, laughing to cover her feelings, hustled me out into the sunlight.

Where was I?

Nattering like a monkey, hiding in branches full of leaves and flowers, leaping from one hiding place to another, we were all monkeys . . .

Stay with me.

He had rosy rings around His eyes.

Rosy eyelids.

He waggled Jyoti closer. Come sit with Me, Jill. Jyoti.

Jyoti came to Me
when she fell off a motorcycle.
It's funny, eh people?
She said it was like a poem in school:
Whose woods these are
I think I know . . .

You know, that poem
is more elegant in Russian.
All snow and quiet.

The snow smelled clean.
Beyond clean.
Like unripe pears,
like stars,
a low-flying dream, Jyoti.
Mark My words.
How can a girl who arrives in My forest
not be one of the Beautifuls?
The snow was smooth
over paths and rocks.
The smell of pine
beyond pine,
these woods are My woods, dear ones.
The woods of the Supreme Being.
Beyond pine,
moss,
snow,
its very coldness:
does God have to say,
I am God?
Skepticism is cold.
Belief is very fiery.
Burn up the ego with Me, Jyoti.

"You know this guy suffers from an acute personality disorder!" the therapist erupts finally. Immediately she flushes. She's not usually in the business of breaching the fourth wall of her profession.

I give her a moment. We face each other. Have I said she's a sisterly, unencumbered thirty? That she uses olive oil on her skin, wears common stones and silver?

As I've said, I've taken it upon myself to peek in a window of her casita.

She likes to think she's native. Not to a place, but to honesty in general. The same way that beauty, to her, means inner beauty.

Her outer beauty visible to characters like me, who think we— she and I—are in this together.

"What about you?" she tries again.

I listened to all of it.

"Can you try telling me how you felt, maybe, listening to all this intimate, grownup—this endless . . . Like you said, babble?"

I, too, was a good listener.

"I'm glad you think I'm a good listener." Is she finally losing patience? "But Jubal, it's your story. Not—Jyoti's!"

You are all My story! He cried out over the zafu population.

Ruth with radish raw parts in the triangles of her eyes, bloody threads, difficulty sleeping. I can see the way her eyes will look when she's older, at once alarmed and tired.

Stay with me—

A lot of breadcrumbs on the birdpath—

My sister was asked to wear white and Ray was amazed, Ray was now in such close proximity to favor. Noa stuck out her foot to trip my sister in the muddy farmyard. The Guru was passing by and He laughed and called my sister a snow angel.

Some angels are afraid of God, and they cower at thunder and lightning.

Other clowns are afraid of God's reason in the face of their cherry noses, their greasepaint, but that's nothing. Try being afraid of God's foolishness.

The crazytalk of the Guru. His pale eyes, His roll of skull fat. I am the enemy of banter! He cried out. I am a seagull, shitting sand, barking orders!

We had seagulls.

Dovorh had seagulls where she came from.

My Own True-Dov. He glittered. You alone invented enchantment. His eyes were stardusted with mica.

My love for you is outstanding!

Some devotees moaned. He was so uninhibited.

He cried, You are so inhabited by ghosts and issues!

I must be looking straight at the therapist, but it takes me a moment to realize she's holding up her wasp-waisted hand to stop me.

I'm getting there, stay with me—

She's not supposed to do what I tell her, but her hand falls.

Do you live alone? I'm stalling.

Do you have air conditioning?

"What?" Smiling uncertainly—

This one-sided conversation. Staged for her benefit, for the benefit of the city of Santa Fe, Texan ladies in turquoise armor, reptilian breasts, blood-soaked sunsets, silver mornings, purple-leaved plum trees. Coyote-dogs shrugging their collars, slipping around the backs of adobes.

The air conditioning fills in around us, hard as an innertube. A life preserver. She's looking at me, and I'm trying to look out the single slider window at ceiling height, or depending on your point of view, ground level.

I have to bend down to see the sky. Falling clouds, earth rising.

"Perspective," she seems to be saying. "I think it might help if we backed up again, got some distance."

She takes a big breath as if to show me.

I close my eyes as she exhales.

I open my eyes.

I take this moment to notice her carnelian and silver pendant, the regional spirit of the high desert, her white shirt like a white feather. As she keeps saying, belief is not part of treatment.

I bow my head.

She stands up as if to get her blood flowing. I stand up too, holding my backpack around the middle. I've kept her sitting too long, it's time to hit the trail.

CHAPTER 6

LONER, CHECK; loiterer, check; lingerer. He really did love alliteration.

Ruth the therapist checking off court-ordered boxes. She looks up, "Who's joining us today, Jubal?"

Does she think I'm trying to get a two-for-one deal? Sneak in a three-for-one, ten-for-one, get them all in for therapy, a Leela choir?

"Sorry."

No one, I say, my palms on my knees. Does she know who I am? I was no one.

Her bell is a guardian tchotchke on the desk behind her. The Guru loved that word. He gave a dharma talk on the English spelling. You are My tchotchkes, people, He babbled, delighted.

The office, for once, is as cold as a root cellar. Vegetable bones, old heatlamps, extra bird crates in the farmhouse basement, Noa took my sister down there. Bare earth that smelled like tinfoil. Here in Santa Fe the dirt is as dry as flour. If you blew away the sky you'd see a net of roots against erosion. The little piñons spiky as discarded Christmas trees. I've seen Christmas trees bundled out of houses here and kicked down ravines by boys the age I was when we found the Guru.

"Your parents found Him," the therapist corrects me.

Letting me off the hook, a therapeutic strategy.

"But at least you're speaking for yourself now."

My sister's skin shivered of its own accord when the lieutenant swept it.

A quick glance—does she dare correct me?

When she was very open from hunger my sister could hear Penny Del Deo laughing gorgeously, charming our mother. Ray was so suggestible. Truly he wanted to be a better human. Our mother's geraniums pressed their leaves against the glass like lily pads— suddenly my sister remembered Halifax. Veils of condensation, water squeezed out of a cheese, earth water. The cold gave my sister's skin a nutty rosy casing.

The world would fall away leaving only the kitchen of the misty house on the misty street with a sky so low Cleary said, Can you feel the sky's feathers? Even before the Guru, Cleary believed in feathers you couldn't see. In believing.

In the fog, the world might drift off without us. We drifted among the telephone, refrigerator, stove, and sink in that house in Halifax; the chocolate powder and the Christmas tree. Curtains like blouses in the windows of the sun porch, laundry in winter, caramel pine walls tacked vertically, ending in a picket row against the ceiling. The floor was the color of a black-and-white photograph. The coats hung in the kitchen, no sense keeping them on the cold sunporch so your hands got colder in the acetate pockets. The pattern of leaves pressed against the windows—

They all wore white shrouds—the Beautifuls—and a whorl of ash on their foreheads like a black-and-white photograph. Whose ash was it? They had all burned with love for the Guru.

My sister gets up off the floor of the Sea of Blankets, a warm sea running down the middle. She's a channel.

You've experienced an invasion of love, of God's love, says the lieutenant. It's potent. You are really lucky.

My sister picks herself up and exits through the neck of her body. She can do that. There is no separate Violet. She is atomic, the atoms in rocks, trees, water—if she is everyone, she is also the lieutenant.

I follow her through Kishkindha but she doesn't see me.

She believes in me, though. She still believes in everything.

I open my eyes; they're already open. My sister is before me. Her legs flopped open in lotus, a bindi of ash on her forehead. Her uniform sweater like a shawl over her shoulders; at some point she must have run back to retrieve it from the holy forest.

"Are you all right, Jubal?"

What have I told her?

"Where were we?"

In the forest. Soft underfoot, you couldn't even hear your own footsteps.

"Can you try breathing?"

I hate breathing.

"What?"

I hate plowing through space with my nostrils. With my tailpipes.

Have I thrown her?

One of the fundamentals of Zen coyness?

Not taking sides. No good, no bad, no parting like oil and water. There was no doubt He had power, even if it was only the power to make us believe He had power.

I slide out of my chair. I get down on the floor, my forehead to the sunflower-seed carpet. A full prostration, singed with carpet.

Dark whorls and whirlpools, I reek of sweat and streamwater.

"Where's your sister now?" she tries, as if to seat me.

We were all joined in His love, we were one body, the human oatmeal, the feelings as shit-colored as dates and raisins.

The same feelings as my sister. Those seagulls used to scare her when they sounded like worldly neighbors.

The same haze of sweat as the lieutenant. I wipe it with my backpack and the canvas scratches my forehead. The therapist glances toward the box of tissues, but she catches herself and looks away quickly.

That box of tissues is everywhere, I say, like He was.

Do I catch her shuddering? Or is it the strings of sunlight untwisting on the wall behind her, listener-untwistener, therapist.

Where's my sister? I'm ahead of myself, I apologize, behind myself, I answer, scattered like crumbs for the Sanctuary chickens. The lieutenant lunging first one way and then another, trying to catch one for the Guru's dinner.

Does she think I do a pretty good imitation of the lieutenant? She has never met the original. He was never original, in his particular pain, or the pain he caused others.

We're all beloved, he reminded Violet.

We were all beloved.

The therapist lifts her eyebrows. Cult-exit behavior. Should she talk to her supervisor? His gray hair is too thick, he wears a bolo, has designs on the attractive young therapist.

When I stop talking it seems as if she has stopped talking too, only she wasn't talking in the first place. Stopped breathing. When she finally takes a breath, I shrink as if she's taken it from me.

I say it again, I hate breathing.

She almost laughs now, "You can't hate breathing!"

As if each breath is subtracted from the life total.

"I never thought about it like that," she concedes. A ruthful if professional smile. She's much more careful with the next one. A straw of air.

A skinny whistle.

She circles her foot as she takes notes, loosely strapped in a sandal. I have the same habit.

· · ·

The same session? Same day or a new one? I'm not keeping track, but she is. Crumbtrack.

"I have a question." Gamely, "Why do you call it a farmtruck?"

It was His truck. He drove it around the farm like it was a dune buggy. Ray was asked to show Him how to change the oil. He ordered the old sludge, like the dairy, dumped out of the pan and into the ocean.

Haven't I told her that we poured the milk out?

Why don't we just go ahead and drown the cows? Ray mumbled later.

Haven't I made it clear to her that we were a closed community? That morality was conventional? He had said it, people were not going to be like their charity ball mothers, there were no Gandhi clichés among us, milk provoked mucous and infantile clinging.

I stand up slowly, lashed to my backpack, cross the room to the window, that rock garden she tends on the sill—

"They're worry rocks," she says. "You can choose one."

Imagine the rockslides, if rocks got worried.

She relinquishes a little smile. "There's a tendency out here, the big sky—" She'd like to let the rest hover in the big turquoise sky, a hanging sentence. But conversation should continue. Conversation with a caseworker should be like asking for directions, drugstores and gas stations on alternating corners. Can you point me to the nearest bathroom? I'm the city's one and only toilet-mongering psycho.

Here we go again! She really takes issue with the colloquial use of the word psycho. Misuse.

She really objects to self-denigration in a patient.

"A client!"

But as I've said before, she needs to think I'm crazy enough to be here.

I don't wash my hair enough. The mountain stream, the messiah . . .

"I don't think you're supposed to use soap," she offers.

The mountain stream, the source of drinking water for the city.

I pick up one of the worry rocks. She's watching. "That one's just polished granite."

It's cooler than the day, though.

CHAPTER 7

OUT OF TOWN toward Aspen Vista. The sun on the highway is shadow-black and the pines are pinched at the vanishing point of the heavens.

Thousands of piñons, busy birds divvying up the nutmeat.

How should I know how to walk among humans?

What does she see in me? Poet? Pariah? Patient?

I see myself: a smaller, birdier version of Ray, beardless, cheekless. If Narcissus saw me, he wouldn't have run into all that trouble.

I see the Guru in the city of Peterborg, as the Huru Gimself called it, a child with a drum full of stomach and God even when other kids were living on vodka.

I get some elevation and the hills fill in with cottonwoods and aspens, footbeds of grassy flowers, depressions of snowmelt.

I lean into the switchbacks. A lot of accidents, a lot of sirens through the thin air, a lot of oxygen-starved balloon heads out here in the high desert.

The sun is a bare bulb up there, I should have told her.

I throw the truck into third gear and it hunkers down, nearly straddling the highway.

The sky is full of sky. The tall pines make the air so sweet you're tricked into thinking it's breathable.

I leave my truck like a solar oven described on public radio and walk into the aspens. The Guru was always popping out of the holy forest, or there He was, in the middle of the raked pathway, the sandy teethmarks on the diagonal, the lichens yellow and gray on antique rocks that made a border.

On the aspen floor, ankle-high blue flowers. Fear is the desire to get out unscathed, I imagine telling her. Have I impressed her enough with my need for therapy?

Soon there's a sunken stream in the weedy understory. I have to be very quiet to hear it. I have to squat down as if the stream were a baby lying in the weavy grasses. I close my eyes. I can see her waiting for me in her pinkskin office.

I can see her hiking with her boyfriend of the peeling nose, moleskinned metatarsals, mirrored sunglasses. They come home dusty. I picture her drinking cups of tea, cardamom and curry, working with her memories—

How does she describe me to her boyfriend? Does she say, Most people use therapy to talk about themselves, but Jubal tells other peoples' stories? Does her boyfriend really listen? Is he dismissive, jealous? Her cool-tiled kitchen, the ceiling fan stirring, is he chopping vegetables? Music on the radio? I turn it on in my truck every once in a while.

Is she buying it or not buying it? How convincing He was, how beautitruthful? How reduced we were, how certain devotees were so thin and hungry they became cannibals—He liked that word—of their own egos?

The sun packed in tight, planet earth hardpacked as adobe.

I'm a puppeteer of the past, a poet of preemptiveness. A pioneer of the particular pull-off where I sleep across the bench seat.

The Guru had Craig R. come up with word lists.

I'm sick of alliteration!

There's no difference between the heat of my organs and the air temperature. The heat of the day is a heart, I imagine telling her.

I've said it already, my truck is an oven.

I pass a group of hikers in canvas shorts and flashing sunglasses ejected at a trailhead. Their dogs look like coyotes.

Motorcycles clog the next pull-off. The air gets even thinner.

I'm twelve thousand feet when I see Him. He's standing in the middle of the highway. He was always a giant. Even a quarter of a mile away I can see His eyes clearly. Flares in the road, air-consuming fire, they are laughing, saying, All this talk about how to live your life, Jubal! All this talk about how you lived with Me, you are really something, Jubal! Let's go back to being regular jerks, My bell-boy, and see if it makes any damn difference.

His face and forearms are tanned and it makes Him look younger and stronger. Everyone is tanned out here in the high desert. He must have been here as long I have. He's wearing Western clothes. He's a Crazy Wise Man, Avadhoot, He can wear anything. Or nothing. I have seen Him a thousand times in His own pink naked. A Buddha with nipples like blemishes.

Come on, Jubal. His lips are moving. His lips are thick and dark. He used to joke around that He was going to outdo Jesus. That's why He had a woodshop. That's why He suffered. Jesus had those big beautiful lips, said the Guru.

His arms are at his sides—He's not waving me down, no signal. I only have a few seconds. I'm rushing closer.

Do Dovorh for Me, Jubal. Should we tell My birdwife we know all about her daughter?

He's wearing His skullcap. His folktale laughter.

Should we tell her daughter? winks the Guru. She's not ready. You're ready, eh Jubal?

He beats His chest. He's not afraid of death. He remembers a hundred deaths and a hundred different bodies like different tunics. Death is a costume party! You idiots. Shudras.

He's so close now His breath fogs my windshield. I can hear the jikki's gong and torture. The sawing pine trees. The shrugging water.

I feel His breath. But He's still in the road, completely relaxed, giant hands doing figure eights, doing mudras. Quiet. Like a heavy dream I can't see out of.

I close my eyes inside the dream, I see spirals and spirals. Light without a color name, except for the daylight coming in through the stitches. Loose gravel spitting in my ears. I'm lying across the bench seat.

One of those hikers is at my window.

I can see the treetops and the sky above. I sit up slowly.

"Hey," says the hiker with his knuckles. Crisp blue eyes, gaunt around the mouth, lips peeling. "You okay in there?"

I look around. The coating on the ceiling of the cab is cracking and it smells like dying plastic. "What happened?" He has to raise his voice.

I've been scared.

"You're white as a ghost. Can you roll down the window?"

My fear-stink clothing.

The hiker says through the window glass, puzzled, "You swerved hard."

I can feel the scared trickle. I am fear of death, my human. My toes are still scared, but now my fingers aren't. I've been so scared my bowels. The shit is hot and granular.

The hiker takes a few backward steps as my window opens. Is the air dream-air? Will I wake up gasping?

But it's so fresh it seems carbonated. The mountain man salutes me. With the window open I can hear the pines on their hinges.

The aspen leaves tinkling. The world reassembles, I imagine telling the therapist. Does she secretly admire my composition?

I imagine her waiting for me—twirling her chair, poking her head once, twice into the hallway—

. . .

I make a tight U-turn and head back down the mountain.

I have work to do. I have to help her.

Now the sky has copper skin like a roasted turkey.

Fear is the same day, over and over. Death is the same day, said the Teachings.

As I make my descent heat fills in, cell by cell, atom by atom.

I cross the parking lot behind her building. The leaves rattle like gourds, the heels of my boots ring the courtyard as if everyone were listening. A runaway, an end run, as Ray said, around human suffering. But it's not wordplay, not a poem or a koan, what I have to tell the therapist.

The courtyard cottonwood rustles.

A plane flies through the sun and shakes the shadows.

The black-bottomed water shuffles.

I close my eyes. In the poetic afterimage of the water I see Dad Ray with his arm around the poet, staggering out of the farmhouse —sometimes they meditated and sometimes they partied. I followed them up the road so late at night it was morning.

The poet on the couch, Ray passed out on the floor alongside him.

The heat is a thousand veils of heat.

There is nothing to say about the sky until a bird slices it open and disappears and comes out the other side again.

It may look like I'm crossing the courtyard but really, I'm getting closer. Those hoofbeats are mine. I catch my reflection in passing —the cottonwood hovers in the heat, gray leaves scratch the black film of water.

Does she think I'm stalking? A question with an answer like a bell around its neck. She doesn't want to think I'm out ahead, either, dropping a zigzag breadpath of birdcrumbs for her to follow. They could be crumbs of anything. As I've said, we weren't regularly on wheat or yeast or even baking.

If I'm stalking her, I'm going backward.

I'm the bellwether of going backward: Dovorh walking back to her cabin in darkness, Ozera was just about the size of the therapist's office—

She walked with her arm out straight so her hand wouldn't touch her body. She had Service to wipe Him.

Like a baby.

She was too caught up in motherstuff. She was too interested in the digestive system. She thought there was purity in starvation, He accused her.

The shit of the Avadhoot is Avadhootshit!

Kai sat down on Dovorh's bed. She swung her legs up. She said, Did Noa sleep here?

Dovorh said, She was supposed to sleep on a little pallet.

Kai narrowed her eyes.

Yes, she slept with me, said Dovorh. She pooped in her blankets.

Down the half-set of stairs, past a directory of names, caseworkers and dentists, hers among them, I follow the half-lit basement hallway with an aperture at the end that turns out to be a mirror.

Ear to the door, I listen for the congested air conditioner. I imagine her hiding from folks like me who think—as I've said before—she and I are in this together.

Hiding? she'd say, with an indignance usually reserved for kitchen sink fights with her dog-jawed hiker boyfriend. He's fifteen years older than she is. Her sad eyes, have I said it?

I give a soft knock—no answer. No phlegmy air conditioning either.

Was Dovorh ever afraid, walking alone, moonless, starless, or did she really believe He was with her always? The memory of her daughter was with her.

Was Dovorh exaggerating when she said a plate of biscuits?

The therapist might believe in one cookie. She's good with crumbs.

What would I counsel her to believe, if I were the therapist? If I were the messiah, how would I visit her in dreams and visions?

What does her bedroom look like? Does she use a long toe to drag her slipper out from underneath the sofa? Her feet are rooty. She grew up running barefoot. She must have got plenty of stickers in the soft arch, as white as cornstarch. And sat down gracefully, without missing a note of her childhood, to pull out the seed-thorn.

I can imagine her doing that. I can see her taking a solitary shortcut, an only child.

I can see Dovorh wandering the bay beach, testing a jellyfish corpse that's taken on the same putrid lilac as the water.

I give her a moment. I knock once more and the door opens.

I bow my head. I don't want to scare her.

I look past her into the office for others.

"It's just me," she answers.

Is this a bad time?

"No! Of course not!" Flustered but insistent.

You must have patients with many more personalities than I do.

"We really don't call them patients." She wipes her palms on her thighs. She adds needlessly, "In the profession."

Be patient.

I don't tell her to be professional.

I take my backpack off and put it under my feet so my knees are jacked up against my stomach. The therapist doesn't hide the fact that she's watching. I'm not an organized personality. I don't collect recipes for Kool-Aid from old Jonestown pamphlets.

Her eyebrows lift, more muscle than fur, a little exception to her beauty.

"I never thought—" she starts, then realizes I'm joking.

No camisole today; a dark pink T-shirt, a color a honeybee would land on. A chocolate brown blazer, those unattractive sandals. Her earrings are a deft mix of beads and silver: they're supposed to look like women made them. With bare hands that could also deliver hundred-years-ago babies.

She feels ridiculous trying to grow her hair. She's not fourteen, she's thirty.

Do you have to get home in time for dinner?

"What?" she exclaims, disoriented.

She answers herself, "Most nights I work through dinner." Gathering her wits, "Many people have to schedule after work." As if it's for my own good that she reminds me I seem to have the privilege of not working.

It's for her own good, I want to tell her.

It's late in the game for a courting ritual. Still, I might as well be a bard of ritual—I could sing her the kiss of the feet of the Guru. My own mother had been asked to rub His flaky feet with sandalwood oil. Stained toenails like shells in an eddy of sea with too much iodine. Purple. Purple sea glass; green, brown, yellow.

Sand through the sieve of life, said Ray. Our lives before we found the Guru.

If the therapist were a bird from her childhood she'd be a

sandpiper. Sandwalker, a million tiny steps like stitches at the line of water.

Our lives were a waste of sand and sieve and life, said the Guru. Of beaches. There was no sand on the bay beach, just rocks in suits of seaweed, pine needles, guano in the gravel. There was no sea glass because it was the Ninth Wife's Service to pick it up for the Guru's collection.

Still, my sister found a lozenge. My sister and Noa passed the honey glass between them: Religion is the garbage of God! said the Guru.

At least in ancient times people used to burn their sacrifices.

The Avadhoot is naked and free, making jokes and sacrifices about dying, people!

Let me tell you how hard it is to come down among fellow men after you've been up on the seawall with the Guru. All shrubbed with coin-sized beach roses. The Guru got such a kick out of sea glass. As if it didn't exist in the Soviet Union.

Piti, the Ninth, broke her wrists and her right leg when the Guru pushed her off the seawall. She finally got pregnant during her convalescence.

I take this moment to note again—have I already noted?—that her earrings are heavy. The hole is a long slit and the heels of her lobes have thinned out with the weight of the silver. My sister heeled like a Hindu demon in Kishkindha Forest.

Phew, I say, as my dad used to say constantly. I am Ray, saying it. I am Violet, shaking under the Guru. I am all devotees, the corporate, the cult, the army of white tunics. We were all Godfolk, through Him we were related, He reblooded our bloodlines, why not, we were one and yet He wanted us to be many.

I am a cannibal of love! I am not here to practice My table manners! I am not incarnated to be some stupid fork-pusher,

napkin-wearer, bank-branch-manager, people! He coughed violently. He had to rest from coughing.

I am only human to love you. Do you understand Me, loved
ones?

Did the therapist not imagine an enlightened being could be so
bronchial? He took antibiotics, but devotees weren't supposed to.

She writes it down. The air conditioning cycles on now, it's just
the fan, she's always cold, the office is breathing. Her notebook on
her lap, we have a human contract.

You and I are among those humans (all humans, whether or not
they know it) looking for God among themselves, looking to pawn
their fear of death off on someone.

"All right," she manages.

All right. She's a slender lady with loose clothing. Her bare toes
are as long as a camel's. This town is full of sandals. Full of earth-
toned feet walking the earth. The Guru used to say, I'd skip straight
to the Seventh if I were you, people. Laughter. I am here to undermine you, people. I am here to get in your way, make a nuisance
with My love for you, you shudras.

The nights are clear and the stars are wicked shards, even in
the summer, here in the high desert. In the winter the sound on
the frozen gravel is weirdly hollow, as if the earth were empty. The
moon is a shell polished by water. How many times have these miracles been disguised by religion?

"What are you trying to say, Jubal?" Each of her eyebrows comes
in two parts, a bite taken out of the middle.

Believe me, the Kishkindhan pathways were damp and springy.
And the wet road around His farm-hermitage-Sanctuary had the
sheen of a mussel shell.

A shell crushed in my pocket. In so many words I tell her: we
call memory the past, and fervently we treat it as time's alibi for
existence.

She shakes her head. "I'm not following you, Jubal."

Time would not exist, I say, without memory.

"If a tree fell in the woods and nobody—?"

I was the tree. I was also the nobody, I tell her.

She might work in words, but again, she's not in the mood for wordplay.

As I said before, the work of the Fifth was to wipe Him.

I catch her eye, all suspect and moisture, but her will is a wall.

No W in Russian, said the Guru.

Of course I stop, I can't walk through walls like He could.

CHAPTER 8

"THERE YOU ARE!" Up go her hands, but she smiles.

"Sit, sit," she fusses. I rest my boots on my backpack. "Okay." Seating herself, "How's the temperature?"

I'm sweating.

"And I feel like we're in a refrigerator!"

She pulls up on the little leash of her teabag. It's not lost on me, a hot beverage.

She and I, in this refrigerator together.

She laughs, a small flock of light across her face, but her spontaneity doesn't seem spontaneous. I picture her with her humorless boyfriend. Even his dog is too serious.

A ring of marbles around her neck, the cold makes her skin finer and paler. She touches the tip of her nose, testing for frostbite. I should show some sign of appreciation for her antics. For example, despite her admonitions for me to sit, she herself doesn't like to, when she could be standing, circling her wrists against carpal tunnel syndrome, discreetly elongating her neck to preempt a headache.

The teabag sways in the cup beside the cup-shaped bell behind her. It never stops swaying. If I were the Guru I would bring the teacup through the air as if it were animated by Walt Disney. Levitation is an understatement. He loved Disney. He would say, Life isn't like anything, you lifey lifey people.

Sing-praise for the ritual veil, for the rocks and crystals and Buddha statuette she finally got rid of. Rise-up-singing for her tarnished silver bracelets, the weight of her earrings, for the way she has been listening for the sake of the local merchants, their vigorous toilets and pump soaps and raffia towels.

She looks at me expectantly. Nervously? We don't have an infinity of sessions.

You timey timey people! He finger-pointed. What is it with your deathbound natures, dear ones? How you fail to see that you are so hooked into it! You will be born again. Do you need My assurance? Is that your big worry, people?

She seems distracted. I'm just babbling, buying time, but she doesn't notice.

"I have to tell you before we get started." She squeezes her eyes shut for a second. "I think I saw you."

I don't help her—I don't not help her.

She pushes ahead. "I did." She checks me quickly. "Your truck. Last week?" She waits for me to say that I saw her, but I remain silent.

"Actually it was probably more like two weeks ago?" One hand hides in her hair. "You were pulled off the road," she says. "Almost to Aspen Vista."

I forgive her for being furtive—her eyes look tired. She's one of those people always getting sand in her eyes. The regular misfortune of walking behind a sand-kicker. Maybe her father.

Did you grow up on the beach? I ask her.

I know the answer. She always forgot to close her eyes when she dove in the water. Her eyes were always red, affronted.

She's not quite thrown, but nudged off course for a moment.

The beach. The carve of sand, the line of silver.

"I guess you did," she reminds me, correcting my trespass, my conversion.

The damp sunshine, as if the sun rose through the water. The trees more gray than green, and frosted white where the sun hit them—

"Well," she knows she has to get it over with. "If it was you up there, you look all right now." A quick nervous smile. "That was my boyfriend at your window. I didn't want to alarm you."

She pauses but I don't say anything. "I've run into clients before, it's not a big deal." She can't quite drop it. "I've found that it's good to just get it out in the open."

She winds her arms across her chest. Her outside wrist is just a skeleton. I can't imagine her hefting the neck of a bag of garbage. I've seen the city bins lined up in the alley behind her casita. I've seen how the weedy cottonwood sheds cotton.

An emerald-green blouse that makes her eyes look less green —strangely. More gray. Like gray in the distance.

"Jubal?"

Is she ready?

Silence but for the vent—I've tested its dragon breath on the outside of her building. I'm not an idiot, I know I have to get to Dovorh who came as Debra.

"Should we talk about why you're stopping, Jubal?"

Why not?

She shakes her head. "Talk or stop?" If the blouse were gray would her eyes look greener? "Don't let me stop you." She can't stop herself: "Let this be your process."

But I still don't say anything.

I see myself—my plan to find her. I'm done with bookstore bathrooms, and vice versa. With candy soap and coffee paper towels. I'm all done with my costume party of crazy. A quiet moment like looking up and seeing birds—you don't have to think anything, I want to tell her.

But you do, your mind birds and scuffs the air around it. Birds like droplets, fountains of birds at the outskirts of vision . . .

I'm almost there. Stay with me.

In His presence the trees were pinwheels and the sky was waves of lushest white and fragrant yellow. He brought Dovorh flowers and He laid them around her head on the pillow. He sang to her and played the piano on the edge of her ribcage. He sang to her that He had come to find her, Remember, Dov-Bird?

Remember the inedible shaggy coconuts?

Yes. It was a dream Dovorh remembered.

He whispered to her that her husband had written Him another letter. Her daughter had gone out West and so on.

She choked on air, tears sprung to her eyes, why hadn't He told her?

He held her chin. Dear Dovorh. He was laughing soundlessly and yet it disrupted the air, she saw windmills.

He lay on His side on her bed in Ozera. From behind His back He took a package. She unwrapped a box of very fine and expensive stationery. The paper was pale pink, almost fabric.

Heavy as silverware, the therapist will have long dark holes in her ears by the time she's sixty. She's not supposed to take sides. A neutral guide. She strives to be opaque, like cloud cover. Rain would be a relief. To be invisible in a world where her hair is the color of dates, and curly . . .

Her hair hasn't been really long since she was fourteen. As I've said. She's trying to grow it.

Do Dovorh! The Guru's high cheeks were caked with tears from laughing. His laughter was a guggling babbling never-before-heard musical instrument.

Holiness was never all still and quiet! When wet wood goes under the power saw it spits and smokes and steers backward!

Just like your Leelas, people!

My Fifth has no harem karma! She is too crazy to live with others. A wounded-insane, a walking-hectic, an inviter-of-starvation—

I was a savant of perfect recall. Of speech patterns.

I was a monkey savant, I stole their chatter, I screeched their Leelas from the rafters, their sing-praise, I could do their regional accents if they had them.

A savant of imitation. I could do Penny Del Deo, she had been an actress, her straight teeth and her small, sharp nose and her ease with flattery. Penny who had missionaried our mother, boggled Ray . . .

I could do Kai, the fact that His lieutenant still wanted to bed her, her lousy relationship with her daughter Noa . . .

All in Leela: Amina once had her own spread in a magazine, a leg on each page, a centerfold starfish.

In Leela, in Open Letter. All in the spirit of openness, centerfold, unfolded.

Jyoti came by motorcycle with a backpack full of dildos.

All in the spirit of turning your back on your own subhuman vulgarity. Why would you turn around and stick your head in death's asshole? said the Fully Realized Being.

Sita came as a midwife. Zoya came from a prominent family. He would pastor their hearts. They should be under the age of thirty-two, thirty-four was the outside limit, with no outstanding health problems.

Birds brought the bird wife, Dovorh.

I glance across at the therapist. I start over. Each one of us, big deal, was born in one way or another. Our mothers cried and bowed and died—or they would, eventually—and held us to their milky pouches. We stanched the flow, and if the Guru could bring someone back to life, He said, He would bring His Own mother.

I should know.

It's hard to lose—to leave your mother.

Should I continue?

Harder to stop than start, unlike death and life, although the Guru would say we only think death is difficult because we're so afraid of it.

The therapist's turn to be silent.

Can she pass it off as the equanimity of her profession? Her training in stillness like still water. But I know how old she was when her mother left her.

I don't mind silence.

As I've said already.

I can sit in silence in my truck for hours. A passing car opens up in my ears, or a yellow jacket, but I'm poised as the universe.

Unconcerned as the universe. Aspen Vista, in the shade, the windows open, I'm not really relaxed but I'm suspended—

Suspension of disbelief, therapy.

Shall I do Dovorh?

"You don't have to ask me," she manages.

Before I breach the fourth wall of being a patient, shall I add that the air conditioner is gasping like a fish? It still smells like cucumbers. It smells like rain when rain hits a body of salt water.

The therapist tilts her head slightly. She imagines—visualizes —water washing down her face, a technique she learned in a workshop.

"Go on."

As I said, training for it. Breathing, spelling four-letter words in her head backwards—

The air conditioning courses between us—

Like a canyon. Of course she doesn't want to fall down there. A sheer drop. Her outdoorsman-boyfriend had a close friend who died rock climbing in—say—Colorado. A vigil was held at the spot where the rock was rotten, there was too much wind for candles.

That's a made-up story.

This is the moment.

Birds brought the bird wife.

But it's to her that I've delivered Dovorh. This is where Dovorh wanted to be, all along, with Ruth, her daughter.

In the early mornings she went down to the beach. Terns hunched watching the sun in its gray sleeve and shifty seagulls worked the shoreline, worrying crabs out of long garlands of burgundy seaweed.

The churny lilac water, eating away the Gulf island.

A lone pelican came winging up the beach. It paused midair and unfolded another set of wings much greater than the first set. Dovorh felt her heart disperse, and she knew without "knowing" that this was her first darshan, her first encounter with the Guru.

Dovorh: We used to say cauliflowers of coral.

She smiled at me, a little guilty over the old gaudiness, poetic materialism, as He called it.

Still, vermilion sea brains.

You see, all this time I'd been keeping track of such garbage! said Dovorh. I was so exhausted by my own garbage! My desires were garbage, my fear, my boredom, my beauty.

He came to find me in Florida. He came for me, Jubal.

Her Master was drawing a half shell through the sand, just like any husband or daughter or normal houseguest. And yet Dovorh's first thought was to gather the sand He had touched. The sand was blessed.

If the sand was blessed, then the whole world was blessed! This, she understood, was happiness.

Yet all in a rush, before she knew what she was saying, Dovorh cried out to her Master, I can't leave my daughter!

Her face became as pliant as a baby's beneath His dabbling fingers.

She tried again, I can't leave my daughter.

He apprehended her with great tenderness. His gaze never left her. You have so much work, Dovorh.

So He called her.

Leave your daughter with this guy, He said. It didn't seem strange at all that He called her husband—whom He'd just spent four days and nights with—"this guy." It was because that's who her husband was to Dovorh. "This guy," already.

But how could she leave her daughter with a spiritual stranger?

Maybe this darshan was too strong for you, My Dov-One. He placed His finger on her chest. Oh you were wide open and now— He clapped once—like a little scallop! He was teasing.

Jubal? said Dovorh. Are you with me?

I nodded.

I felt that my love for my daughter was so dense inside my heart that it had become my heart, said Dovorh. My chest was so heavy. I fell back on my elbows, as if my daughter had pushed me.

I've already dreamed you, Dovorh. I've dreamed you in birds. If you come with Me we will have birds, that is My promise.

His sweetness! He looked out over the water. The water would rise or recede if He wanted. And yet she wanted Him to show her that He knew her completely. She was silent.

If this is how it is with you, He said sadly.

She dug her bare toes into the sand and saw two pelicans rise and bank. Their wings were black gloves and the empty fingers almost brushed the surface.

Snowfields under the therapist's eyes, even her lips have lost color. Her throat locks and her stomach is as choppy as an open ocean.

I stumble backward for her benefit, dragging my backpack, I want her to believe me, and yet belief is the corruption of the human spirit. Despite the air conditioning the brass-painted doorknob is blood temperature.

That mirror at the end of the hallway makes me look less extraordinary than I feel. Medium height, my dark hair not yet long enough for a ponytail. I step back into the doorframe. I've done it. I bow foolishly—she doesn't have to know I'm bowing to her—and cult exit out of her office.

CHAPTER 9

OUT OF TOWN and into the daylight.

A collage: sky, trees, birds, buildings.

Sharp relief, sharp scissors. One thing against the other.

I head up toward the Rio Chia land, the long-deserted commune.

Past the stream where I wash my clothes and my body, my body in clothes, I refuse my own plasticky scars, my very own pink naked. Twinkling leaves on strings— Past the scoop-out where I went off the road when I saw the Guru.

I pull off and stutter against some potholes at the turnoff for the old commune. I catch a glimpse of a dog with a weathered hind trotting away down the long dirt driveway. A lot of stray dogs here in the high desert. An ugly chain droops across the entrance. I pull up the stake the chain is chained to. The powder earth doesn't hold.

Ray would have liked to tour the defunct Rio Chia. His curiosity and candor, his badge of belief that could get him into or out of anything. I can see him fingering the crimples in his forehead. I can see him rolling the master bead of his mala between his thumb and finger. And the Guru with His divine unargument: Belief is just a bone, MacFarland. That's why we bury our dead. The Guru's forehead was smooth and polished. Eh people?

I bump along the private road. Those Rio Chians were supposed to have planted an orchard. Almond trees and apricot. I see stick figures, wicker ghosts, a few leaves curled with disease or mortification. They used to make their own almond butter. I'm a mile deep. I feel buried.

I take her name apart, it spells the rapist. Someone should fix that.

I should. I tracked her down. Sat her down, told her our story.

How her mother loved her—I spoke for her mother.

There's a washed-out lot and a few dirty stucco buildings that look like old sheepdogs. Llama dogs, I'm sure they had llamas. A screen of cottonwoods, an underground spring, the hidden delta of the Chia.

Of course it's quiet. I'd like to unzip and piss against that shedding stucco. I hate the way they lived all together. I hate humans falling for the human idea of God. Grownups swooning over other grownups—

Grownups like children, the way they think they're unseen when they themselves are unseeing, I imagine telling the therapist. She has to know I can see her toes in those Jesus-was-a-fisherman sandals. I can see her small breasts in those camisoles.

Peripheral vision.

There's a shelter at the end of the long row of cottonwoods with a metal roof that keeps blinking. The clouds are magnetic. They must be, the sky is metal. I'm quiet.

Does she understand I was trying to help her?

Trying to help her help me—speak for myself.

Does she think I'm finished?

I can see Him shambling down the lawn of the farmhouse, holding His staff, His small feet in Indian leather sandals. It's summer and His back is bare. He's wearing underpants.

Did I help her?

Her training in post-traumatic-stress-disorder, I've studied the framed certificate—does she see right through me? Will she see me one last time in her air-conditioned office?

I close my eyes and imagine she intercepts me at the door of her building. Her eyes peek out from behind her feelings.

Obviously I can't keep seeing you, Jubal. I have a wonderful colleague—

Will she be able to meet my eyes?

If you want to continue.

She'll pause, second-guessing herself. Do you?

I don't want a colleague. I don't want a cult of therapists, of Bird Daughters. I don't want anotherapist.

I want to wring God's neck as if He were a peacock. They thought they owned the Sanctuary, those peacocks, gods in disguise, haughty, sleepless. Underneath the long wands of feathers, just another putty carcass.

God is a grid. Not a peacock. God is the organization of life into time spent till death, I want to tell the therapist.

One last session?

What did I expect? You can't just spring one on your caseworker. You can't ambush her with her own sadness. You can't force your way into her story.

What if I was too convincing? Does she think I'm a real crackpot? A coil pot, gray-sky clay, a new figurine on her windowsill? I have no idea if her father remarried. Maybe she has a little half-brother who sends her his school ceramics wrapped in newspaper. A half-sister she helped raise, maybe she's all mothered out, having acted, herself, as a mother. Maybe her mother was dead to her already.

Still, I imagine she ushers me in like leaves in a peaceful forest. Her sweeping skirts, open-toed feet, long jewelry. Come in, Jubal. She'll gesture around us, the office is a burrow, cool as the heartmost heart of the forest. Go on, she'll say, and she'll let it trail, an ivory shell path that turns and finally disappears between earthmounds of memory.

Things are poetic but not realistic. Why would she invite me back to her office? She has no obligation to see me. To see God in me, to root out the Guru.

If the roots were rotten,
if the tree fell,
if we toppled from the spiritual ladder . . .

I fall forward in a full prostration on the grounds of the abandoned commune.

She must have wanted her mother to think she was the most wonderful person in the world. Not the Guru. She must have wanted her mother to believe everything she said: Come back to me.

. . .

I ride my truck back down the mountain.

I've come this far!

She crosses the courtyard from her office.

Did someone tell her I was out here waiting?

Nobody else out here in the heat, in the courtyard. She gestures toward the granite ledge around the pool and we sit down together, separate planets with the night between us.

Her earth-colored moon face.

She appears so open. Is it something she learned in therapy school? In the mirror?

It's what I've been saying all along but it's still true. I'm not quite finished.

Silence.

Does she think of silence as recovery from loss? As the ability to sit under a tree— We could have been friends, if I'd approached her under the willow where I first saw her.

"Thank you for telling me about my mother."

I can't quite look at her, so I don't know if she's looking at me, either.

"My dad used to say she was touched. You know, that she was better off elsewhere. At first I wanted to know where she went—

"But then I was so angry at her that I didn't.

"I never knew my dad wrote letters." She closes her eyes. "Of course I missed her."

I close my eyes—

"I can see how it might be hard for you to believe, but I've moved on. Years ago. I've had to."

—savant of premeditation.

"I guess I'd like to know how you found me, though.

"Jubal?"

That's easy.

The Fifth got hold of the letter He had taunted her with, the one written on fancy pink paper.

Now that Ruth says she likes it out there in Santa Fe, I'm getting rid of the girlhood stuff in her old bedroom. I just thought Debra might like to have something. I remember she gave Ruth this stationery.

Dovorh's eyes were shining.

What should I do, Jubal?

The therapist holds up her hand—she's crying. She smiles through her tears. "Sorry."

She looks so sad even though she's smiling. Her eyes are heavy. The beautiful green is sediment: sand. Gold, silver, and iron.

A deep breath.

I don't say I hate breathing but I do. She can read my mind, now that we've recognized each other: "I'm listening, Jubal. If it will help you to keep telling me your story."

Yes, Rutherapist, it will help me.

As I've said already, stay with me. I'm almost finished.

The Guru came forth from the pole barn where He had been prodding Masha the cow for mastitis. He wore tall boots and a Woolrich. A mane-like scarf. He was not some swami-mendicant. He
did not revile milk.

Have I said not one single practitioner could hand-milk? The
Guru pushed up His sleeves and pulled Irinka's nipples. His eyes
were full of black sparks, pinpricks in a blanket. He tugged some
more and Irinka's milk gushed like spigots.

So the children were on milk now, and there were a lot of mu-
cousy children but at least they quit crying. My sister passed the
pole barn to Kishkindhan Service and the Guru called out to her.

We are all evolving! Not just you leetle children!

She performed a full where she stood.

Grownups should quit avoiding their kids as if they were missing
out on some ego fulfillment! cried the Guru. Some consoling of
the ego!

Stasis is for the birds! The scribal ancients!

Birds printing their feet in our gravel.

My sister's forehead in the gravel. The Guru squatted down beside her. He was as rough as a cat's tongue. He was the whip of a
hunting cat's tale. Nine lives, nine wives, King Cat Ivanovich.

He hissed in her ear, Are you assimilating to your lady powers?
What is going on at the heart-root, Violet?

Can you tell Me now? His attentional force, His all-encompassing
energy, the devouring fire of His love, His possession of her was so
profound—

The therapist puts her hands over her ears, although I suspect her
earrings prevent her hands from making a really tight seal.

Finally she can admit it: "It's hard for me to hear this." Her hands flatfooted—"In my parlance—" she finally lets herself sound self-important, "It's child abuse."

She takes a breath. "How can I help you see that you shouldn't have to bear any of this? You didn't ask for it, and you didn't deserve it." Self-righteously, "These are very damaged people."

Children are blessed, Violet, whispered the Guru. Blessed, placid, remote as sky. When you get to the sky there is no sky, Violet.

My sister followed the Guru's gaze upward. They rose together. For a moment she saw the world as He did: smaller.

Listen.

We sat in tiers of zafus in the dim and cedar zendo. It was always cool inside the zendo; in late winter it was freezing. There was Violet, her mind an empty shell, a breath vessel. There was Ray, pulling on his beard, nervous, excited, flushed out before the Guru, Gautama the new parrot with the same name as the old one yakking from the Guru's forefinger: You have to be idiotic to love Me, MacFarland!

There was laughter. Violet startled. There was no shortage of lovelaughter.

People are out for themselves! squawked the parrot.

Individuated lives are a waste of time, energy, and attention.

Your house, car, child.

Independence is a refusal to surrender!

Why are you all in love with the grueling affair of the ego?

Why are you all in love with your egos as if they were your children? Cute egos, yeah people?

Everyone was in love with his or her own Practice. His or her own Practice was adorable, like a bubble-bottomed diapered baby. Belief was diapered and robed like the Guru.

Some people were now saying a line had been crossed with the Loving Monkey. Those who really knew Him would not say that, would know that He had crossed all lines already, had made a wild weave of lines and crosses, of three-pronged bird prints in the snow, in the dirt, there were the long curves of dirty foam from the gorge of the bay, and the clatter when He dropped His staff and Piti, clattering after it, broke her ankle.

He liked to sit on the old scarred seawall, there would be a row of disciples. Not so fine Germanmade after all, Piti, said the Guru.

Those who really knew Him—but the problem was He had distanced Himself, and there were now those who did not know Him. Who judged Him on their own, human terms, said the Inner Circle. Who glommed on hastily, greedily, thinking they could get something out of it.

Sita went to see the lieutenant.

The Loving Monkey was not in any way a cover for inappropriate behavior, she told him. You should know this. She seemed at a loss for words.

She said again, You should know this.

The lieutenant saw that she was not comfortable standing on the threshold of the Sea of Blankets.

The lieutenant dropped in on Kai. Noa was undermining the whole Practice. Noa was tribe of Narcissus, a whore of self, of self-contraction, a jealous enemy of the Guru. He paused and his fury only gathered.

It was Noa, wasn't it, who was snooping around, who took it upon herself to *report* . . . To fabricate some so-called inappropriate involvement.

Who else, Kai? Who else—he had to stop himself. His voice was rising. Who has always undermined me, my Practice? Who has always come between us?

Although even as he said it he knew it had long been over

between him and the First Beautiful. Making such young, gentle love during the Loving Monkey, he wasn't thinking of Kai. He wasn't thinking at all. The bliss, finally, of doing what the Guru told him to do. Not thinking. Doing nothing.

The lieutenant wore one of the bulky, stained Farm Life jackets even though it was mild. In fact it had turned out to be such an early, mild spring that Kai had already served the miniscule leaves of the wild chickweed plant she found on the south side against the pole barn. He hated chores and smells. He wanted a higher plane. The Guru was always teasing him and making him go to livestock auctions and county fairs to barter off the ram lambs and the little bullocks.

He noted that Kai was watching his hand nose around in the pocket of the ugly jacket. He could hardly look at her. He was repulsed by the thwarted love he'd suffered. He was humiliated. He slid a small Mason jar of the kind she used for pickles out of his pocket.

Red pepper flakes, plum paste, peppercorns, rice vinegar: Kai thought of the discerning Roshi mincing her pickles, his parallel gaze and ritualized grunting. Giving birth to Noa, the Roshi had spiraled through her. The Roshi was in Kyoto, but Kai had already known her child wasn't going to come out looking like her, a teenage runaway from Lost Angeles. She had wanted to give the baby a Japanese name. She had asked Him formally. But birth was no island with plum trees and a Zen government. The Beloved had touched the baby's forehead with a finger the size of a small penis. Kai's insides twisted like a washcloth and out gushed the placenta.

The jar the lieutenant held out to her had a dollop on the bottom that looked like grain mustard. It was warm from his hand, from his pocket.

There you go, Kai, he said. Taste it.

He wanted to watch her eat. She always caught him watching. She unscrewed the gold lid—the canning top came apart in two pieces. She turned in to the kitchen to get a spoon. He stood there watching.

The First Beautiful dipped the spoon and she brought it to her lips and she put her tongue to it. She never asked what it was or why he brought it. She never asked anything. She submitted to all aspects of the life of Practice. She ate excrement, now, in her would-be lover's presence.

They did it in His name. All of it. Life in God's name—how else?

The therapist doesn't want to be in a room with God's name, not even an open courtyard. I'm sorry, I say. It's understandable.

Again, I'm sorry. Suddenly I feel revulsion, as big as a cow's head, birthing through me. I'm outraged as a bull, I open my mouth to so wide it rips at the corners—

My eyes fall upon the dark crimps of the therapist's hair. Shiny as obsidian, she must have oiled it. I've seen those arrowheads in museum cases. She touches her breastplate.

I know I'm not crazy like He was. The power of power is not enlargement, I say. But distortion.

The sky is darker at the hem; just like that, a strange calm creeps up on me in a dark watchcap.

I don't know if Noa became the Tenth Beautiful, I doubt it, or if Cleary was chosen. I don't know who was thrown out of the basket. I left. I'm about to leave, in that lifetime. In the story.

One more false start, I'm sorry.

"Don't be sorry!"

I'm almost finished.

Bluejays screeched through the forest toward evening, seeding wild blueberries in their oily white droppings. I listened for the dinner gong. Violet had been invited to eat with the Guru. Strict Kalma; it was necessary not to gorge after purification when the body was like a sponge. When the heart was a sponge it could take up happiness. She had fasted for seven days but He said it was merely an imitation of purification. Everyone who had been involved with the Loving Monkey had fasted.

The Guru looked around the dining room with a provider's abstracted contentment. It was generally a good time to be in His presence. You could expect tidbits, as if you were the family dog. Vash the dog was not allowed in the farmhouse.

Spiritual Life is not about being crafty, the Guru began. Being sneaky.

He wrinkled His nose. Being semantic, people. Hypnotic, cosmographic, not like Hindu paintings of droopy bears and monkeys with porky breasts and human noses. He winked at Violet.

Not like tangkas, He said, yantras, people. Not like chopsticks.

People around Him started laughing. He was so funny! People bent over, splitting their sides, always keeping an eye on the Guru.

Spiritual Life was SL when the Guru was in a Period of attention to the alphabet.

He carried on. SL is not hidden or complex! He snorted. It is not animated by visions! All this chanting, these morbid paradoxical koans, people, why not sing the alphabet!

He was so funny! Loosen up, He demanded, He was right to demand it!

The innermost said Savings and Loans. Devotees could be jesters. Little cupids of the Avadhoot. Twisted little arrows.

I am going to be a nuisance, people, until you realize this. The

Avadhoot is clowning around, do you hear Me? The Crazy Guy is making obscene gestures!

He was always poking His fingers in our faces. He touched Violet with His gaze and she trembled with happiness. He laughed—she opened her mouth, too, and His laughter coursed through her like pebbly water. She was lightheaded—she had hardly eaten—she floated. The Guru touched sticky dates and varnished persimmons and they became Prasad. The Guru nodded to the jikki and the jikki rubbed his finger on her forehead.

She was preformal, chaotic, canceled out, a blackness as rich and varied as any color in the two caves of her eye sockets. She was the Guru's own Zen coyness in logic, she was the Teachings of inside-out, the vanishing act of surrender. The Guru threw His mighty head back with laughter.

She was so light she could be blown. A loose cluster of atoms! The same atoms that made the breath of the Guru. Ray had said He was fundamentally practical, it all made sense, people had said it checked out against physics, but I made no sense to myself. My existence.

His phenomenal force, His magnetism in full evidence, His musician's face, the pale, canted gray eyes, Slavic—His sudden gaze, this state of inimitable attention.

Let the whole thing drop, people! This and this and this—that, and the other thing!

He settled with His broad back to us, as if to say, There's nothing to see, people, so close your eyes and get on with your enlightenment.

There was Ray, watching the Ninth Beautiful, Piti, naked. Come party with us! Piti had a tinny voice, straight hips, flat breasts, nipples like little dark necks, craning outward.

The Guru got up and poked Ray's chest with a cigar, a cigar had materialized. Loosen up, MacFarland.

The rumor was the Guru had the largest collection of dildos in America. Ray was watching Piti handle an eggplant-shaped papaya. Messner grabbed it and sliced it lengthwise with a machete.

Give us a bite, Piti! cried Amina. Its meat was mushy like cooked apple. I almost gagged. I passed the skin boat back to Piti. Piti passed it to the Seventh, the *Playboy* centerfold, Amina who was Amy, bimbo of God, but it was Jyoti who'd fallen off a motorcycle and dragged herself through a snowy poem.

The rumor was Ray was picking up finish carpentry work off the Sanctuary, MacFarland wasn't starving on Kalma.

That glow in the marble of Cleary's navel? Jelly knees, jelly ankles? Of course she wasn't enlightened, but with the possibility of becoming the Tenth Beautiful, she was no longer afraid of death, either.

Cleary performed a full prostration and came up off the rug with cat hair stenciled to the front of her tunic.

Ray said, Our marriage is on the rocks, Master.

Marriage! cried the Guru, really guffawing.

Full-time job to shut out the world so you can hear your own breath, Ray, added the lieutenant, asana of crouch, in a corner. Sometimes, he said, you breathe out your asshole.

In the style of the Guru, the lieutenant grunted. In the style of shitting in a hole in the woods with an outhouse shack plonked over it.

I closed my eyes. A kaleidoscopic cartoon-scape, like the Disney movie *Fantasia*, the Guru's new favorite. I heard Mozart. I stretched, and divided, a banyan tree at Dharamasala. I was a mite in the feather of a bird. I was humble before piebald guinea hens and dancing cranes with orange Mohawks. They were always watching.

I was always watching my sister. She closed her eyes—

All My birds are Buddhas, said the Guru. Their baggy necks and shiny slides of shit, the mites in their feathers, Buddha mites, Buddha feathers.

He was mounted on Chinese silk, His stomach was a torpedo, a colicky king, the Life Force in His intestines.

The Bimbo of God called out to me and I prostrated. As I came up He caught my eye, a cosmic joke between us. Then He pointed. I felt the focus like a blade buzzing through a log in the woodshop.

He said, I have been waiting. He climbed down and boated Himself across three cushions. Bandy legs, the bodily proportions of an infant, blown up to tremendous scale. He patted a cushion and I knelt alongside His vessel. Do you think I forget you from one day to another? He said. How could I forget My Own face, Jubal? He touched His face as if it were disembodied. Somewhere, a stone skull toppled off an ancient statue.

Look at you, He said. He waved His arms and the air clouded. He said, All you cloudy people.

He startled the clouds between us and regarded me through their feathers.

We are now headed toward the Period of the Psychological, said the Guru. He paused. He cleared the air. Go tell everyone I said it. He put His hand out. He wore no rings, the wives wore no rings, His hand was a swollen starfish. He said, Go get Me an orange.

There was a basket overflowing with Prasad on a small table. A cornucopia of fruit had been blessed, oranges, kiwis, avocados. He was watching. He was grinning. Love filled the room, stuffed it like a pillow. He wiggled His starfish for me to come closer.

He threw off His cloak. A child must be rewarded rather than missionaried, their black-and-white photos of stick huts, mud ovens. He cried, Go get Me an apple!

I scuttled to the fruit basket. Golden Delicious were His favorite. I was past hungry, no-headed, there were monks somewhere who lived like sheep on alfalfa and water.

I was just a slanted line, slanting toward Him. I came bearing an apple. I bowed. He received it and He smiled. When He touched it, it became an orange.

He laughed.

I laughed.

He handed back the orange.

In my hand it was an apple.

He stroked its yellow apple breast and it was an orange. Thick pitty jungle skin. He threw it to me and by some miracle I caught it. An apple.

He whispered, If only you had brought an orange.

Students were to let go regular Service in preparation for Celebration. The Period of the Psychological was the silent night between the waxing and the waning. Sitting Practice was also abandoned.

This was the Period of the clearheadedness of the Buddha, Jesus turning the other cheek, this was what the infant Moses was thinking as he bobbed by in his reed basket. Nothing.

This was the sadhana of Crazy Wisdom.

All devotees were invited on His Hermitage-Sanctuary, even Ray, who the Guru now called Judas. The Celebration was upon us.

Ray drove the Sanctuary station wagon fifty miles to the health food co-op to purchase pintos and lentils, dried apricots, and big oily Brazil nuts. He was asked to come up with pocket money and he went around begging funds from the newer students. Pritam went down to Boston, on to New York City, for the serious donations.

My sister and Noa crossed the farmyard eating a handful each of dates rolled in coconut. The Guru stuck His head out of the pole barn and beckoned. My sister followed Noa. The Guru put His arm around the Roshi's daughter.

What are you eating, Noy?

Noa opened her fist for Him and He poked around in it. He popped one in His mouth. He swarmed my sister and Noa. He lifted His arms and His armpits opened in hairy mouthfuls. Noa stumbled around laughing, hanging on to the rails as she doubled over, but my sister was frozen. The Guru cocked His head at her.

Warm milk from the shaved-looking udder made her sick. Rare ducks and a mangy ostrich milled around them. Peacocks with be-jeweled tails competed outside in bone-scoring falsetto. The Guru said playfully, coaxingly, again eyeing my sister, Irinka-cow is off in a mucky corner.

My sister knew the cow was pregnant. The Guru slapped Dasha when she swatted with her hempy tail. He sat down beneath her belly. He knocked it with His fist. Your belly is an old drum, Dash, He said, rubbing out the places He'd hit, moving His hands down to her udder.

My sister couldn't help it. She took a step back. Did He know she'd been through the Loving Monkey? That she was unable to —let go, as the lieutenant instructed? Did He know she was full of self-preservation and self-justification? Of ego?

If it's a bull baby will we name it Roshi? said the Guru.

My sister, taking another step backward, caught Noa's eye across the humid milk house.

Eh Noy? After Papa? The Guru giggled. His whole big body trembled like homemade yogurt.

He would formalize the Celebration with a lavish spread on the sloping lawn of the farmhouse. The maples had flowered a mineral red in April, and now, in June, the leaves were so green they were wet and shining. The grass was globbed with dandelions.

All were to be garbed in white, ladies should wear flowers in their hair, white jasmine at the temples: even from the wholesale florist, Ray marveled, exorbitant. Ladies should wear mascara, flaking clay bindis. The Beautifuls should wear burkhas, as should Dharmakaya ladies.

The Guru moved among us. He wore a white Punjabi, white silk cape around His massive shoulders. He bent to touch the children's heads, He was beaming. He sampled everything. He loved potato salad and cold cuts, Davai, He said, Give Me strawberries, grapes, bananas, oranges. He scooped up the peels to steep in vodka. He stuffed them in His pockets.

Devotees collapsed at His feet and He raised them. He held Margaritka's hand for a while; China came to Him and He stopped and blessed her. He would have blessed anyone. Everyone. No Kalma now. No tamari, forget the dates and the coconut. The Guru had taken a look at Ray's kidney beans and kicked the burlap with His blunted zori till it burst open. The birds beat their wings, tottered on stick legs, would kill each other for the litter.

This was the time to let go of sadhana!

He gazed allknowingly across the sangha, effortlessly encompassing the particle of a particle that was each and every one of us. He was incarnated to shine for us, how could we forget it? He opened His mouth and all mouths were on Him. He laughed His wonderful, wonderful laugh for us, His laugh was in our bellies.

Tell Me how you came to love Me so desperately! He cried, and my ear was the loudspeaker, sparking with sound, resonating with the million particles of His lovevoice.

I am yours, now, people. He signaled to the jikki. The bell was primed, and sounded. He closed His eyes. The bell was rings in water.

He opened His eyes.

Time to let go of life in all its falsity and its feeble! Its so-called rules and restrictions! The fear of death! The sky dumped the sun behind the low hills where devotees used to pick blueberries.

Piti handed Him His goblet. Za nasha zdarova! To your libido, people! He took a long draught, then screwed up His face and spat out water. Piti murmured something into His great fluffy white sideburn. His belly was a hard cone full of life juice.

What is this pure spring water? He howled. Who here is innocent?

He looked around—He found me.

How old are you, Jubal?

I was seventeen now.

Too old for all this piddling innocence!

Sita and Kai disappeared into the kitchen. They came back bearing trays of glasses. The children's vodka was watered down with orange juice.

. . .

The concert barn was streaked with the medicinal smoke from citronella candles, flames like exotic plumage, firebird of one thousand years, phoenix. No sleepers now. Wandering fowl crooned outside the open doors or mingled like society. Bats swooped from the black rafters of night and snatched insects in midair. There were no lights in the outbuildings, only a dim bulb over the door of the farmhouse ambered by moth wings, big floury moth torsos.

Not just people's stomachs but their whole frames were taut with the treats they'd gorged on. The air was taut too; all lips were wet, all eyes polished. Wicks were lit in kerosene in red tin houses. Zafus placed so close they were touching. People's lotus knees were touching. I caught sight of Cleary moving as one with the wives when the wives came in and took their places.

We waited. It must have been almost midnight when the Guru entered. He could enter us. There was no bombast. He almost shuffled to the piano, and yet we knew He could take us. He could take us gently and completely with the familiarity and symmetry of Mozart. It had been said He played these same pieces as a boy, and

His only fault had been a very subtle acceleration even His constant Elizaveta Dimitrinova had not detected. He had to have a fault to be human. He played jauntily, marchingly, now, as if He were making fun of musical convention, or of His love for His mother. His prancing hands made dark shadows on the scrim of air flickering with smoke and lamplight, and all we had to do, all we had ever had to do was open.

My sister sat beside Noa. Her eyes must have felt low, like mine did, her hands heavy. On Noa's other side, Kai's face was contorted between bliss and grief, as if Kai would smile at death when it came for her—

There was a sense of worship, but release also. Fear becomes Surrender. Who was merely listening? Everyone was played like the Guru's instrument.

I could see Cleary's small, even features, the veneer of loveliness, God-longing just beneath the surface. She fixed her mouth and lowered her eyes. The rumor was He had praised Cleary's eyes as little violets.

But there was no condoning attachment. No pride in violets. We were all free-falling. Gautama, the Guru's parrot, fell nine times out of an arthritic pine tree. Then the next Gautama. We had all made offerings to the knotted delta roots, Prasad of dates rolled in coconut.

It seemed like the music would go on forever. In her exhaustion my sister felt Happiness Spreading, leveling like water. A black hole, an eye turned inside-out, that was a koan. My sister opened her eyes again, I opened my eyes. She saw a sleepless guinea fowl pick across the splintery barn floor in front of the piano.

Now the Guru's hands rounded their backs: after Mozart, the braveheartedness of Beethoven. The Guru had said the soldiering, conquering of Beethoven exhausted Him, and there was always a break following "Emperor." The Concert Barn stayed hushed.

The Guru Himself would not allow anyone to wipe the sweat from His neck, not Dorothy, or His forehead, and He sat slumped at the piano. Moments passed, the air was crossed and countercrossed with its own phantom music.

Without warning He raised Himself and veered into Prokofiev. No sleepers!

My sister might have been woken and slammed by a wave—not here, the bay was a pond—but a lifetime ago in Halifax. The Guru jerked back violently with the accents and impulses, as if He were receiving blows to His protruding stomach. Prokofiev—percussive shards, charged with dissonance. Every time there was a tune we recognized, the Guru seemed to pry the harmony apart so that themes and refrains became ominous, whole chunks of melody broke off into nonsense. Dorothy was forced to shuffle pages, and her wattle became red and replete with effort.

He began to sing along with His music. There were no words, but it was weirdly conversational. At once sad, and taunting. The wobble of a human voice against the pure chimes of the piano made us ache all over. The Guru had said that He suffered greatly to produce this music.

The loose guinea fowl, all ratty grays and tans like an old sweater, hopped smartly to perch on the piano, its knobhead nodding to keep up with the Guru's traveling fingers.

The Guru loved birds and beasts. Why else would He be a farmer? He could be anything. As if choreographed, with poised asshole, the bird pivoted and expelled a jet of thick juice onto the keyboard.

The Guru's hands were covered with milky green splatter.

But without missing a note, with the back of one hand, He catapulted the guinea fowl clear off the piano.

The music became gibberish. It seemed like He should have stopped playing. The hen, in slow motion, was dark and bulky in the air, like a small dog kicked for yapping. But then, against all the odds, it whapped its stunted, squared wings, and took flight above us.

How was it possible? Who in that sangha could resist watching?

My sister couldn't. She remembered the rare chicks under the heat lamp in Kai's room in the farmhouse. The gray, attic light from the high dormer. Even now she could see Noa swinging around the room with a day-old crane in the palm of her hand—a day old, or an hour. My sister, sickened by the thought of that tiny bird's death for months afterward. She could still smell the fatty casserole of wood shavings.

Now. She could smell it. I could smell it.

The Guru stopped playing.

Everyone could hear the beating air—all eyes lifted to the deep rafters. One last breath held together.

And the bird dropped. Straight into my lap. As if I had commanded it.

I heard myself making sounds like the Guru made when He vocalized Prokofiev. Someone behind me hiccupped. Ray tried to suppress his sounds through his nostrils. My whimper was laughter, and it was catching. A chirping came from another disciple, and in a few seconds there was laughter through the whole sangha.

My sister's laughter welled up uncontrollably, communally, inside her. She was in the presence of one of His miracles. He had cut the bird's wings, and He had made the bird fly again. Here was the Teaching of opposites, made manifest. Everyone must be laughing in Celebration! thought my sister.

But the Guru shoved backward on His bench, and His wide meaty face was filled with blood like an organ. The laughter fell away in strangled coughs and clearings as He rose: He bared His teeth and let out a long *sssss* in the tradition of Kyoto.

The bird was surprisingly light in my arms, and quiet.

You dare interrupt Me!

Idiots! Fools!

The bird in my arms—Buddha mites, Buddha feathers.

I put one hand on its silky shoulders. My hand sunk. Where was the body? For a moment I had the feeling that it wasn't there at all. That I could pass my hand through feathers. Then I felt the motor and I kept my palm pressed against it.

Let Me see if what I have taught has made any damned difference! Even your souls are shitty, American!

His rejection could turn devotees to stone, all white stone around me. It was their fault, it always was, they cowered. The Guru would ream them and refuse them. They had been so open. Had been opened.

The bird was purring. Not from its throat—the sound filled my hand, I could feel the sound where the bird sided against my stomach.

Mark My words! the Guru bellowed. This is the time I have been awaiting! The Time of True Division! Not just a little Schism! This is the time I make My final retreat with My only trueloves, My higher people! They will know Me now! You others with your material shrivel—

The cape had slipped off His shoulders.

Those who would be Mine—I saw the silk underneath the piano. I couldn't take my eyes off it. Those of the Living One, the time is now upon you!

The warm bird shifted.

I loved you others but you could not receive it! Truly you belong in the sandmine, anthill, pissants, truly you are of no consequence.

Was He finished?

He marched stiffly across the stage toward the door where moths were spinning out their last midnight.

Was He serious? Wasn't the bird a symbol, a miracle, hadn't He worked in birds before, weren't they scratching and shitting all over His Sanctuary? Some people around me were still craning to see the miraclebird I was holding. Was it a test? Should they remain seated? They wanted to. They had been awake for so many days and delirious nights in preparation for Celebration.

But then Sita followed Him, draped with leis of calla lilies. Piti rose, so did Arthur, the jikki. Zoya, Tamsen, Jyoti, Heidi, Amina, all in burkhas.

No Dovorh.

The Inner Circle behind the ladies, the lieutenant first, those cracked hips, then Messner, and Pritam. Zoya turned back and gathered the Sanctuary Children. When they had cleared out I saw my sister. She sat alone among zafus like tussocks in an empty forest.

The lanterns flickered after the wind of departing students. The Concert Barn seemed more hollowed out than ever. Ray had once, unpopularly, suggested the possibility that it might cave in on them. He had said there was a reason for cross beams. I watched my sister, standing now, scanning the hall, gathering up its cushions and corners.

The purring of the bird was getting louder. More people began to look around, trying to see where it was coming from. My sister was looking.

Where was Cleary? The dancing shadows were lamps on dark, lively water.

My sister had flowers in her hair and the ash of flowers on her forehead. Where was Cleary? Enough people were standing that it was hard to see around them. Ray was standing, shaking his head in wonder, catching someone's eye, and pointing to me—I was still holding the fowl. It adjusted one partial wing and then the other.

If my sister waited too long, she would have to run in the dark to catch up to our mother. It seemed entirely possible the Guru would manifest as the screech of a parrot from a high pine perch or the mist of a ghost in a white veil. What if it were too late? What if disciples had become dark poles of trees, trees slipping into other trees into that final void, cones and rods, inside-out, what if there was still fear, after fearlessness?

I saw her turn between grownups. I lost her for a second.

The bird was warm, and I did not want to unseat it. I saw my sister nearing the doorway. I willed the bird to thrill my sister. I took my hands off its shoulders. Its legs were rickety. It flapped once and resettled.

I thought I saw my sister's white flash in the dark doorway.

CHAPTER 10

I CROSS THE COBBLED square, just a one-pigeon parade, passing itself off as purple. I'm out of crumbs, bird. I was always hungry.

Down the stairs, it's hot in her underground hallway.

She meets me at the door.

"What do you mean, Jubal, no Dovorh?"

If I close my eyes I can still see the bird wife, ghosting behind me across the courtyard. Her beautiful deep-set eyes. Her hands ornate with tendons.

I don't have to say anything.

The therapist has known all along, but she didn't know she knew until this moment. That's how it feels.

"Didn't anybody help her?" She knows the answer to that one too. And she knows, and says flatly, "It was anorexia."

Her Master called it spiritual starvation.

I can see her as a child, balanced on one leg like a heron.

She would have spent hours alone on the beach. The little street, a tunnel through palm and bougainvillea, petered out in cracked blond shells and the long ropes of a thorn plant sewn through the footpath to the ocean.

She crosses the cell to the window, sweeps her worry rocks into one hand. Punctuation like a loud, brief rainstorm.

Is she angry? Is she relieved because now she'll never have to be angry?

I can see her taking a shortcut through the Jurassic interior of her island.

I know she was at school, the morning Dovorh left with the Visitor-Guru. It seemed like such an ordinary morning.

No motion in the pink-brown office where light comes in at ground level: daylight spreads out like an ocean floor above us.

Ray said, You know what? Although he didn't look like he knew anything.

He shook his head, he was chronically bewildered. His hands looked lifeless at his sides.

I heard someone say a bonfire on the beach, he said, burn us off, you know, but we've already been through it.

Was the whole thing an anticlimax?

I guess I quit, Jubal. He said my name with trademark wonder. As if even after all that it was a wonderful name and wonderfully we had no idea of its meaning. No words of wisdom. He shook his head again, still vivid, pigment leaching only at the temples. We sat in the kitchen. If my sister were there she would have leaned with her back flat against the wall, a flower pressed in a dictionary. Cleary used to do that in Halifax.

Ray could pull his beard into batwings. Cut the bullshit, yeah Ray? I could hear the lieutenant saying.

And Ray, chuckling, self-approving, I've always had a bat's radar for respect, and bullshit.

If my sister were there she would have pushed herself off the wall and moved toward the staircase.

I was so tired. I turned toward the stairs. Up to bed already? said Ray, suddenly disappointed.

I stopped but didn't answer. The overhead light in the kitchen was brighter than usual, as if the night were deeper. Ray blew all the breath out of his body. He stuck his hands in his pants pockets. He stirred the car keys.

Hey Jubal, he said. Keys and stars, rattling together. I'm going to go get the old station wagon.

It was on the Sanctuary.

You coming?

Come on, said Ray, already going.

Back down the dark road, chips of silver mica pushed into black velvet. Ditch frogs creaking, pale columbine drained of color.

We got over into the snarls of crown vetch when a car passed us. Another car hard on the heels of the first one, they always seemed to go faster in duos. I was glad to walk single file.

Balmy June, we hardly disturbed the night walking through it.

There were lights on in the farmhouse, but we didn't see anybody in the windows, the screened porch like an empty bird-cage. Ray whispered, He made it clear He was a fool tonight, didn't He.

I said nothing.

Ray said, I saw it coming. It came out sounding like he couldn't decide between apologetic and heroic at the last minute.

The Sanctuary station wagon was stowed in maple shadows. The little white farmtruck was beside it. Ray put his arm across my chest and we paused for a moment, listening, feeling the dark for humans. He stood thinking. He put his hand in his pocket.

Coming with me?

I didn't answer.

He gave me a moment.

Suit yourself. He reached for my shoulder and he grasped me to him.

He pulled a second set of keys from his pocket. He passed them to me as if we'd already discussed it.

If we were already dead, as He said we would be if we left Him, then the two vehicles were our coffins. A Living God must die. All living things must die, and a God who dies is the God of Death.

Again Ray blew his air out. He shrugged, and I watched him fade away, then disappear inside our old station wagon. It was never his way to hold on to much of anything. I climbed into the farmtruck. Browned blue upholstery, worn to skin, someone's old Farm Life jacket stuffed down under the glove compartment.

That's all, I tell her.

That's how we left that farm with its promiscuous peacocks, raspy wind, cockeyed roofs, and cocks with shingles. We left that hermitage, where we had moated rocks and idoled pinecones.

We had blown a flake from a treetrunk, a powdery moth, we had adored the mossbeds in His image. We had opened paths so He could reach us. Opened sky to the wings of fir trees.

The cackling birds with their monstrous hangnails, pebbles for eyes, pebbles for brains, adored Him.

The beasts and the human beasts adored Him.

I was awake now.

Really Awake.

Ray went one way and I went another, that simple.

Forty days and forty nights to reach the high desert.

I watch Ruth take a moment and inwardly remind herself to relax her shoulders.

Her face has been painstakingly cleared. Her face is just for me, a mirror for my face.

The sky is pulpy in the window. If it rains all the good dirt will be washed off the hills onto the highways. The few scrub piñons around the parking lot are too small to cast shadows.

I put on my backpack as if I'm ready. Burn scars stretched tight like plastic. Those maples, I tell her, in winter, on the lawn of the farmhouse: it got so boring to look at bare trees, so boring you stopped thinking about bare trees and started thinking about enlightenment. You weren't even a dirty pink bird body with bleeding pores, you had never been as blue and green as a peacock, not a bird, or a monkey, in His mind you weren't even a fucking monkey.

She takes a breath. I'm not surprised to see it doesn't help her either.

We left that night. We left Cleary. The night licked us like a mother animal. The swaying trees on the swaying planet.

Ruth the gleaner, the good listener: it's taken her a while, exactly as long as I wanted it to take her. "There's no sister, is there," she says quietly.

Both sandal soles make contact with the ashy carpet.

"It all happened to you."

I'm quiet.

"I'm so sorry."

She is. Beyond the confines of her profession.

The air conditioner is off, the office is quiet.

She walks me out, or I walk her, it doesn't matter. Black pool with black bubbles like pebbles. The heat has broken like a glass bell—

The light shines through the sky window. I'm a one-bell-boy flock now, my own bellwether, fall weather, cool enough to drive anywhere.

She says, "Is that what you'll do?"

The whole sky is still, though we're directly beneath the flight path of jets to Albuquerque, frozen in flight, wearing leis of lights.

If I had a sister she would love the little back streets—here in the high desert. The acequias, the driveways that are drawbridges, the dusky sage-leaved trees that sponge the water. In the summer there are plums and apricots on crooked alleys lined with adobes and stick fences. Generous cottonwoods and weeping willows.

Wind in the giant townsquare tree. Louder than usual, the leaves are drier, at last the rain is racing toward us.

Acknowledgments

Thank you

to editor Harry Stecopoulos at Iowa, for plunging into the strange world of this novel and coming out with a meticulous report, great insight, and constant encouragement;

to the following literary magazines and their generous editors, who originally published excerpts as: "Icarus," in *Witness*, and reprinted in *The Literary Review*; "Buddhist Tales for Western Children," in *The Southern Review*; "The Lieutenant," in *Southwest Review*; "The Guru," in *Cutbank*; "Named," in *Guernica*;

to the Howard Foundation at Brown University, for a fellowship in 2015–16; to the MacDowell Colony for a snowy fellowship and the warmth of family in 2017;

to Thalia Field for a crucial, soul-sustaining read;

and to Michael Allio, who read, questioned, and supported this novel with his own genius and grace, at every turn.